WORTH YOUR WHILE

SEATTLE ELEMENTALS, BOOK TWO

CONNIE SUTTLE

Published by:
SubtleDemon Publishing, LLC
PO Box 95696
Oklahoma City, OK 73143

Cover art by Renee Barratt @ The Cover Counts

To Walter, Joe, Larry, Lee, Dianne, Sarah, Mark and Denise.
Thank you.

For "the Fat,"
the ginger kitty extraordinaire.
Rest in Peace

ACKNOWLEDGMENTS

As always, this book is the result of collaboration. If it weren't for the support of my editor, my cover artist and my beta readers, it would be less than it is. All mistakes, as usual, are mine and no other's.

About the Author:
Connie Suttle lives in Oklahoma with her husband and a conglomerate of cats. They have finally banded together to make their demands, which has proven disconcerting to all humans involved.

You may find Connie in the following ways:
Facebook: Connie Suttle Author
Twitter: @subtledemon
Website and Blog: subtledemon.com

Demon Revealed

Demon's King

Demon's Quest

Demon's Revenge

Demon's Dream

God Wars Series:

Blood Double

Blood Trouble

Blood Revolution

Blood Love

Blood Finale

Saa Thalarr Series:

Hope and Vengeance

Wyvern and Company

Observe and Protect*

First Ordinance Series:

Finder

Keeper

BlackWing

SpellBreaker

WhiteWing

Queen of Thorns and Roses

Other Titles from SubtleDemon Publishing:

Malefactor

Transgressor

Underhanded*

by Joe Scholes

*Forthcoming

CHAPTER 1

oyal Palace, Sirena
Randl Gage

"I know BlackWing X is in the area," Zaria informed me. "Zarigar told me so. It won't be a stretch for him or the others to check on an anomaly that happened on Earth IV."

I knew Zarigar could do the checking on his own. For some reason, Zaria wanted the ship and its full crew to go with her son. Zaria never asked for favors or made these decisions lightly.

Something was up.

"What, exactly, are they looking into?" I asked.

"Well, there's a coup attempt going on—a race hidden for centuries is trying to take over."

"That's happened too many times to count—on too many other worlds. Why this one?"

"The anomaly."

"Which is?"

"Let's just say that one of Earth IV's inhabitants appears to be special. So special that she recreated herself after an incident that took her life. Now, you and I know that's impossible—or close enough."

1

"Not without help, anyway," I agreed. "How did you learn about this?"

"Through Conner. Someone escorted this person to the other side, and then watched as she turned, on her own, and went right back where she came from."

"That can't be done without help, either."

"There may be someone taking credit for it, but he had no control over what happened, no matter what he thinks."

"Why do you think this happened?" I asked. "Are you concerned she'll cause trouble for us?"

"On the contrary. I think she may be able to help us. As for why this happened, well, she may have something in her lineage that is unknown and unexpected."

"So you want Zarigar to send you images and information."

"I want Zarigar to send images and information to both of us. Then we'll know for sure."

Hidden Base, Deserted Planet Earth V
Ver'Dak Dis'rai

"My Lord Ver'Dak." Hannet, my Third-In-Command, approached. He'd perfected the art of walking and cringing at the same time. The crab-like result didn't please me as much as he thought.

"What is it, Hannet?" I growled at him.

"Ah, it has come to my attention that Ruudann is ah, deceased. On ah, Earth IV."

Several seconds passed while I quelled my anger and the urge to strike Hannet. "What did that fool do this time?" I asked, without pretending to be civil.

"He was destroyed by the uh, only known and capable uh, fire demon."

"Did the fire demon survive?"

"She did not."

"Good. Who has taken Ruudann's place? Have all the Shakkor

Agdah communities in the Northern and Southern Americas accepted their rule?"

"Vaalenn has stepped into Ruudann's place—it was at his request, should he die."

"Is she competent?"

"She is untried, my Lord."

"Keep an eye on her. If she does anything stupid, let me know."

"I will, my Lord. Is there anything in particular I should watch for?"

"Exposure of her kind. They work better in secret, just as we do, remember?"

"Yes, my Lord. What should we do if Shakkor Agdah is exposed?"

"We go in and take over, of course. We've given them as many chances as they deserve to destroy that planet, and why they haven't succeeded is beyond my imagination. They can become my useful tools elsewhere, just as anyone else might. Taking Earth IV will bring the other three down swiftly, will it not?"

"The final three do not have the protections in place as IV does."

"Exactly my point. Keep watching them and send regular reports."

"Of course, my Lord."

❧

Gulfport, Mississippi

Cassie

"Thanks for picking me up." I shut the door on Gina's small import and flipped the sun-visor mirror open to check my hair.

I'd been walking for three days before deciding to call her—after leaving Will and New Orleans behind. Gina was shocked to hear my voice on her cell phone. I'd had to explain my absence for three months, thanks to Will the asshole wizard, who'd used me to kill a bunch of Shakkor Agdah.

Will thought I was dead, too, at first. That's what happened all the other times he'd used a fire demon to kill those fuckers.

"All those fire demons—used as a sacrifice," I grumbled as Gina pulled out of the Walmart parking lot in Gulfport, Mississippi.

"Cliff told me," Gina confessed. "After he sent Rob packing."

"Yeah. I heard the sprites knew." My words were flat. I'd cared for Rob. Thought of him as a friend. Yet he'd stood aside and let Will haul me to my death, without telling me anything.

"Have you talked to Parke?"

"Do you see a cell phone here?" I patted the shift I'd awakened in three days earlier. "I was in a fucking crypt in New Orleans. No access to electricity there—or phones or shoes. I had to beg to borrow someone's phone in Walmart's restroom to call you."

"I'll get you home in about four hours; you can clean up and call Parke from there," Gina sighed while turning onto the highway.

"Yeah." Frankly, I wanted to turn to fire demon and burn down the house, I was still so mad at Will, Rob and every other fucking sprite in existence. Plus, I looked like a homeless person dressed in a dirty shift, no shoes and my hair matted from lying on a crypt shelf. That crypt shelf had held rotting bones before Will dumped me there.

"He's so proud of himself, for putting me back together."

"Will?" Gina turned swiftly toward me, her eyes wide with shock.

"Yeah. Then he informed me that the others he'd done this to died. All of them. All these centuries, and everybody's waged war on the fire demon population. Who knows if there are any left?"

"Except you," Gina said, her voice soft.

"Yeah. Now I need a fucking therapist to deal with my fucking life."

"Will you be glad to see Cliff, at least?"

"Yeah. You, too. Sorry I'm so grumpy, but you see how things turned out. I should be dead. I'm not."

"I'm glad you're not. Somebody else is Prince of Alabama, though. Parke and the others said it was important to put somebody in that slot, in case Shakkor Agdah shows up again."

"I don't care about that," I blew out a sigh. "I wasn't really comfortable in that position anyway."

"Everybody says you did a great job."

"They were being nice because I was *dead*." My laugh was

humorless.

"Are you hungry?" Gina changed the subject.

"Yeah."

We pulled into a McDonald's just off the highway ten minutes later, going through the drive-through. Gina ordered two cheeseburgers for me, with a large Coke. For three days, I'd lived off handouts and restaurant Dumpster finds. At least the state was moving toward normal, after the poisoned escapee problem was eliminated.

All of that happened during the three months I was unconscious in a New Orleans crypt. "Do they know more about the poison disease?" I asked around a mouthful of cheeseburger.

"Not much. They're working on it—that's all I hear," Gina shrugged.

"The U.S. Government; finding new ways to move even more slowly and mysteriously than before," I quipped before sucking on my soda straw.

"Yeah, I know." I walked through the door and past Cliff, who blinked in disbelief at my appearance. "After I have a bath, I hope a few things are back to normal."

"Should I, ah, warn the Chancellor?" he drawled.

"You can if you want. Tell him I needed a bath. I don't feel clean enough to have a decent conversation with anybody."

"I'll pass that along."

"Thanks."

"No problem. Cassie?"

"Yeah?" I turned back to look at him.

"I'm really glad you're not dead."

"I have mixed feelings about it," I said and resumed my journey to the bedroom and shower.

Cliff Young

"Chancellor, I have news," I said when Parke answered his cell phone.

"What news is that?"

"Well, it's about Cassie."

He hesitated, then said in a gruffer voice, "What about Cassie?"

"This will come as a shock, because it certainly did to me, but she's alive."

"What the fuck? Cliff, if you're lying, I'll have your wolf strung up on a barbed-wire fence."

"I'm not lying. Gina picked her up in Gulfport a few hours ago. Seems the wizard found a way to pull her back and she's been in a New Orleans crypt while her body recovered."

"Where's the wizard now?" Parke growled.

"We don't know. Cassie told him to fuck off and walked out. She's been walking for three days, until some kind soul lent her a phone in a Walmart restroom. She called Gina to come get her."

"I'll be traveling to Alabama the moment Jon can get me on a plane," Parke snapped. "Don't let her go anywhere, all right?"

I heard the sounds of desk drawers opening and then Parke's shout for his personal assistant before he spoke again. "Is Cassie planning to call me?" he asked.

"That's what she said—when she got out of the shower. She hasn't bathed in more than three months, so I can't say I blame her."

"Good. I'll let you know when I'm headed that way."

"You do that," I said, my tone flat.

Cassie

It should have come as no surprise that I'd find a finger bone stuck in my hair after spending three months in a fucking crypt. I dropped it on the floor, where it ticked and bounced across the tile before coming to rest at the base of the toilet.

"Fuck." I bent over to retrieve it before tossing it in the

wastebasket, on top of the dirty shift I'd peeled off my body. A part of me said I should feel bad about tossing somebody's bone in a wastebasket, but I sure as hell didn't plan on making a trip back to New Orleans to return it to the crypt.

Will could still be creeping around the place, wandering in and out of the concrete walls like they were air instead of solid material.

I considered that my mood hadn't improved since I'd died.

"Fuck you, Will," I huffed. "Fuck you, too, Rob." Jerking on the shower handle, I turned on the spray and waited a few seconds for the water to warm up before stepping inside. It surprised me that the drain didn't clog from so much dust and dirt flowing down it.

Will could have cleaned me up a little. He hadn't even bothered with that.

The asshat.

$\sim$

Seattle

Parke

"Mom, I don't really know how to explain it, because Cliff didn't know either. He said something about the wizard putting her back together, or some strange thing like that. I'll get more information when Cassie calls. I have a flight to Alabama scheduled first thing in the morning, too."

My mother looked at me as if I'd grown another head. "They better not be lying about this," she snapped. "Destiny still thinks her sister's dead, and I'm not telling her otherwise until I know it's true."

"Look, I feel the same way," I said. "It's too much to process at the moment." Opening a drawer of a chest, I lifted a stack of clean underwear and tossed it into the open suitcase on my bed.

My cell phone rang, then. It was Cliff's number, but I considered that Cassie probably had no personal belongings with her—her cell phone was in her purse at the house in Alabama when Will performed his act of murderous treachery.

I had the purse, clothes and Cassie's other things here at the house, neatly packed up by Gina and mailed from Tuscaloosa. I wondered if Cassie had found something to wear after bathing. Shoving that thought aside, I punched the button on the phone and said hello.

"Parke?" Her voice wobbled, as if she wanted to cry at hearing my voice.

"What, baby? Are you all right?" I wanted to shout at her, hug her and soothe her at the same time.

I reminded myself that none of this was her fault.

"Do not ask her about that fucking wizard," Mom hissed at me. I blinked at her—she never used profanity.

"I'm—okay," Cassie hesitated.

"Sweetheart, you sound like you're anything but," I said as gently as I could. "Are you hurt? Have Gina take a look, all right?" *Don'taskaboutWill, don'taskaboutWill*, I mentally chided myself.

"Has there been any news—anything new about my uh, father and grandfather?" she asked.

Thank goodness, a safer topic. "Dan is looking, baby—he's got several working with him, and even a few from the NSA are helping, because of all the murdered humans," I breathed. "They may have gone back to Mexico, or farther south, even. We haven't picked up a trail yet, because they haven't killed anyone since they left."

"Good and bad news," Cassie sighed.

"Yeah. Baby, I have a plane ticket to fly to Alabama tomorrow morning. I'll be there around two. I'll get a rental and get to the house as quick as I can."

"Have you heard from any of the sprite royalty?" Her voice had turned bitter.

I had—they'd sent me condolence notes. I'd ripped them up and fed them to the fire in my fireplace. I hadn't heard anything since; I believe they knew what happened to the notes and had no desire to approach the Chancellor again about his dead wife—especially since they'd known all along she'd been marked for death.

"We can talk about that tomorrow," I said. "When I see you. All right?"

"How's Destiny?"

"She took your ah, *disappearance* really hard. I was waiting to hear from you before telling her the good news."

"Good? Huh. That remains to be seen."

"This has been hard for everyone," I said. "Let me try to help you through this, all right? This is something we've never seen or experienced before, so we'll be charting new territory."

"Yeah." She was back to tears and had added a pile of depression to the burden on her shoulders.

"Do you have clothes to wear?" I asked, changing the subject.

"A few things—sweats and stuff."

"I'll have Mom pack a bag or two of your things—they're here at the house."

"Do you have the pyramid?"

I had no idea why she'd ask about that, but I did have it. "I do," I replied.

"Can you bring it with you?"

"Sure."

"Thank you. I need to go."

Her last words were barely a whisper before the call ended.

Cassie

Gina hadn't warned me about my missing wardrobe and personal things—she'd packed most of it up and shipped it to Parke in Seattle. She'd even tossed in the broken pyramid that Aunt Shelby sent to me.

I had no idea I'd miss it as much or more than my clothes and personal things. Even Shelby's jewelry chest had been shipped to Parke. Maybe Destiny had gone through it—I hadn't been able.

Shelby's home was nothing more than an empty lot, now, after my murderous relatives had burned it to the ground. I'd be lying if I said I didn't feel—well, *untethered* was the best description I could come up with.

Perhaps I should be grateful I was alive, but I was still too numb to feel that emotion. Too angry, too—and betrayed. "Don't forget betrayed," I whispered to myself and wrapped my arms tightly about my waist.

Rob—I'd loved him as a friend, when all along, he'd *known.*

All the sprites had known.

And they'd smiled and made nice all that time, knowing I was a dead woman—meant as a sacrifice to save them and multitudes of others from the evils of Shakkor Agdah.

As for Will—I couldn't think of him without white-hot anger blazing through my veins and my fire demon threatening to reveal itself. So far, I'd kept it safely hidden, but that could change. I worried that I'd lost control—or would lose it if provoked even the slightest bit.

I found myself stomping toward the kitchen—where Gina and I had fed those treasonous, ungrateful, murderous—I couldn't come up with an appropriate term to describe my anger at all of them.

"I'd ask if you wanted some coffee," Cliff drawled, "But you look wide awake enough to burn down Atlanta."

That brought me up short, just before I reached the massive kitchen counter. I blinked in confusion at Cliff for a few seconds before my brain engaged well enough to ask a question.

"Why Atlanta?" I asked.

"Because it's not in Alabama," he noted and sipped from his mug of fresh-brewed coffee. "Although some geographically-challenged individuals would probably argue about it. Sit down. If you want coffee, I'll make some for you."

"It smells good," I admitted.

"Then you'll have some."

I took a seat at the kitchen table and waited while Cliff made a mug of coffee for me, thickly-laced with cream and sugar.

"Are you back at the PD's office?" I asked as he set the mug in front of me and took a seat on the opposite side of the table.

"No. They asked. I said I needed some time. There's a temporary in place right now, but it looks like I have a friend somewhere who's willing to let me have a sabbatical."

"Who?" I asked, curious.

"I figure it's somebody at the State Department, who knows somebody at the NSA," Cliff shrugged. "You bought us some clout somewhere with those guys."

"I didn't do it by myself," I said and sipped my coffee. It was creamy and sweet and *coffee*. Like heaven-in-a-cup coffee.

"No word on any Shakkor Agdah survivors—not yet, anyway, although I got the idea from Rob before I tossed him out of the house that there could be more in hiding," Cliff had ignored my comment.

"Great. I'm really not in the mood to play sacrifice again, you know."

"I know. If I'd guessed at it to begin with, I'd have fought all of them about it, too. There has to be another way to get a handle on this. No wonder there aren't any fire demons left. They fucking sacrificed or killed all of them."

"Nothing like being a target." I did my best to hide the sarcasm. It showed, anyway. "I can't say whether it's a good or bad thing that I know about it, now."

"When will the Chancellor arrive?"

"Tomorrow afternoon. He says he'll get a rental."

"Is he coming unguarded?" Cliff almost growled the words.

"He didn't say."

"I'll find out." He whipped out his cell and punched a number. Parke was on the line in seconds. Cliff put the call on speaker, so I could hear the conversation.

"You better have guards with you." Cliff did growl, this time.

"I'm bringing Daniel and a rock demon with me, and Jon is coming too, to handle business. We'll have a meeting with the new Prince while I'm there."

"Sounds good. Just wanted to check."

"Thanks. How's Cassie?"

"Having coffee for the first time in three months. She likes the coffee. Her situation not so much."

"Understood. I'll see you tomorrow."

Cliff ended the call and pocketed the phone with a long sigh. "Can't be too careful," he said.

~

Robin Newbourne

"Why are you here?" I asked. Well, that was a stupid question. I knew why he'd come. The wizard had sent a message, asking me to meet him on neutral ground.

Neutral. It meant away from the King of the Earth sprites.

He'd chosen a coffee shop, where he sat at a window table, consuming a croissant and coffee as if it were a commonplace thing for him to do.

"What should I call you?" I pulled out the empty chair at his table and sat, feeling weary and sick to death of the world. "Will is a bit—mundane, don't you think?"

"Zedarius," he mumbled around a mouthful of food. "Will is better. It doesn't make me—stand out."

"I know of one person who will always recognize what you are, no matter which name you use," I snapped.

"Feeling it, too? What shall we call it—shame? Remorse? Self-loathing? All of the above?"

"*Theer-re-kibrus,*" I growled at him.

"Ah. Wishing you were dead, eh?" He knew the sprite language, too. It didn't surprise me. "She'll speak to you before she'll ever speak to me again, and that could be never," he shrugged. "Want something to drink?"

"I'm not in the mood to exchange pleasantries or share a beverage. I want to know how to get my friends back," I challenged.

"There's something my mentor used to say to me," he said, before lifting his paper cup to drink.

"What's that?"

"Forgiveness is the richest of gifts, and one we do not deserve."

"Thanks for nothing, then," I scooted the chair back to rise and walk away.

"Start with a truce and a promise to help. Keep your promises, sprite—from now on, or you'll lose everything."

"Seriously? That's what you have? Bastard." I did stand, then, and turned to walk away.

I am farther from forgiveness than you will ever be, because of the shortsightedness of my kind, he silently informed me. *Fire demons are nearly extinct, in a time when we need them more than ever. I—slept, when I should have been working to protect them.*

That's when I walked out—there was more than enough guilt of that sort to go around, and the sprites held their share of it.

We'd been awake all that time, and we'd done nothing, too.

Aimlessly, I wandered down a sidewalk in Tuscaloosa, my feet automatically steering me toward the courthouse. Construction crews were on-site, putting a new building together. Trucks and a mobile office were parked nearby, and would be until the work was completed.

Across the street, at one of the churches, a couple was getting married.

Must be Saturday afternoon—it was the best day of the week to have a wedding and still find parking for a crowd of people.

It made me wonder how Cassie was doing—the wizard said in his initial message that she was alive—and angry.

Because we'd used her. Led her on.

Killed her.

Except she didn't die.

Will was just as surprised as anyone else. I would carry the message of Cassie's survival to the King, but it wasn't because I wanted to. Averill would be more than angry if I withheld the information.

What he'd do with it, however, was anyone's guess. Likely, he'd extend the knowledge to the other sprite kingdoms, but I wanted to be left out of that.

Mostly, I wanted to go back into hiding and feel sorry for myself, because my friends were no longer my friends.

As if it weren't bad enough that communication between the Chancellor and the sprites had come to an abrupt halt. Cliff would call that *poor planning on somebody's part.*

He'd add that it was poor timing, too, when we needed to stand together to eradicate the threat of Shakkor Agdah completely. We couldn't act in splintered groups; Shakkor Agdah would take us down, piece by piece.

The only time we'd truly acted in concert was while Cassie was alive—and unaware that she'd become a sacrifice in the end. Perhaps it was guilt that drove the sprites to become allies—to assist the others who were hunting the evil that Shakkor Agdah had become. Not only had they regrouped, they'd learned to use new technology to attack us in ways we hadn't imagined.

It didn't matter—what Cassie had become was an unexpected pivotal point, and we'd rallied around her.

Someone else had become Prince of Alabama in her place, and Averill didn't care two cents for him—or any of the others. While effective enough, nobody would come together around water demon Ralph Greenville—that was a given.

Cassie had pulled everyone into her wake, even those who'd refused to cooperate before. I sighed and considered how to break the news of her survival to Averill.

Cassie

"The burned remains of your aunt's house have been cleared away, and the insurance money paid out to Destiny, as your heir," Cliff informed me over a second cup of coffee. "Parke was working on the tech company shares last I heard, to put those in Destiny's name, too. I doubt that's been finalized, so you have that much left, at least."

"Yay, me."

"There is one advantage you have that you didn't before," Cliff pointed his coffee mug in my direction.

"What's that?"

"They think you're dead—*Shakkor Agdah*, and your father and grandfather. No fire demon has ever survived being exploited the way you were. I'd say that can be used to your advantage."

"I'm sure a celebration was had somewhere."

"Cassie, I'm not good with stuff like this, but I do know a werewolf shrink, if you want to talk to him. He's well aware of all things supernatural. Maybe a visit or two with him will help."

"Is he in Alabama?"

"Atlanta. Not a long trip by plane or car, by any stretch. I can get him here, or I'll go with you there, your choice."

"You know, I wouldn't mind getting away from Alabama for a while."

"Well, let me find a way to get us there—after the Chancellor arrives here, of course."

"He has no hold on me—not only did I die, but the annulment is still in effect."

"I doubt he'd try to stop you from seeing the doctor. I'm sure he realizes that this has taken a terrible toll on you. Frankly, the rest of us are still in disbelief over what happened, too."

"I think I'd prefer to drive to Atlanta," I told Cliff. "If you're still willing to go with me."

"I'll get you there, however you want to go."

"It's funny how they leave a hole in you, isn't it?"

"Who?"

"Rob. Will. Even when you learn that they betrayed you, there's a part of you that doesn't want to let them go."

"Love is a hard thing to turn off. It's the same when somebody dies —your love doesn't die with them. You keep loving them, even when they're gone. Eventually, you'll be able to deal with the scars. Trust me, Rob left a hole in me, too. We'd worked together for years, after all."

"Has he tried to contact you?"

"Maybe a couple of times. I refused to reply."

"Then I hope they have holes, too," I mumbled.

"I reckon they do. I found the original caretaker for the lawns and such; he says he never got the message from the previous owners, so Will must have intercepted it. The original is here, now, living in the boathouse like he did before."

"The real William Berry?"

"That would be him, only he goes by Bill and pretty much keeps to himself."

"Thank goodness."

"The ah, new Prince of Alabama isn't much to see or to speak of; although he does have a faction behind him. They sent his nomination to the Chancellor, and his name was the only one put forward. Not much of a contest, really; Parke couldn't find anything criminal in his background, and he'd served as a city councilman for six terms, so he has some kind of experience."

"Ross had a faction behind him, too."

"Greenville may be too afraid to step out of line; I think Parke laid it on pretty thick when the appointment was made. It's a cinch that he won't be able to bring all the sprites together for a common goal; only one person I know has ever pulled that off."

"What about the prisons? Are they still planning to use the private ones? Shakkor Agdah has their fingerprints all over that."

"We know that, but the human legislators in this state are a bit asinine in the matter.

There are some who want it put to a vote, but that hasn't been decided, yet. That's one of the things I've been working on since you ah, were gone for three months. I've been tracking the money. I confess it hasn't been easy, and I usually end up with nothing tangible. The feds are working on it, too, so we've taken to sharing information."

"They've probably routed it through so many banks, and had it laundered way too many times to make it obvious," I sighed.

"Too true," Cliff conceded. "We keep hitting dead ends, all the while waiting for the new leader or leaders of Black Myth to let us know they're in charge, now."

"They may be waiting to spring plan B on us, to announce their promotion," I said.

"We worry about that, too. I wish we had information on who was killed three months ago, and how many died with him or her."

"I think I may know somebody with that information," I said.

"Who's that?"

"Morton and Dalton King."

CHAPTER 2

*P*arke

"She's right," I told Cliff over the phone. "Maybe we ought to step up our search for those two. I have a few contacts in Mexico that may help."

"Wave a reward in their direction. I hear money talks loudly there."

"I'll consider it. What's Cassie doing right now? Can she talk?"

"Gina sent her to bed. I doubt she's gotten more than a few hours' sleep since she left New Orleans. There's something else, too. I know a werewolf psychiatrist in Atlanta. Cassie wants to see him. This has affected her significantly, and there's a lot to sort out."

"Understood. How quickly can he see her?"

"I can get her in after the full moon, if I pull a few strings."

"Then pull away. I can get plane reservations for her."

"She said she'd prefer to drive," Cliff said. "I offered to take her."

"Find a place in Atlanta, then. Something to rent that's suitable and has room for us to have an office."

"You serious?"

"I've cleared out my caseload; others will handle court appearances. I can stay for a month or more. Doesn't matter whether I'm in Alabama or Georgia to handle business."

"I'll get on that now," Cliff said. "I have other contacts in Atlanta. I think we can find something that will work."

"Good. I'll grab a rental at the airport, so you won't have to pick me up."

"If it's all the same to you, I'd prefer to have two wolves waiting for you—for extra protection."

"That's fine; they can tail us on the way to the house. I've put in a call to Trey and his boss; I'm asking for his help and maybe that of one or two other vamps."

"Good idea. I'll make sure we can house vamps in Atlanta."

"If nothing else, they'll have access to safe houses there."

"True. I'll look for something with a basement or a cellar that can be locked from the inside. They prefer security, in my experience."

"I agree. Do what you can, and we'll make arrangements for payment when I arrive."

∾

Cliff

"We have two that are suitable," I handed printed pages, complete with photos of executive rentals, to Gina after getting off the phone with a friend in Atlanta. "We can rent either one—take a look at the pictures and tell me what you think."

"Nice," she studied the exterior photos side by side.

"Both are in the Temperance Acres addition of Buckhead."

"Well, why don't we go for the one on Alys Drive with sixteen thousand square feet, then?" Gina swiftly ran through photos of the massive house, which included an olympic-size pool, a wine cellar, eight bedrooms and four living spaces, three of which could be converted to offices or extra bedrooms.

"We can put the vamps in the wine cellar, it's big enough," I said, looking over Gina's shoulder.

"I was thinking the same thing. They can lock themselves in, there are no windows and they don't need a bathroom. What's not to love?"

"I'll call Jake back, then, and tell him we want to rent it for a couple of months. He may want a six-month lease, but we'll work around that."

"I guess it's on the market, then?"

"It is, but nobody's jumped at the exorbitant price tag, so it's been empty for nearly two years. The sellers won't mind the income, and it won't be like we're staying there forever."

"I suggest renting a post office box while we're there," Cassie shuffled into my office. "I don't want any mail forwarded to a specific address."

"Good idea," I told her. She looked as if the nap hadn't gone well, but I held that back.

"At least it's furnished," Gina sighed. "We won't have to buy anything, and we can rent office furniture and equipment."

"I can arrange to have some groceries delivered and waiting when we get there," I said. "I just need a list for the delivery service."

"Living in a city has its perks, I guess," Cassie yawned.

"I can put the list together," Gina told me.

"Good. I figure we'll leave day after tomorrow; I doubt the Chancellor will want to be on the road right after a long flight."

"Pack for heat and humidity," Cassie said. "Because we'll have that for sure."

Gina

"I have a few errands to run at the pharmacy—my med kit needs supplies," I told Cassie. "Want me to pick up soap and shampoo for you?"

"Yeah. Let me make a list," she said, searching through kitchen drawers for paper and pen. "I need deodorant, lotion, hairspray, shampoo and conditioner," she pulled a small pad of paper out of a drawer, followed by a pen. "I'll write down the makeup list, too, if you don't mind."

"I don't mind. Cliff is buying, so it's no trouble."

"I can pay him back when I get my stuff from Seattle—if Parke remembers to bring my purse. You're not going out alone, are you?" She lifted her eyes from the list she was writing to study me.

"No, Kent is picking me up. We'll grab a burger while we're out and bring back pizza for you and Cliff."

"Oh, my gosh, I haven't had a pizza in—never mind. I'd love a pizza. Thank you."

"You ready?" Kent walked into the kitchen. "Oh, hey, Cassie. Glad to see you," he said.

"Likewise," Cassie told him. "I wrote down the kind of pizza I'd like," she added, handing me the list.

"Good enough. We'll be back in two hours or so."

Kent had a hand on the small of my back as he walked me out of the house. We climbed into his Chevy truck and buckled ourselves in. "Want food first, or shop first?"

"Let's eat," I said. "I'm hungry and it's been a long day."

Later, after we'd eaten three and a half double cheeseburgers between us, we headed for the twenty-four-hour pharmacy. I preferred to go at night; the drug store tended to be less crowded and my spots less pronounced.

"Will you be okay here if I run to the liquor store down the block?" Kent asked.

"Sure. Get a few bottles of wine, okay?"

"I will. Cliff wants some Scotch, actually."

He left for the liquor store; I headed for the makeup aisle on the far side of the pharmacy. That's where Rob caught up with me.

"How is she?" he asked right away.

"Physically, she looks a little thin. Well, gaunt may be a better term. No surprise, since it took three months for her to wake up after that debacle."

"Emotionally?"

"Defensive. I suppose that's no surprise either, since she was betrayed and nearly killed." I jerked two tubes of mascara off the peg in front of me, in the brand and color Cassie requested.

"I'm searching for signs of Shakkor Agdah's regrouping, but they're lying low," Rob muttered, shaking his head.

"Cassie says they're probably perfecting plan B, since plan A was thwarted, for the most part."

"Under new leadership, too, and that could take time to put in place. Do you think she'll ever forgive me?"

"Rob, a lot of people will have to forgive you, not just Cassie. She did say that there's a hole left behind, where you were—before. She said that she hopes there are holes in you and in Will, too, that are just as painful."

"I can't speak for the wizard, but the hole in my heart feels as big as the sky."

"It's funny how love works, isn't it?"

"We try not to love humans, it's far too painful. It's mostly the same with other supernaturals, although they have extended lives in most cases."

"But Cassie was different, huh? Especially since she pulled your ass out of the fire more than once. A few bits of jewelry are no consolation for betrayal, Robin. You'll be happy to know that those things didn't survive the fire that burned for two days."

"I don't doubt it, since that fire was combined with a wizard's spell. The sprite kingdoms don't think much of the new Prince of Alabama."

"Hmmph," I snorted. "Greenville couldn't defend himself against a class of angry third-graders. The human variety and not the other kind." I moved down the wall, finding the other items Cassie wrote on her list.

"Averill feels the same. I informed him that Cassie survived. I received the information from the wizard. It wasn't a congenial meeting."

"So. All that time, the solution against Shakkor Agdah was murdering a fire demon. Huh." I wasn't complimentary in my description. "You'd think that somebody, somewhere, would have been working on a different solution, rather than painting a target on every fire demon's back."

"I know." Rob ducked his head and sounded guilty. "We're down to three fire demons, total, and that includes Cassie. Until she woke, that number had been reduced to just two."

"Will needs to stay the hell away from them, then," I snapped.

"I think he understands that, now."

"Does he understand that the Chancellor has a kill-on-sight warrant out for him?"

"It isn't easy to kill a wizard," Robin whispered. "The Chancellor should rethink that warrant. Perhaps he should issue an invitation to talk with him. I agreed to meet with Will so I could unload my feelings on the matter."

"And how did that turn out?"

"I think he feels guilt—and emptiness, too. I unloaded on him anyway."

"Because he deserved it."

"He said as much."

"Is there something else?" I asked before heading toward the soap and shampoo aisle.

"I have a letter for the Chancellor from my King. It's important that he read it, as we recognize the need to stand together to survive the next wave of Shakkor Agdah attacks. And, as Cassie lived, we hope she may be able to adjust the method used last time, to hunt for Shakkor Agdah."

"In other words, you want to use her for a rallying point, like we did last time."

"Her name is even more revered among the sprite kingdoms. They saw her as one who could save the Earth with her death. Now, she has become even more of an icon."

"Please note my previous comment about bits of jewelry." I stuffed two bottles of lotion into the basket I carried.

"Understood. If we cannot obtain her forgiveness, then at least we must beg for her cooperation. I don't see us surviving the next wave of attacks otherwise."

"What about Will? Does the same go for him?"

"In the spirit of truthfulness that I wish to carry forward, yes."

"In the spirit of truthfulness, I'll tell you now that Cassie has agreed to see a shrink, because she needs the help. Tell me about Will's and your part in that."

Rob went still with that news. "This—I am so sorry," he breathed while pinching the bridge of his nose. "She's had nothing but misery, since her mother's disappearance and her father sold her to Ross Diablo."

"Have you ever been treated like that, General?"

"No."

"Nuff said, then."

"I must go, Kent is returning. Please deliver this to the Chancellor." He held out a heavy white envelope that bore the crest of the Earth sprite King.

"I'll give it to him, to honor a past friendship," I said, slipping it into my purse. When I turned to find the deodorant Cassie wanted, Rob slipped away.

Cassie

"Pizza's awesome," I bit off the point of a slice and chewed with satisfaction.

"We asked for extra everything you wanted," Gina grinned as she unloaded the bag containing her med supplies into her kit.

Two other bags, containing the items on my list, lay on the kitchen counter. I'd take them to my bathroom when I finished eating. Surely Parke knew to pack for Hotlanta, when he put clothes together for both of us.

"Pizza is good; so is the Scotch," Cliff lifted his glass in a toast to Gina.

"Kent got the Scotch; you can thank him next time you see him," she said.

"I'd like for him to come with us to Atlanta," Cliff said. "I think I can wangle a leave of absence and pay his salary while he's gone."

"Have you mentioned it to him? He didn't say anything to me."

"I asked him not to until I could get clearance from his boss."

"It would be nice to have him close by," Gina agreed.

"I may be pulling others in as bodyguards, too. I'm going through a list of volunteers now."

"Demon, werewolf and otherwise?"

"Yes. I sent the word out earlier today to Packmasters, Princes and Princesses. I outlined lists of requirements and the types we'd like to hire. Names came pouring in shortly after."

"Did Parke get the memo?"

"He was on the list. He made a few suggestions of his own. The property is on three acres and part of it is wooded. We'll need three shifts of guards. Vamps, of course, are the most desirable for graveyard shifts."

"No pun intended, I'm sure," I said.

"Are you dismissing my tendency to do just that?"

"Why no," I teased. "Why ever would I do that?"

"Is Parke bringing your swimsuit? There's a huge pool behind the house," Gina said.

"I have no idea what he's bringing, and I'm really too tired to call and give him a list of clothes that he can't find," I replied.

"We'll get what you need that he doesn't bring," Cliff soothed.

Zedarius

So they were going to Atlanta. I stood outside the kitchen window, hidden behind a spell and listening to their plans. I still had a spell around the perimeter of this property; I'd place another one in Atlanta. And, while Cliff was eating in the kitchen, now was a good time to steal inside his office for information on the new location.

I could get there in advance and set up as many protection spells as I wanted, without their knowledge. Whether they knew it or not, we were all targets of the next wave of attacks, and it paid to be as well-guarded as possible.

Zedarius?

I froze. I hadn't heard that voice in a very long time. Coming to me now meant only one thing—the limits placed on Shakkor Agdah's power were unraveling further. Two of us awake at once was a strong warning. Three would mean the situation was dire.

Four of us awake meant the destruction of the bridge connecting Earth IV to Earth III was the only answer to saving those remaining worlds.

Yosuke? I responded.

Surely you feel the unraveling, he sent.

I do. Much has happened, my friend. Tell me where I can find you.

Meet me at the always open restaurant on the eastern edge of the city of Tuscaloosa. I am there, now. They do not have decent tea. Yosuke sent an image of a pancake restaurant off the highway.

I will be there shortly, I told him. I had information to acquire, first.

"I have never dreamed of such—that the population of fire demons would be destroyed, or that one could survive the immolation."

"I helped gather her sparks, but she may have come back together eventually on her own. I cannot say that for certain, but the strength was there."

"How long did she burn?"

"Two days."

Yosuke sat back against the leatherette booth, while a thoughtful expression touched his features. "Quite remarkable," he nodded. "I wish to meet her."

"You have an advantage," I grumbled. "She doesn't know you, yet."

"Ah. The betrayal," he nodded. "As this is the first time anything like this has occurred, I imagine it is quite enervating."

"Before, I grieved and moved on, considering the necessity of it in my mind. Things are very different, this time."

"Because we need her, do we not?"

"We do. She brought the sprite kingdoms together and devised a way to remove a threat through them. The method was quite effective; we should build upon that innovation to find a way to eliminate Shakkor Agdah, should they step upon the ground."

"Explain this method, and then tell me how she managed to get water and earth to speak to one another."

"It's rather complicated, so I'll start from the beginning."

Parke

"Louise is interning at an animal hospital in Bellevue, as of two days ago," I answered Daniel's question. "She has an apartment, and two rock demon guards," I added.

He considered my answer for several seconds before nodding his acceptance. "Where are we on getting Trey to help us?" Daniel asked his next question.

"He's on board, and the Council is sending one vamp with him and two others after we arrive in Atlanta. Cliff says the wine cellar is more than large enough for four beds, two on each end."

"Three acres guarded by four vamps at night? Sounds good. I hope it's enough."

"The Council says they can supply more if they're needed, but I believe Trey is the one they'll depend on to tell them that."

"Then I figure the supernatural FBI and the Council will expect updates on information as it comes in," Daniel sighed. "I'd do the same in their shoes."

"That's the idea—to keep them informed. Are you packed and ready to go?"

"Yeah. I had to buy a few things—when we were in Alabama last time, it was wintertime and the weather was close to what I'm used to. I'm not prepared for Alabama or Georgia in the middle of summer."

"I had to repack after Mom reminded me of that," I confessed. "And I had to go through Cassie's stuff a second time."

"Well, I'm going to turn in," Daniel ran a hand through his hair. "We have an early flight."

"Yeah." I didn't mention what worried me the most—would Cassie be comfortable sleeping with me, or would she ask for a separate room?

Zedarius

Yosuke and I took our time laying perimeter spells around the property in Atlanta, leaving out a set perimeter of lawn and the portion where automobiles would drive in to park. Those would be set and modified for recognizable vehicles once Cassie and her entourage arrived. Yosuke and I would know if anyone crossed onto the property who shouldn't.

We'd discussed the fourth pyramid, too. Like me, he'd double-checked it, making sure it was still safely buried.

Cassie had the third one; Shakkor Agdah held the first and second. They could have found a way to destroy them—they were hidden behind so many dark spells that I couldn't feel their pulse any longer.

All four were necessary to keep Shakkor Agdah fully in check. Now, two were expected to do the work of all four, and we'd seen already how they'd gotten around that limitation.

"Tell me more about the ice demons connected to the fire demon," Yosuke said after we'd finished our last spells.

"Murderous miscreants. I've considered tracking them."

"If the situation here is contained, I'd suggest you look for them, too. It could perhaps ease your way into rejoining the fire demon's forces."

"I hadn't considered that," I admitted.

"I'm here to help," Yosuke gave me a rare smile.

Rob

Will's spell hadn't been altered to keep me out. I studied Cassie through the kitchen window. She looked gaunt, just as Gina said. I'd follow them to Atlanta, too; part of the grounds was just that—ground, and I could find any of them who stepped upon it.

I'd pass the information to Averill, too. Perhaps he'd notify the other sprite kingdoms, so they could keep an eye on her. At least

Averill and his son were speaking again, even if it was stilted conversation more often than not.

Re-Anne's frostiness had also thawed somewhat. Most likely due to the guilt that gnawed at all of us after Cassie's near-death.

Of course, we hadn't known it was a near-death for three months. Earth sprite scholars were already searching records and writing new ones regarding this miracle and wanted more than anything to speak with Cassie and the wizard, to glean firsthand information.

They kept asking me if Will did anything different with his spell, or whether Cassie was responsible for her own recovery. If that were true, they wanted to delve into the matter, to find the difference between her and so many other fire demons before her.

I doubted Cassie was in the proper state of mind to answer their questions. I jumped when I heard Will's voice in my head. *Sprite, we need to talk*, he said.

About what? I kept my reply even; I had no desire to let him know he'd startled me.

About Dalton and Morton King, and how their capture could put us back in the Chancellor's good graces.

That possibility hit me like a brick wall. *That's a wonderful idea. Good thinking.*

It wasn't my idea. Yosuke came up with it.

Oh, no. A second wizard had awakened. That meant even more bindings on Shakkor Agdah's power were loosening.

Then we should get on the trail of those two quickly. Where can I find you, and where were they last seen?

The last I heard was New Orleans, but I wasn't interested in tracking them while I was there recently.

Understood. Is there any place in particular where you'd like to meet?

Meet me at the Rue des Morts *cemetery tomorrow at sundown.*

I'll be there.

~

Cassie

A part of me didn't want to see Parke. Another part wanted to run somewhere and hide—from him, from Alabama, from Shakkor Agdah and from my murderous relatives. Mostly I felt uncomfortable, as if my skin no longer fit what was left of me after the incident with Will.

"The full moon is in three days," Cliff pointed out. He'd found me standing on the back porch of the house, staring at the lake behind it. He was right; the moon was certainly nearing full as it shone across the water. I merely hadn't paid attention until now.

"Cliff, I hope there's a safe place for you to run on the full moon," I turned toward him. Only then did I realize I was hugging myself, as if attempting to keep my soul inside me, rather than winging its way into the atmosphere.

"We change locations every time, now," he said, his voice low. "We don't need more surprises. I've already made arrangements for after the move to Atlanta."

"Yeah. I get that. I think I've had my fill of death—mine and others," I admitted.

"*Study the past if you would define the future*," Cliff quoted. "That's not mine—Confucius said it."

"Will is the only one I know who can tell me about the past fire demons, and I really don't want to talk to him again. Ever."

"That is for sure a fucked-up way of dealing with an enemy—deliberately sacrificing your friends every time, rather than looking for a new way to defeat them." Cliff's words ended with a growl.

"The sprite kingdoms may have the information, too, but I don't want to ask them, either."

"See my previous complaint," Cliff said.

"Yeah."

"Well, I'm off to bed. I have a few things to do before the Chancellor gets here tomorrow. Good-night, Cassie. It's good to have you back."

Cliff

I stopped by my office to get my phone before heading to bed. I had a missed text. With mixed feelings, I opened it, because it was from Rob.

I know you never wanted to hear from me again, but I thought you should know that the wizard and I are now hunting Morton and Dalton King. If you have current information, I'd be glad to have it—Rob.

Before I could stop myself, I replied.

South of the border, last I heard. If you find either of those bastards, we need questions answered.

Understood, his reply came swiftly. *Will keep you advised. How is Cassie?*

It took me a while to respond. *Lost,* I finally tapped out. *Trying to get her help.*

I'm sorry. Have no way to make this right.

"You're damn right about that," I growled at the screen before shutting the phone off.

Parke

Destiny and I are coming with you. Have already made reservations on same flight. The text from my mother as I was getting ready for bed shocked the hell out of me.

"Dammit," I cursed before dialing her number. If she wanted to text instead of coming in person, then I'd one-up her and call.

"She needs people around her that she knows and loves," Mom snapped at me rather than saying hello. "Destiny is her sister and is currently out of school. We can stay for a week or two, then come home if we have to."

"Like she doesn't know and love me?" I asked. I caught sight of my face in a cheval mirror in my bedroom; my eyes were going dark. Working to calm my temper so my rock demon wouldn't tear the house down, I added, "Mom, it could be dangerous for you and Destiny. I think you're safer here."

"I disagree. I doubt we're safe anywhere, nowadays."

"Fine. Did you make reservations for Jerry, too?" I named the rock demon who guarded the house at night.

"I did."

"Then fine. Go if you want to."

"I will."

"I said fine."

"Fine."

"Mom, the full moon is in three days," I reminded her.

"I know that. I suspect we'll be going wherever it is you and Cassie go."

With great effort, I kept my fist from crushing the phone in my hand. "All right. We'll discuss this tomorrow."

"Good." Mom ended the call, and not a second too soon.

"Damn," I rumbled before texting Cliff. He'd need to know that three more were coming with me.

～

Cassie

I just got a text from Parke, Cliff texted me. *Your sister and mother-in-law are coming with him. Seems they really want to see you.*

Tears came; I stifled a sob at the thought of seeing Destiny. Yes, I knew it was dangerous for her to be anywhere near me, but I so wanted to see her.

Thank you, I replied to Cliff's text, through blurred vision. *I'll be so glad to see them both.*

I thought so. Get some sleep; they'll be here soon enough.

Sleep would be welcome, but I doubted it would come soon, if at all. Maybe the dull roar of a television turned low would help. Lifting the remote from the nightstand, I flipped it on. A late-night talk show host was making political jokes during his stand-up section of the program. I tuned it out—mostly it was the same sort of thing as was always done.

Until the image shifted to a local Birmingham news station. "We have just received confirmation that the Lieutenant Governor and his family, who were on vacation at their cabin on Lewis Smith Lake, are now dead. The bodies were discovered earlier today by a bodyguard returning from a scheduled weekend vacation. The area has been sealed and quarantined, with only investigators in HAZMAT suits allowed in or out. An unconfirmed source says it may be the same disease that affected so many others during the massive prison breaks in March."

I was out the bedroom door and shouting Cliff's name in seconds.

CHAPTER 3

assie

"We need to ask questions, that's why," Cliff struggled to keep his voice civil as he spoke with someone on the phone. "Let me speak with the Governor."

I'd found him in the kitchen with a cup of coffee in one hand, his phone in the other. He looked as if he'd gotten as much sleep as I did, which wasn't much.

Silently, I went to the fridge to grab the carton of eggs and a package of bacon. Cliff would be hungry, whether I was or not.

When the Governor of Alabama came on the line, Cliff put the call on speaker.

"Cliff, you think you can help us with this?" the Governor asked.

"I may be able to, yes."

"What do you need from me?"

"I need to ask the guard questions. I assume he's in quarantine right now?"

"He is, but you can talk to him through a speaker. He's at a hospital in Birmingham."

"Good. I have a couple others who'll be with me when I go; one or two from the FBI and maybe someone from Homeland Security."

33

"How soon can you get there? We need answers fast," the Governor sighed. "We're in the process of rounding up anybody who had any contact with the family two or three days before. The emergency lines are swamped with calls, and this time of year, that lake area is packed with tourists. For now, we're advising everyone to stay indoors, but we may have to evacuate the entire area."

"Has the guard shown any signs of the disease?"

"Not yet. He says he didn't touch anything, but we have to be sure."

"Understood. I'll let you know when I head that way."

"Call my private number—I'll have it sent to you," the Governor said. "If this is a new outbreak, we're in for a rough time. A couple of friends tell me you were in on getting this shut down the last time."

"I was, but the enemy may have upped their game in this round. I'll keep you advised."

"Thank you, Cliff."

"You're welcome, Governor." Cliff ended the call with a sigh.

"Eggs and bacon will be ready in a minute," I told him, as Gina slouched into the kitchen, covering a yawn.

"I love you," Gina hugged me while I attempted to pour a cup of coffee for her.

"I love you, too. Sit down, I'm cooking today."

"Are you packed up?" Cliff turned to Gina as I plated food.

"Yeah. Took me half the night, but I'm ready to go."

"We're ah, moving today, right after the Chancellor arrives," Cliff informed me. "He called late last night and said it didn't make sense to unpack for a single day. Besides, we need to be on the road to Birmingham soon; he's flying there to meet us, so he can help question the guard."

"I'm pretty much ready, too, I guess," I said, setting plates in front of Gina and Cliff, before taking a chair and sitting with my cup of coffee in hand.

"You're not hungry?" Gina frowned at me.

"Not right now. I'll eat later."

"Don't let this upset you," Cliff pointed his fork at me. "Besides, you need all the strength you can muster. Eating helps."

"I don't know how to deal with Parke," I blurted.

"Talk to him, that's all you have to do. If you're not comfortable with anything else, then tell him that." Cliff wiped up a bit of over-easy egg with his toast before stuffing it in his mouth.

"You're no longer Princess of Alabama—you can set aside the annulment," Gina said.

"I'm not sure I want to."

Cliff's head jerked up and he blinked at me. "It can be sorted," he said after a few seconds, before going back to his food.

"Maybe that's something to discuss with the doctor," Gina sighed. "A third party, with no outside interest."

"Yeah." I turned my coffee cup on the table, toying with it while trepidation grew. I did and didn't want to see Parke. I was looking forward to seeing Destiny and Parke's mother, though. What did that mean?

"Trey and two other vamps flew to Atlanta last night," Cliff said. "They'll be waiting to hear from us. I've left a message for Trey to meet us in Birmingham to talk to the guard, so it may be late before we get to the house. Fortunately, the owners are leaving a cook and a housekeeper, plus the groundskeepers on for us, so that shouldn't be a concern. I told them we had someone to help the cook and enough staff, otherwise."

"At least it's only a two-hour drive or so between Birmingham and Atlanta," Gina pointed out. "Still, with the vamps coming that way after nightfall, it could turn into a really long night."

"I expect it will." Cliff sipped his coffee.

Parke

At least there were enough seats in first class for Mom and Destiny's last-minute reservations. As it turned out, this was Destiny's first plane trip and she was unusually wide-eyed and mostly silent while she took everything in.

It was ungodly early, too, so I was thankful the first-class flight attendants were already pouring coffee while the plane was loading. Mom and Destiny were given orange juice at their request; they could sleep on the trip to Birmingham.

I had work to do, as did Jon, and Daniel, out of habit, would be awake and guarding us. Peter and Jerry, the rock demon guards, were in business class right behind first class. They'd be awake and watchful, too, throughout the flight.

Cliff's text regarding the quarantined guard in a Birmingham hospital came during the drive to the airport; we'd arranged to meet him at the hospital to ask the guard questions.

He'd also arranged to have Trey come for the questioning as quickly as he could get there after sundown. I would know if the guard was lying, but I couldn't force him to tell the truth as Trey could.

So far, there were no signs of the disease in the man, so I was cautiously optimistic about his truthfulness. All the other guards were dead from the disease.

Either way, I'd know the truth when I saw him. I was a truth demon, after all. I merely needed Trey to place compulsion to ensure we got the truth from the man, and for the official record.

Behind the curtain in the first-class galley, our flight attendants were busy getting things ready to serve us breakfast once we were in the air and at a proper elevation. I waited for the announcement telling us the plane was loaded and we'd be on our way soon.

I wanted to see Cassie. I wanted to put my hands on her and reassure myself that she was real—that I hadn't spoken to a ghost. I had her purse, wallet, cell phone and the broken pyramid in my briefcase, which was shoved into the overhead bin. She'd asked for those things.

At least I hadn't deactivated her phone; I'd added her to my plan after we married, and I'd never changed that. She'd have to charge it up to use it; I hadn't bothered.

"Destiny, is your phone turned off, baby?" I heard Mom ask.

"It's on airplane mode," Destiny replied.

Kids. Destiny knew as much or more about this stuff than any of us, even if it were her first flight.

A flight attendant made the announcement that the door was closing and we'd be taking off, soon. I leaned back in my seat and sipped coffee, hoping we'd have an easy time in the air and a good tail wind to send us to Alabama.

~

Cassie

"It's an hour drive to Birmingham, and maybe twenty minutes more to get to Saint Christopher's Hospital," Cliff said as I dropped my single bag in the foyer, alongside his three and Gina's four—one of hers was filled with medical supplies.

Two of Cliff's werewolves were scheduled to meet Parke at the airport; he was bringing Jon and Daniel, plus two rock demons who'd serve as guards, and his mother, Kate, and Destiny.

Would we have enough room for all of them?

"Stop worrying," Cliff said.

"How did you know?"

"I recognize the look."

"Fine. I'll stop worrying."

"Kent's here," Gina checked her phone when it buzzed. "He can help with the bags."

Cliff decided to take his shiny, new black Escalade for this trip; it would hold us and all our luggage, too.

Kent walked in the door as Cliff lifted his briefcase and largest bag. I pulled up my small duffle and borrowed purse, which had little in it except lotion, lip balm, a comb and a small mirror. Parke was bringing my wallet, phone and the pyramid.

"You okay?" Kent studied me for a moment.

"Yeah. As okay as I can be," I told him. If he wanted to know more, Gina could fill him in on the trip to Birmingham. Weariness had draped itself over me like a heavy blanket, attempting to stifle any desire to do anything other than what was absolutely necessary. That included talking about how I felt.

"Let's go," Cliff sighed and stepped out the front door first.

~

New Orleans

Rob

"You picked quite the place here," I told Will. I wasn't being complimentary. The crypt where he'd kept Cassie was so old it was sinking into the ground, and only a few flakes of white paint remained on it, making it look as if it were covered in lichen.

The top of it came to a rounded point, with the name Grant-Allen near the apex. Will touched the side; I stepped back when smoke poured through a crack, inadvertently bumping into the Mays crypt beside it.

"What are you doing?" I demanded, silently apologizing to the Mays family for running into their final resting place.

Will wasn't done, though. The smoke became so thick, I couldn't see the McDonald name on the crypt opposite Grant-Allen. Wondering if coughing and waving smoke away would do any good at all, I settled for crossing arms over my chest and waiting for the wizard to finish whatever confounded spell he was casting.

"I had to cleanse the crypt of any sign we were there," he blinked at me. "Now, everything has been returned to its proper place and there are no signs that it was ever occupied by anyone other than the Grant-Allens."

"Where to now?" I asked, wondering if he had other business in a New Orleans cemetery besides this.

"There's a house on the corner of Welker and Morgan to visit. I believe our quarry may have stayed there for a while. If they've gone to Mexico or farther south, getting any sort of evidence from them will help me with a location spell."

"You mean hair or fingernails?"

"Yes, if there's anything like that. Even clothing they've worn can be a huge help."

"Sounds easy enough."

"Except for the Ice and Water demons who live there permanently."

"Well, why didn't you say that in the beginning?"

"Are you annoyed?"

"Hell, yes."

"Ah. Good. With your help, we may be able to incapacitate both while we search their home."

"Now I remember why I was never close friends with a wizard in the past."

"Why is that?"

"They're fucking crazy."

Instead of being angry, or firing back with an insult, Will laughed. "Astute observation," he clapped me on the back. "Come on, we'll search the house and then go for lunch."

"Now you're talking," I growled and followed him toward the cemetery gates.

"This is it?" I stared in disbelief at the house on the corner of Welker and Morgan. It still bore water marks from the last hurricane that flooded the city, and that was years ago.

"I never said it was a mansion, and probably looks worse on the inside. At least you won't be destroying a manicured lawn when you make a hole in the back yard."

"I'm making a hole?" I tapped my chest in disbelief.

"One deep enough to force them to work hard to climb out of it."

"Do you know how close the water table is beneath the soil?"

"You haven't checked this area in more than a century, have you?" Will frowned deeply at me. "You don't know that all those levees and the water pumping systems they've added are causing the land beneath the city to dry up more than it should, and has resulted in the city's gradual sinking? Every day, it's falling a little more below sea level. A good half or more is already there. I figure you have a hundred and fifty feet of ground—of one type or another, before you hit rock."

"How long do you think it'll take them to climb out of there, if they go full demon?" I demanded.

"At least half an hour if I replace the dirt over their heads."

"Right. How do you propose we get them to fall in the hole to begin with?"

"Dig the hole and leave the last few inches of topsoil intact."

"Have you been watching too many action movies recently?"

"I thought all movies had action. That's why they call them movies."

"Look—never mind. Let's get this over with."

"You look like hell," Will whispered.

"You try digging a hundred-and-fifty-foot hole big enough to accommodate two demons in their larger forms," I hissed at the wizard. "How are you getting them out of the house?"

Will and I had hidden behind an untrimmed hedge at the back of the yard, after I'd finished the hole. I hoped he had a spell to clean my clothing; I was covered in mud and stray rootlets.

"I'll set a fire over the hole," Will said. "Right about now." Lifting his hands, he cast the spell, causing a grass fire to spring up directly over the hole.

We waited.

Nothing happened.

"They're either playing video games or they're the most inattentive demons I've ever heard of," I drawled.

"Then I'll make noise," Will said. Moments later, you'd have thought a banshee screamed in the back yard, the shriek was so loud.

Still nothing.

"What the hell?" Will muttered. "Go to the front door. I'll check the back."

"You want me to knock and tell them their backyard is on fire?'

"It's as good as anything else I can think of. Here." He waved a hand again and cleaned my clothing.

"Right. Because I need to look good when I'm jumped by a demon."

"Tell me you don't have your own ways to deal with dirt and with demons."

"Fine. I do. I just wanted you to see how hard I worked to make that hole."

"Duly noted. Go to the front door. Now."

Twenty seconds later, I was at the front door, ringing the doorbell. When there was no answer, I rang again and knocked. Still there was no answer.

"They're not going to answer," Will opened the front door and stepped aside to let me in. "They're dead."

I followed him into the kitchen, where ice had shattered across the tile floor. Most of it had melted already and had mixed with the water from the water demon.

"Who do you suppose did this?" My eyes met Will's.

"Two ice demons could have," Will said.

"Do you suppose?" I didn't finish my question.

"I think they're back in the states, if that's what you were about to say."

"Then we need to look for the evidence we came here for."

"Check the closets. They had to hang clothes somewhere. I'll check the bedrooms and under the sofa."

The closet in the back bedroom yielded the best results, because two of the shirts smelled like gasoline. Had they worn those shirts to destroy Cassie's aunt's house?

"I have something," I yelled to Will.

"Good. I have hair, I think."

Thirty minutes later, with the clothes and other items stuffed in a small grocery tote, Will and I sat in a restaurant to have lunch.

"How long will it take to get a lock on those two?"

"It depends."

"On what?" I asked as our server set plates of food in front of us.

"On whether they're hidden by Shakkor Agdah or not."

My hands stilled; the fork dangled from my fingers for several seconds. "You think that's why they're back, don't you?"

"Why else would the come back? Why else would they kill friends who'd hidden them from those on their trail? It makes no sense."

"Tying up loose ends?"

"Among other things. Shakkor Agdah wants those responsible for the big blowup. That's me, you, Cliff, the Chancellor, and, if they find out Cassie's still alive, they'll really be hunting for her. That means pulling in every slave they have and setting them on our trail."

"We never found out who was in charge of Shakkor Agdah last time. We're just as much in the dark this time, too. Any suggestions?" I stabbed the barbecued brisket on my plate as if it were an enemy.

"And killing off a politician in Georgia by giving him their disease is a good way of pulling us back in, isn't it?"

"Except they don't know we're scattered, but that may not hold true for long."

"Scattered may mean easier to kill. Putting us all together may be the same. What's the answer, Will?"

"We are stronger together." He tore a roll in half and buttered it.

"How do we accomplish that, then?"

"Stay on the trail of the ice demons. That could ultimately result in a reunion of sorts, especially if we let the others know. It would be better if we haul in Morton and Dalton when we meet."

"And promise never to sacrifice someone we love again?"

"Yes. Definitely that."

"Good, because I can't go through that again."

"I admit, I don't have the stomach for it myself."

"Add that to the fact that Cassie will see you coming from a mile away next time."

"There won't be a next time. I've made that promise. I'll sacrifice myself before I'll do that to her again. There's something else you should know, too."

"What's that?"

"The second wizard who's awake and stepping into the fray. He knows everything that happened, including the part you and I played in it."

"What's his name? You think we can hold the line with two in this fight?"

"I have no idea, and he calls himself Yosuke."

"Sounds Asian."

"He looks Asian, too."

"I know you can change your features to suit yourself, or to fit in," I shifted on my chair.

"That is correct, but at times, we choose to resemble what we admire in humans, too. If you met Yosuke, you'd swear he was an ancient philosopher."

"Where is he, and why isn't he here helping us?"

"He has made himself a member of the groundskeeping staff at the house the others have chosen to rent in Atlanta."

"Why are they renting a house there?"

"Because they believe they are targets where they are, which is likely correct, and also because Cassie is in need of a, ah, therapist, I think you call them. The werewolf is recommending a friend who lives in Atlanta to provide that service."

"I know about the therapist. It worries me."

"As it does me. We need her strong—it was her strength that carried us through last time."

"Well, I've never come back from the dead. I suppose it would cause huge problems, which could take years of therapy," I breathed, suddenly becoming more alarmed than I already was.

"Calm yourself, General. We have plans to prepare, and frantic participants make terrible decisions."

～

Birmingham, Alabama
   Gina

"We just got to the hospital. Cliff and Cassie have already gone up to the isolation ward to talk with the security guard." Trust Rob to pick the worst time to call; I had to walk into the ladies' room to answer my phone.

"I have news, and it isn't good." Rob ignored everything I'd just said.

"What news is that?"

"Dalton and Morton are back in the U.S., and they killed the ice demon and water demon they holed up with in New Orleans."

"How long ago?"

"Early this morning, according to Will. We think they may be heading back to Alabama, at the ah, urgings of Shakkor Agdah. We'll make an attempt to follow them, but wanted you to know that they're probably looking for revenge—for all those who died when Cassie— well, when she almost died with them."

"This isn't good, and now it's looking more and more like a trap," I said. "They know we'll investigate the deaths from the disease they spread, so we're likely walking right into their waiting arms. I have to tell Cliff about this."

"Good. Tell him what we know so far and that we're tracking Morton and Dalton. If we find them, we'll do what we can to make a capture, but I can't guarantee anything if it comes down to a fight."

"I understand that. Look, I have to go. The sooner Cliff knows about this, the better I'll feel."

"Then go. I'll call if there's anything new on this end."

"Thanks, Rob."

"Any time."

Cassie

"He doesn't look sick to me," Cliff said as he and I walked up to the window where the speaker was located. On the door, a biohazard sign warned anyone away who wasn't authorized to enter the room. Inside the room, we could see Nate Millburn sitting in a chair watching television. So far, he hadn't noticed our arrival.

"He doesn't look sick to me, either," I sighed. "I think he's probably telling the truth."

"I want to know where the Lieutenant Governor went before this happened, and who he saw, talked to, touched, whatever," Cliff waved an arm. "We could have more cases of the disease out there and we haven't found them, yet."

"I know."

"We have a problem," Gina rushed toward us with Kent right behind her.

"What problem? Have they found more victims?" Cliff asked, his body stiffening, as if he were ready for a fight.

"Not from the disease. It looks like Dalton and Morton King are back in the country, and they killed an ice demon and a water demon in New Orleans early this morning. My ah, source says that they may be heading toward Alabama, at the request of Shakkor Agdah."

"Source?" Cliff frowned, and his eyes narrowed as he studied Gina. I was curious, too, but it appeared that Cliff had suspicions where I had none.

"Well, uh," Gina suddenly sounded uncomfortable.

"Don't—I think I know," Cliff stopped her with a gesture. "We'll talk about this later. Anything else to report?"

"That the attack on the Lieutenant Governor, and the Kings coming this way could mean they're laying a trap for us, to take revenge."

"Fuck," Cliff muttered.

"I guess it's a good time to leave Alabama, then," Trey walked in with another vampire behind him.

"Not before we talk to that one in there," Cliff pointed toward the only occupant of the isolation ward.

"Have you heard from the Chancellor?" Trey asked as he and the other vamp scrutinized Nate Millburn.

"On the way," Cliff replied. "Should be here anytime. We've had news that the Kings are back in the states and headed this way, most likely."

"That's not good news," the new vamp spoke for the first time. "Grim Norton," he introduced himself. "I'm with the NSA. Trey and I've worked together before."

I couldn't decide whether to ask him about his name or just snicker. As it turned out, I did neither, because Parke chose that moment to walk out of the elevator and come toward us at a near-run.

"Parke, I," he hit me like a storm, and his mouth was on mine before I could say anything else. I thought his arms would crush me before I could go to prelim.

"Oh, lord." Cliff's words were the only ones I heard as Parke showed me how much he'd missed me.

CHAPTER 4

*C*liff

"Trey and Grim had to place compulsion on three nurses and one doctor after that little display," I lifted my cup of coffee and drank. When the hug-and-kiss-fest was over, we'd finally gotten around to questioning Nate Millburn, who'd told us the Lieutenant Governor had played a few rounds of golf the same day he'd left for the scheduled three-day vacation. Currently, we were in the process of getting security footage from the golf resort involved.

"Now," I locked eyes with Gina. "How many times have you spoken to Rob?"

"Twice," she admitted. "He found me in the pharmacy when I went to get a few things for Cassie the other night. Then he called me shortly before I came looking for you—to tell you what he and Will found out about Dalton and Morton."

"He and Will are tracking the Kings." I'd known that already, but thought they were on their way to Mexico or places farther south. I considered the killings for a moment. "Why did they kill their friends—Dalton and Morton, that is?"

"I don't really know," Gina shook her head.

"Why did the sprite and the wizard decide to go after Dalton and Morton in the first place?" Trey asked.

"I think they want to make amends," Gina blushed under his scrutiny. "Rob really feels the separation. I don't know what Will feels. I haven't spoken to him and don't intend to."

"Does Rob understand that's a steep hill to climb?" I asked.

"He knows you, Cliff—probably better than anybody. He understands that."

"What about the water demon and ice demon the Kings killed?" Trey asked. "Were they involved with Shakkor Agdah in any way?"

He and Grim were only pretending to have coffee in the diner we'd chosen close to the hospital. Parke had taken Cassie with him; they were heading to Atlanta while the rest of us sat here and discussed the events of the day.

"I think those two only helped the Kings when they got to New Orleans earlier in the year; I have no idea why they'd kill them now," I shrugged. "It makes no sense."

"Unless they refused to help them again, perhaps?" Grim lifted an eyebrow. That was more expression than most people got from a vamp, so it intrigued me.

"That could be it, I suppose," I agreed. "Help, money, looking at them cross-eyed—the Kings aren't picky about their reasons for killing."

"Hard to understand why they're not friends with everybody," Grim noted.

Had a vamp just cracked a joke? I must have blinked several times before I snorted a laugh.

"You'll get used to it," Trey deadpanned.

Cassie

"Do they have Mellow Mushroom pizza in Atlanta?" Destiny asked me. She, Kate and I sat in the back of the van Parke had rented, while

Jon, Parke's assistant, and Pete and Jerry, the two rock demon guards, sat in the middle row. Daniel drove; Parke rode shotgun.

Destiny hadn't let go of my hand since I'd gotten in the van. She and Kate asked questions at first, most of them the kind I couldn't answer. I couldn't recall anything except dying and then waking up in a crypt, and both those things still troubled me.

"I think they have more than one," I squeezed her fingers before pulling my hand away and putting an arm around her for a hug.

"Good. I haven't had any in so long."

"We'll put 'em on speed dial," I told her.

"We're twenty minutes away from the house," Parke repeated the navigation system's announcement. "Does anyone need anything from a convenience store before we get there?"

"Do we have stuff in the fridge?" Destiny snuggled closer against me.

"I think Cliff said someone would stock essentials. Milk, coffee, bread—that kind of thing."

"Good. I want a glass of milk and then I want to sleep for two days."

"We'll get you fixed up," I said. "Nineteen minutes and counting."

She was asleep against me when Daniel pulled the van into the drive at the back of the massive house. A garage door lifted, revealing a man who waited for us to pull inside and park.

"I can carry Destiny," Peter, one of the rock demons, offered. I nodded; he got out of his seat and pulled it forward so he could reach her.

The man who'd opened the garage door for us was talking to Parke and Daniel when I stepped out of the van. He was Asian, I think. After studying him for a moment, I turned away and straightened my clothes; I felt unsettled and frumpy after the day's journey.

Kate did the same after Jerry, the second rock demon guard, helped her out of the van. "I'll take you to the bedrooms they've set up," the Asian man said while leading Parke, Jon and Daniel in my direction. "I'm Yosuke," he introduced himself to me and held out his right hand. I shook with him, then took Parke's offered arm to walk into the house.

We got Destiny settled in a bedroom first; Kate and I removed her shoes and socks before covering her up; she was sleeping the sleep of the young and exhausted. I couldn't recall when I'd slept like that last, or whether I'd ever done it.

Kate took the bedroom across the hall; she only wanted to get in bed, she told us. The master bedroom came next, and that's where Parke delivered me before going with Daniel and Yosuke to collect bags from the van and Jon went looking for a room suitable for Parke's office.

I imagined Parke and Daniel had questions for Yosuke, too, and I didn't want to interfere with that. Parke was a truth demon; he'd know if anyone were lying to him.

I was too tired to be interested in anything they talked about; I just wanted to crawl into bed and hoped my case of the willies would go away. After learning that Dalton and Morton were back in the country and probably hunting for Cliff and Parke, the unsettled feeling wouldn't leave.

"Here you go," Parke was back, carrying two large bags himself, with Daniel bringing a third into the massive suite. "Your purse, phone and the pyramid are in this one," he patted the one on his left after setting it down. "I think Mom put shampoo, brushes, combs and pajamas in there, too."

"Thank you," I sighed. "Maybe having my own stuff will make me feel more like myself."

"Stop worrying, sweetheart," Parke stepped forward and took my face between his hands. "Right now, I feel like the luckiest person alive." He leaned in to give me a lingering kiss, then pulled away.

"Daniel and I want to talk to Yosuke," he said. "Get in bed, baby. You look exhausted."

"I will. I just want to sleep."

"I know. I'll be back after a while. I'll try not to wake you."

"All right."

I watched as he and Daniel left the suite, closing the door softly behind them. Then, I reached for the bag containing my pajamas. Time to go to bed.

～

Parke

"The housekeepers stay in the apartments over the garages," Yosuke explained. "They've stocked the refrigerator and pantry with staples, but they'll shop for anything else required by you and your guests."

"We'll have some night guards coming in; will that be a problem?" Daniel asked.

"Not at all. There's a small guard house at the back of the property, if they want to take breaks. I also have the alarm codes for the house and the keypad outside the garages." He handed Daniel a folded slip of paper. "These can be changed whenever you want."

My cell phone dinged with a text from Cliff. "They're here," I said.

"I'll show you the codes now, when I open the garage door for them," Yosuke said, taking a direct route from the kitchen to a hallway and then to a mudroom just off the space for the first of five garages. We'd parked in the first bay; Cliff was getting the second one.

Daniel and I watched as Yosuke tapped in the code, then hit the lift button for the second garage. We went through the door at the back of the bay; Cliff's headlights nearly blinded us as he drove into the space and parked his Escalade.

"Nice car," Yosuke breathed.

"Rain headed this way," Cliff said as he stepped out of the car. Other doors opened; Kent, Gina, Trey and Grim got out. "We'll get the bags," Grim offered with a wave. "The rest of you, go to bed. We've got this."

"Night guards?" Yosuke turned toward me.

"Yeah. Grim and Trey," I pointed out the proper ones. "Another van is coming with two more in thirty minutes or so. This is Gina, Kent, and this is Cliff," I introduced the others.

"Very pleased to meet you," Yosuke shook hands. "I'll show you to the bedrooms; you can make your choices from what's left."

"We'll share," Gina indicated Kent. I wasn't surprised.

"The cots in the wine cellar are for those two, and two others who haven't arrived yet," Cliff leaned his head toward Trey and Grim. "Since they're day sleepers."

"It's the quietest place in the house for that," Yosuke nodded.

"We'll handle the others when they get here, if you'd like to go to bed," Trey offered.

"Fine with me," I said and turned to go back in the house.

"I'll rent office furniture for you and Cliff tomorrow," Jon said. He'd met me in the kitchen, where Daniel and I were discussing where the rock demons and the werewolves would sleep.

"We need to have a talk, Jon," I told him. "You're about to be privy to information most humans will never know."

"Why are you talking about humans like you're not one?" Jon frowned.

"He's not," Cliff set his shaving kit on the kitchen island. "Neither am I."

"But," Jon began.

"Kid, you're not in danger," Cliff gruffed. "You're probably safer with Parke and the rest of us than with the neighbors next door, who *are* human. What we're about to tell you is the truth, and nothing but. Just bear in mind that without the folks currently in this house, every human in the country would be dead of that foul disease earlier this year."

"I ought to give you this now," Gina walked in and handed me a heavy envelope that bore the crest of the Earth sprite King. "May as well give him the whole picture while you're explaining things, huh?"

"You think Averill just wants more pizza?" Cliff deadpanned. I bit back a laugh.

❧

"Those guys—they're really vampires?" Jon wasn't sure what to do about myths that had suddenly become reality.

"They drink bagged blood. Stop worrying about it," Gina soothed. "I've been around vamps, werewolves, shapeshifters and demons all my life. I'm still in one piece, although I'm only half human."

"The only reason I'm telling you this now is because you have to be careful here, and make sure that you're never alone if you leave the property. Trust me, you're better off if Trey, Cliff or I are with you."

"You have a lock on your bedroom door," Cliff patted his shoulder. "You won't need it, though. You're safe and among friends."

Jon frowned his misgivings, but didn't say anything. "If you need to talk to somebody about this who *is* human, don't," Cliff added.

"What about my husband?"

"We'll consider him and decide whether we think he can keep secrets. Trust me—you're better off never breathing a word about this to anyone else."

We watched as he walked unsteadily toward his bed. "We're gonna have to place compulsion," Cliff mumbled.

"I'll get Trey," I nodded.

❧

Cassie

Parke was still asleep when I woke; the sun was rising on the Atlanta metro, and I was hungry. I had no idea when he'd come to bed the night before, so I slipped out of bed as quietly as I could and headed for the bathroom.

After going through the usual and throwing on clothes, I found Destiny and Kate in the kitchen, eating scrambled eggs and bacon at the massive island. The cook was cleaning up after making their breakfast. She turned, smiled at me and offered to make more eggs.

"I'll take it, and thank you," I told her. "I'm Cassie," I added.

"Beverly," she smiled at me. "You like your scrambled eggs soft-cooked or all the way done?"

"All the way," I said, liking her already. "Need help? I usually do this for myself."

"Nah—I heard you were recovering from a short illness," she waved a hand. Beverly's teeth were white against dark skin and her smile, with deep dimples, would light up any room. Her hair was pulled back in a tight, coiled braid, and she struck me as the kind of person who should be nominated for sainthood by somebody.

"I'm really okay, now," I told her. "Just a bit scrawnier than before, that's all. I'll pour my own coffee, since you're cooking."

"Help yourself," she said, leaning her head toward the corner counter where a coffee station had been arranged.

"She put cheese in my eggs," Destiny said as I found a mug and lifted the coffee pot to fill it.

"And you liked it," I teased her.

"They were awesome."

"I'm putting a grocery list together," Kate said. "If there's something you want, I'll add it. Beverly says we have an empty fridge and a big freezer in the butler's pantry, so we can fill those up if we want."

"Who's going to the store?" I asked after taking my first sip of coffee heaven.

"Gemma," Beverly said. "She loves shopping of any kind, so that's her job."

"I smell breakfast," Gina shuffled into the kitchen, only half-awake.

"Beverly is making," I told her. "Sit down, I'll bring your coffee."

Beverly didn't blink an eye as she set two plates of eggs and bacon on the island for us; Gina hadn't bothered to hide her spots from anyone. It made me wonder if Trey had been busy already.

"I'll bet you don't like the stares you get when you go out," Beverly set a glass of orange juice in front of Gina. Gina's head slowly rose until her eyes met Beverly's. "Mr. Trey told me things, and I told him some things, too, so he let me be."

"What things?" Gina breathed.

"About you folks, and I told him my brother-in-law is a werewolf.

Nice man—my sister loves him more than anything. Gemma, on the other hand," Beverly shrugged. "I figure she won't understand what anybody is talking about, because Trey told her to ignore it."

"Seriously? Your sister married a werewolf?" Jon's steps were hesitant as he walked into the kitchen.

"For twenty years. Let me tell you," Beverly waved her spatula for a moment. "I like Benjamin Stokes more than most humans I know."

"Have a seat, Jon," I told him. "I'll get you coffee. There's no need to treat anybody any different than you did before. We're actually civilized—at least most of us," I teased.

"Some family not included," Destiny pointed out.

"Who?" Jon looked ready to flee.

"Cassie and Destiny's father and grandfather," Kate told him. "Did you overhear any of the conversation about Morton and Dalton King?"

"I heard something, but had no idea what was going on," Jon sighed and settled on a barstool.

"Those two killed our mother and our aunt, I'm sure of it," I replied, setting a fresh cup of coffee near his hand. "They're homicidal ice demons, so stay the hell away from them if you can."

"Are you sure we're safe here?" Jon still wasn't convinced.

"You're as safe here as you can be anywhere," I told him. "We're not helpless, you know."

"Just let it sink in for a while," Beverly advised. "Stop worrying, and figure out how you can help, instead."

"We have video from the golf club the Lieutenant Governor visited before he died," Parke announced. He and Daniel walked in together, both looking rumpled and sleep-deprived.

"What did you find?" Kate asked.

"A woman and a possible dalliance," Daniel slumped onto a barstool and shook his head. "The FBI can't get an ID on the woman, and nobody remembers seeing her. She and the Lieutenant Governor left together, though. We have images from the parking lot, showing them getting in his vehicle together, while the two guards who were with him stayed behind.

"Then, an hour later, they show up again, the Lieutenant Governor drops her off, and he and the guards drive away. The woman walks out of camera range and disappears. All the camera images have been searched, and none of them picked her up again."

"Nobody remembers her being there?" I poured coffee for Daniel and Parke while Beverly fixed breakfast for them.

"The guards with him that day are dead, so they can't tell us anything," Parke grumped before sipping coffee.

"Did she ever touch grass—or the ground?" I asked.

"We're not calling the Earth sprite," Parke's stance was unrelenting.

"He owes us," I muttered and went back to my breakfast, which was getting cold. "They all owe us."

Parke

"I'm only saying that the wizard may be able to identify the woman," Daniel argued. "Cliff and Gina have Rob's number. We could call."

"What will that do to Cassie?" I demanded. "That we contacted the enemy?"

"I can send it to Rob, if you don't want to."

My rock demon wanted out—to smash things. Daniel was right.

And so was I.

Averill's letter, too, weighed on my mind; he promised help, in nearly any form, if it were needed.

Especially if Cassie needed it.

I thought about asking him to pay for her therapy, but discarded that idea. Averill said to contact him through Rob.

Of course.

"Find out where they are and send them the images if they're agreeable." I stalked off, considering where I could go to work out frustrations. The full moon was too close, and my rock demon wasn't pleased with the way things were going.

All I had to do, now, was keep this hidden from Cassie and Cliff;

they were the ones most severely betrayed by Rob and Will. Maybe I should ask for another, more suitable Earth sprite to work with us. Rob would be fuming if we passed that message to Averill through him.

Something to think about.

Too bad there wasn't another wizard to work with us—one who actually had a heart instead of a chunk of coal.

Robin

"I didn't expect to hear from you," I said when I answered Daniel's call. If anyone would contact me, I figured it would be Gina.

"We have our own set of problems to deal with," Daniel rumbled. "One of those is identifying a woman that even the FBI can't find."

"You have images, I take it?"

"Yes. We'd like you and the wizard to take a look. We think she may have had something to do with the Lieutenant Governor's death, but we're not sure what or how. If she had the disease, she's likely dead, now, but we really need to know how she got it."

"And where, no doubt," I agreed. "We'll take a look and let you know. Out of curiosity, where did this woman meet with the Lieutenant Governor?"

"A golf resort twenty miles from his cabin," Daniel replied. "Pleasant Hills Country Club," he rattled off the name.

"Not far from where we are," I mused.

"Where are you?"

"At the lake house outside Tuscaloosa. Will says Morton and Dalton were here recently."

"How recently? Did they damage anything?"

"Recently as in last night, and so far, we haven't found signs of damage to the house. The boat house, on the other hand, is a complete loss. Be grateful the groundskeeper is visiting out-of-state relatives after Cliff gave him vacation time. They'd have destroyed him with the boathouse if he'd been there."

"Did they burn it down?"

"They ah, froze inside all the cracks and worked their way outward —I imagine it was to illustrate their displeasure that the rest of you weren't dumb enough to stay there and wait for them."

"How remiss of us. Remind me to pay them back in kind."

"Only if we don't get to them first."

"Sprite, if you can take them down, I will dance at your wedding."

"That may be quite a wait on your part, then. We'll let you know if we determine anything about the woman, and keep you advised as to the continued health of Dalton and Morton King."

"You do that." Daniel ended the call. Seconds later, images showed up on my phone.

"What did he send?" Will stepped to my side to look at the photos of an attractive woman, dressed to lure a man to her side. She'd certainly lured the Lieutenant Governor; I saw the photos of her getting into his car.

"Oh," was all Will said as I thumbed through the images Daniel sent.

"What's that supposed to mean?" I demanded.

"Let's just say Shakkor Agdah found a way to drive the knife deeper. Sprite, if we can't find the Kings in the next twenty-four hours, then we need to travel to Atlanta with all haste."

Temperance Acres, Atlanta

Yosuke

The authorities believe the Shakkor Agdah woman to be dead, Zedarius informed me. *She likely won't wear the same disguise twice—that would be stupid.*

What if there are others? I responded. *Several females could cause just as much damage as the infected prisoners.*

I sincerely hope that's not the case. Even one female can do enough damage on her own. Vampires and Werewolves may recognize a Shakkor Agdah, but that depends on whether she masks her scent. The sprites may be able to discern one of her kind; an Earth sprite would, should she ever step on grass or ground within range. Air and water may be more helpful, but they need to know about her, first. Fire will only wound her—perhaps enough that one of ours could reach her and deliver her death.

Has Robin contacted Averill?

Yes, and sent images to his King. The distribution of this information must be faster than it has been in the past. If not, we will see masses of outbreaks, and many of those infected can be in very high positions.

Have you informed Daniel?

That's Rob's next call—to let them know what they're dealing with. I'm sure they'll want to go over those security videos again, just to make sure she didn't touch anyone else. If so, we could find more bodies and more people infected.

What about the Kings?

Rob and I plan to track them on the full moon tonight; we want to destroy them before they can do more harm. I have no doubt they are still taking orders from the enemy, and that makes them doubly dangerous.

Let me know if you need help.

How is Cassie doing?

She sounds fine, but there is a haunted look in her eyes at times. Her first appointment with the werewolf therapist is two days after the full moon.

I will carry this guilt the rest of my days. It is one thing to kill a fire demon you barely know. It is another to kill one—or intend to do so, when I not only knew her well, but she showed me kindness I didn't deserve.

I've considered this since we last spoke, Yosuke told me. Without her, your mission would have failed completely.

Yes.

I will watch her carefully. I believe we may see one another sooner than you think. Above all else, we must keep her survival a secret.

The full moon is coming, I began.

Then you understand my warning. Do not underestimate the two you follow. They have not survived so long by being foolish, and they may have other friends they haven't murdered as yet.

Yosuke was right. We didn't know all of Morton or Dalton's

contacts, or how easily they could place pressure here or there to get what they wanted—money, information, or a hiding place.

"We need to track the Kings closely, and leave nothing to chance," I turned to my sprite companion. "Yosuke believes they may have contacts, and he worries about Cassie's continued safety."

Rob frowned in concentration. I understood he was having a conversation with his King. "You're right," he nodded after a while. "All it will take is a small slip of the tongue, and Shakkor Agdah will do everything in their power to hunt her down."

"Do we have a list of those who know—or suspect, even?"

"We do not."

"Does the Chancellor have such a list?"

"I'll send a text to Daniel."

Atlanta

Parke

"She's Shakkor Agdah?" I must have repeated that question twice; Daniel didn't bother to answer it again. "This is worse than we imagined."

"He says she can change her appearance and ah, lure many into her trap, infecting all of them." Daniel paced through my study, sounding as if he were about to explode at the news Rob gave him.

"More damage may have been done already, and we won't know until the body count rises," I agreed. "Did he have any suggestions on how to stop this?"

"He didn't send any."

"Fuck. You know this means we have to alert all the Princes and Princesses," I growled. Again, my rock demon wanted out to smash something. I struggled to retain control; this was a rented property, after all.

"I say we let them know after the full moon."

"Yeah. I can see the sense in that. I'll let Trey know when he wakes; he can pass the information to his people. Right now, we need to get the Governor of Alabama on the phone and let him know. He can call the Governors of surrounding states and pull them in on this. Did Rob say anything else?"

"He asked if there was a list of people who knew Cassie is still alive. He says that she'll be in immediate danger if the enemy learns she survived."

"I'm not sure I like the idea of a list," I countered. "A list is something somebody can steal."

"Still, it's not a bad idea," Daniel told me. "Maybe we should put a coded list together, and then manage it as well as we can."

"Include the sprites on that list, then."

"I'll do that before we go out tonight. Are you sure the space is safe enough?"

"Cliff arranged it through the local pack; there's a small creek that runs through the property, with wide, muddy banks on both sides for Cassie if she wants to turn. Mom and Destiny will be on one side of it; we can work on the other side. Cliff says there are some large rocks there the owner wouldn't mind having broken down a bit."

"Smaller is easier to move," Daniel agreed.

"And we can have some fun doing it. I've been wanting to smash something all day."

"I'll just freeze them in the cracks and break them apart."

"Like the Kings did to our boathouse."

"I really want our hands on those two," Daniel clenched his fists.

"Yeah. And not just for the boathouse."

Cassie

I'd only pulled out pajamas and a few things from one suitcase the night before, because I was too tired to unpack everything. At least I felt better now and leaving clothes too long in bags was never a good idea.

Hefting the bags onto the bed, I unzipped them and stared at the contents. Parke or Kate had rolled the pyramid in bubble wrap and stuffed it into a corner of the smaller bag. At least I felt better, knowing it was close and under my control. Aunt Shelby had died to get it to me, after all.

The packing tape holding the bubble wrap securely around it had been liberally applied, and, since my nails were barely above the tips of my fingers, it took a while to peel it away.

Once the tape was removed, I unwrapped the plastic around the pyramid to hold it in my hands.

The subsequent flash of light and stab of pain to my head was the last thing I remembered for a while.

assie

With no idea how long I'd been unconscious, I pulled myself off the floor and felt a wave of dizziness wash over me.

What the hell happened?

I only recalled unwrapping the pyramid, and then blinding light and pain.

Did I have a stroke? Where was the pyramid?

Frantically I began to search, until I knelt beside the bed and reached beneath it. My hand touched the tip of the pyramid, and I froze.

The *tip* of the pyramid. The top of it, that was broken—was now in one piece and whole. Jerking the pyramid from beneath the bed, I stared at it—it looked as if it had never been damaged. Script covered the parts that were missing before—script I couldn't read.

Not then, anyway.

Earth sprite scholars had examined it the first time, and they'd only deciphered parts of it. I wasn't about to ask them to look at it again. In fact, I was reluctant to tell anyone about this.

With shaking hands and trembling breaths, I wrapped it in the bubble wrap again, then went looking for a safe place to keep it. If

Shakkor Agdah learned of it, they'd come looking for the pyramid—and for me.

"Is it too late to add to the shopping list?" I asked Gina, when I passed her in the hallway later.

"No—but Gemma will be leaving in about fifteen," she said.

"Good. I have a short list to add. Where can I find her?"

"In the kitchen. Beverly has a long list of groceries, so Jerry is going with her to help."

"Can't go wrong with a rock demon to fetch and carry," I said. "I'll go catch them before they leave." I sprinted along the hallway on my way to the kitchen; it would take five minutes to get there from where I currently was in the house.

"I have a few things to add," I said when I skidded into the kitchen a few minutes later. I waved the slip of paper I'd written my requests on; Gemma held out her hand to take it.

Gemma was in her early thirties, had light-brown hair and wore makeup that covered a wealth of natural beauty, in my opinion. I didn't say anything while she scanned my list. "For sure," she nodded at the last item I'd added. "I'll get you taken care of, don't worry."

"Thanks," I said. "You're a life saver."

"I'd say that remains to be seen," she offered a luminous smile. "Are you ready, Jerry?" she asked her guardian rock demon.

"Ready," he agreed. "Who's driving?"

"You mean you're not going to insist on taking the wheel?"

"First time in Atlanta," he grinned. "You'd have to tell me where we're going anyway."

"In that case, I'll be happy to drive," Gemma said. "Come on, these groceries won't buy themselves."

"Noooo," Jerry teased on their way out the door.

"Well if that don't beat all," Beverly settled fists on her hips when the door closed behind them. "Gemma usually doesn't get too close to anything male-oriented."

"Seriously?" I turned toward Beverly.

"Yep. When the owners are here, she makes sure to stay out of their way—especially the mister."

"You think maybe he's a," I hesitated, wondering whether I should keep going with this train of thought.

"A womanizer?" Beverly hmmphed. "I don't think so. She came here like that—shy of anything male. No idea what Jerry has that the others didn't, or vice-versa."

I wondered if Trey's compulsion had anything to do with Gemma's new mood. I made a mental note to ask Parke about it later.

Did Jerry leave to get groceries yet? Parke asked me.

He and Gemma left a few minutes ago. You can call him if you want to add to the list.

I'll do that.

Wait—I have a question about Gemma and the compulsion Trey placed on her. What, exactly, did he say to her?

That if she saw anything unusual, to treat it as normal, and to trust us.

I think you may have done a misdeed, then.

How so?

Beverly says that she's very shy around males, and I figure there's a good reason for that. Now she's acting out of character. If Beverly notices, somebody else could, too.

Who is she going to see that will notice, outside Beverly?

No idea, but it could happen.

I think you're worrying about nothing. We don't need her afraid of anybody here, okay? If it turns into a problem, we'll deal with it.

Fine. Call Jerry and tell him you want extra-soft toilet paper.

How did you know? he teased.

Hmmph.

Lilith Sloane

I turned down Alys Drive in Temperance Acres, driving slowly past houses that most people could only dream about.

So.

This was where that treacherous little bitch had holed up, after sending my Doyle to prison. Well, I knew somebody. Her days were numbered now. Too bad she'd made me hunt for her all these months.

"We'll be back for you, you trollop," I promised under my breath and drove past the massive house. Anybody who lived there ought to watch out—she'd probably accuse them of rape and torture, too.

All I had to do was place a call and pay half up front. Somebody would be watching the house from now on, looking for an opportunity to make Gemma Chandler dead.

Cassie

"What are you doing?" Parke walked into the bedroom just as I was putting the last of my new toiletries away.

"Just putting up stuff that Gemma and Jerry picked up for me," I said. "Do you need something?"

"It's going to take an hour or longer to get to the location, so we need to eat in about half an hour, then get ready to go. Traffic is brutal in Atlanta—at least that's what more than two dozen people have told me today."

"And we don't need to be held up with werewolves in the car."

"Or rock demons, ice demons, or anybody else who changes on a full moon."

"Understood. Has somebody told Jon that he'll be here with the vamps and the other staff tonight?"

"Trey told him last night, and also told him to keep his eyes and ears open for anything out of the ordinary, and to go straight to Trey or Grim with what he knows."

"A good shriek will send the vamps running in the right direction," I pointed out.

"That, too."

"I'm not sure I'll be making the change," I told him, meeting his gaze from across the room. "Does that bother you?"

"You may want to anyway—just to make sure."

"Sure of what?"

"That you ah, still *can* change, I guess."

"You're worried that the asshole wizard may have done more damage than we already think?"

"I just want to make sure everything is as fine as it can be."

Unsure how to take all this, I kept the growing worries to myself. Why wouldn't that part be fine? Granted, I hadn't attempted the change, but there really hadn't been a good opportunity—or a reason for it.

Was he worried I was more than broken emotionally? What would that mean if I were?

"I can see I've upset you, when I didn't mean to," he began to walk toward me.

"No," I held up a hand to stop him. "I'll sort this out on my own, thanks." Stalking past him, I went through the door, heading for the kitchen. Maybe Beverly had something I could pound into submission, like mashed potatoes or other, surly vegetables.

Less than two hours later, after a rather uncomfortable dinner where Parke talked and I didn't, we loaded into SUVs for the trek to the location. I still didn't know where we were going, but Cliff and Parke did.

I sat in the back with Destiny, while Kate rode in the middle row with Gina and Kent. "You okay?" Destiny's hand closed around mine as Daniel drove us onto Alys Drive and turned right.

"Yeah, I'm okay," I sighed. "You and Kate hanging out with Jerry and Pete?" I asked.

"Supposed to," she said. "So they can keep an eye on us. What about you?"

"I'm still trying to decide whether I want to change," I replied.

"I can't believe you spent all those years not changing," she leaned her head against my shoulder.

"Aunt Shelby said it was important, so I learned to squelch the urge."

"I miss her."

"Me, too."

"Sometimes, I try to remember anything about Mom, but nothing comes."

"Baby girl, you were too little," I put an arm around her. "I used to stand beside the counter in the mornings when she made biscuits and watch as she just threw everything together. They always came out perfect, too."

"Like Aunt Shelby's?"

"Like that," I agreed. I didn't add that Mom would smile at me while she worked the dough and rolled it out on a pastry sheet. Those smiles were tiny gifts I tucked in my memory, holding onto them tightly so they wouldn't escape.

"Gran Kate says my ice demon is strong," Destiny said. "Really strong."

"Hon, I knew that the second you defended yourself against an older water demon, and came out on top."

"She shouldn't have done what she did."

"None of those people on the other side that night should have done what they did. They started a war; we fought back. I'm not sorry they lost."

"I'm not sorry Shakkor Agdah lost last time, either. Two girls I went to school with in Alabama died from that awful disease. I thought you were gone, too."

"So did I, honey. So did I."

Douglasville, Georgia
Dalton King

"Hurry up, I'm getting itchy," I snapped at my son. "It'll be too bad that we left our tail back in Tuscaloosa. They won't know we hitched a ride with Ralph Greenville, courtesy of Vaalenn."

"Did Greenville say where he planned to go tonight? He has to change somewhere," Morton growled at me.

"Why? You want to be under Greenville's thumb instead of Vaalenn's?"

"Wouldn't hurt. He has money hidden—you can bet on that."

"Somebody's tired of eating fast food," I pointed out.

"And what if I am? Hell, we've gone to bat for Vaalenn, just like we did for Ruudann. At least Ruudann got what he wanted, even if he did have to die for it. The girl's dead, and there won't be another they can lay their hands on so easy. Black Myth's star is rising, boy, and we're gonna rise with it."

"First, we have a few assassinations to deal out, or did you forget about those?"

"We've got help coming, or did you forget about them?"

"I'm not risking my life against rock demons until I know the help's arrived."

"Sensible plan. Make sure the backup is there before we take on whatever they've got to throw against us. Without Cassie, they won't stand a chance, when Black Myth shows up with demon killers."

"They better show up with those weapons. I want assurances that we'll survive this."

"Trust me—we're too important for them to just toss away. We've carried the ball for them too many times."

"Tell that to Ruudann. Oh, I forgot—*he's dead.*"

Fairfield, Alabama

Rob

"How the hell did they get away from us?" I demanded. Will ignored my question regarding Dalton and Morton's disappearance; instead, he stood beneath a tree next to a restaurant parking lot, with his eyes closed.

"We're needed in Atlanta. Yosuke says there's danger," Will's eyes and mouth popped open simultaneously.

"Damn," I hissed.

"We don't have time to dither; they checked out of the motel behind us about four hours ago—and their tracking trace ended abruptly just off the sidewalk outside it," Will said. "That means someone gave them a ride, and they're in Georgia by now. Just as well, I suppose; I used up the last of the clothing and hair we found in New Orleans to track them this far. If they've learned somehow where the Chancellor intends to spend the full moon, then we'll have trouble.

"As in Black Myth trouble?"

"Undoubtedly. Come. I will take you to Yosuke, who will help us find our quarry. I hope."

"You hope?" My words turned into garbled porridge as Will grasped my arm and moved us, employing the uncomfortable displacement trick that he uses. It never failed to leave me ruffled and feeling as if I'd left something behind—such as my ass or my feet.

Averill, I managed to send a message after my initial disorientation, *help is needed.*

～

Privately-owned land, south of Big Haynes Creek Recreational Area, Georgia

Parke

"Chancellor, this is Mac Harbour, Packmaster for the Eastern Atlanta Pack," Cliff introduced us.

"Chancellor, it's an honor to meet you," he shook my hand. "I do want to discuss something in private with you and Cliff before we ah, get started tonight."

"All right." I knew that he was beginning to feel the moon's pull, just as Cliff did, so we had to hurry. "We'll step over here," I pointed to a spot nearby, within a narrow clump of trees.

We strode the distance quickly, before Mac drew to a stop. "I got a call from the Prince of Alabama two hours ago," he said softly. "He finally got around to talking about the full moon and where you might end up, tonight, Chancellor. I want you to know I lied to him and told him that the Douglasville Pack was playing host. I worry now that I may have placed them in danger."

"Why would Greenville even want that information?" Cliff frowned at me.

"There's no need for him to have it," I growled. "Is it too late to get the Douglasville Packmaster on the phone?"

"I'll try now," Cliff said, although his words sounded as if his werewolf wanted loose.

"Give me your phone," I held my hand out, although my prelim was the one accepting the device. The moon was getting to all of us, now.

Cassie, I sent to her, *the Douglasville Pack may be in trouble. Can you take Cliff's phone and keep trying to reach them?*

Cassie came running toward me; Cliff and Mac changed in front of me, fought their way out of clothing and ran into the nearby wooded area, howling. The rest of Mac's pack answered.

I was on my way to becoming full rock demon by the time Cassie reached me. Dropping the phone into her hand before I crushed it by merely holding it, I stalked away so I wouldn't disturb her call. Pete and Jerry were waiting for me, beside Mom and Destiny.

We'd be close enough, though, to help Cassie if help were needed.

Cassie

The phone rang on the other end and kept ringing until it went to voicemail. It meant the Douglasville Packmaster was running and hunting with his pack. I hung up without leaving a message and stood beneath a sycamore, staring at Cliff's phone.

That's when it rang, and the number displayed I recognized at once.

Rob.

Rob was calling Cliff. *Why?* I couldn't imagine he'd do that unless it was something important.

"What is it, Rob?" I answered, my voice angry and waspish.

"Shakkor Agdah is attacking the Douglasville Pack," he sounded out of breath. "We're outnumbered and overrun."

Where the hell was Douglasville in Georgia? I wasn't as familiar with this state as I was with Alabama.

Until it popped into my head with perfect clarity—as if I could see the pack fighting for its life against two ice demons and others dressed in dark robes.

Go, my conscience urged me. Without demanding a how or why, I dropped Cliff's phone in the grass and *went*.

Parke

Destiny's ice demon shouted a strangled cry of alarm when Cassie disappeared in front of us. At our current location, we were east of Atlanta. Douglasville was west of Atlanta, with a huge distance between us.

Had Cassie been sucked away from us by something evil?

"We can't change back," Mom wept, her tears freezing on her cheeks.

She was right—I couldn't change to drive a car or use any other form of transportation. In our current state, we were helpless to look for her or to travel toward Douglasville.

Cassie? I sent to her.

She's busy, Will's voice growled into my mind.

Wizard, if anything happens to her, I'll kill you myself.

And I'll allow it. I'm needed, now. We'll contact you later.

Robin

Eight Earth sprite warriors arrived to do battle—they were closest to the area and employed a great deal of energy to get here. Twenty more were on the way, but Averill warned they might not arrive in time.

Parrying a blow from an enemy who decided to attack me, I swung my blade in an arc immediately after, removing his head. Will and Yosuke, fighting in tandem across the field, struggled to keep half the Douglasville Pack alive.

The other half was already dead—in Shakkor Agdah's well-planned initial attack. *Why attack these wolves?* There was nothing to be gained here, except to put the rest of the supernatural community on notice.

In the distance, behind too many Black Myth soldiers to count, I caught glimpses of two ice demons. There was no doubt in my mind as to their identity. Wearing full battle gear in the heat of a Georgia summer night drenched me and my eight sprite warriors in sweat. I worried it would blur our vision while we battled on.

When the huge fireball hit the ground in the center of Black Myth's troops, black-cloaked bodies were flung high in the air from the impact. Their screams and death cries reached my ears as I swung my blade at yet another opponent. *Where did the fire come from?* Will's shout sounded in my mind.

No idea, I replied, jerking my blade with difficulty from an enemy's chest. Besides, ordinary fire would only kill Shakkor Agdah if it fell directly on them and they failed to put it out. Whoever sent the fire had probably killed a few, but I expected the flames to die back after only a few moments.

I hope there's more fire coming, Will hissed mentally. *We need around twenty fireballs that size to cut the enemy down to numbers we can handle. Wait, is that,* his sending tapered off.

This was no ordinary fireball. This fireball rose from the ground and grew in stature and in fury, until the arms it possessed began lobbing fireballs into the attackers, making them scatter while shrieking. Many of them ran while burning, their black robes dripping bits of fiery cloth that hung in the air as they fled.

Cassie.

Cassie had come, in a way I couldn't determine, and she'd grown so huge, standing at the center of our attackers, that those close enough were consumed by her initial landing. Tossing fireball after fireball, she killed swaths of Shakkor Agdah, who couldn't run fast enough to escape her wrath.

To your left, General, a newly-arrived sprite warrior shouted. Eons of battle training had deserted me while I watched Cassie's fire demon do battle. I deserved to be reprimanded for such a gaffe.

Instead, I whirled swiftly enough to block a well-aimed blow, then delivered a death wound to my assailant. That blow was followed by the removal of his head before he could crumple to the ground.

More fireballs rained on the invading army, spraying black-robed bodies into the air and deafening anyone who battled on while shaking the ground with their intensity. How had Cassie come by this much strength—to continue fighting in this way? I'd never seen anything like it.

That's when three Black Myth troops ran in my direction, weapons in their hands and trained on me.

Those weren't swords—they were demon killers.

They had demon killers. Feet away, they stopped to take aim at me and the sprite warriors about me.

"Retreat," I shouted at my troops. "Demon killers," I screamed as they stopped to look at me in confusion.

The weapons were raised and trained on us. The one in the center was aimed at my chest.

The firebolt that seared through his body from behind was like an arrow of flame. Two others followed quickly—for the two Shakkor Agdah on either side. In slow motion, I watched as three Black Myth captains dropped to the ground where they'd stood, their demon killer weapons dropping from lifeless hands.

How? As I watched, Cassie destroyed the three weapons with well-aimed blasts. The meadow filled with smoke from her fire as I recalled I could still move. With haste, I began searching for more of the enemy. All I found were blackened corpses strewn across the field. Eventually, I discovered bodies of werewolves who'd died as wolves, caught in a trap laid by Shakkor Agdah and who knew what else.

Wait.

"Where are the Kings?" I spoke my question aloud, as thick smoke drifted across my path and obscured my vision.

"They ran, like the cowards they are," Cassie snapped an answer at me. Smoke cleared between us; she stood there scowling at me, both naked and furious, with arms crossed over her breasts. "Just because I saved your ass—and Will's ass, too—doesn't mean I've forgiven either of you." Her glare could melt ice, it was so hot and intense.

"Assholes."

She turned and stalked away from me, her body stiff with anger. I still had to determine how she'd arrived to protect us, or we'd have been overrun by the sheer number of Shakkor Agdah sent to destroy anyone in the area, werewolf pack included.

"Why did they attack here?" I flung at Cassie's retreating backside.

"They thought Parke would be here, you idiot."

"Someone gave them false information? Intentionally?"

"That about sums it up."

"Fucking hell," I breathed. Removing my helmet, I let it drop to the ground with a clank before wiping sweat off my face and forehead.

"We've shielded the area so we won't get curious human visitors," Will and Yosuke walked up to me. "I imagine the Chancellor will want to see all this before we destroy the remains."

"Where is the fire demon?" Yosuke asked. "Is she well?"

"She looked fine to me, and she's pissed," I told him. "What worries me is that Morton and Dalton got away. If they suspect she was the one shooting fireballs, then Shakkor Agdah will have that information in no time."

"You think they could identify her in that form?" Will asked softly. "I've never seen a fire demon grow so large."

"Let's hope Black Myth thinks she's a male, then, but it still won't erase the target on her back. They'll be looking for a fire demon from now on. Her cover's blown, one way or another, and she did it to save our asses."

"If my calculations are correct, there were at least a thousand Shakkor Agdah here tonight," Yosuke sounded thoughtful. "They planned to destroy the Chancellor and the Grand Master, didn't they?"

"Cassie says that they were intentionally given false information as to where the Chancellor would be tonight," I agreed. "She didn't say who gave the information, though."

"The Chancellor will also be pissed, then," Yosuke agreed.

"I figure he's on his way here, somehow," Will sighed. "Especially if he knows that Cassie came."

"Well, I guess I shouldn't be surprised that you'd stick a mole in our midst," Cassie walked toward us, wrapped in a purloined shirt that hung almost to her knees. I imagined the werewolf who'd left it in the woods wouldn't need it any longer.

She'd pointed her words at Will, but her gaze had fallen on Yosuke.

"I am Yosuke," he introduced himself. "I am at your service, lady demon," Yosuke bowed to her. "I pray you do not include me in the anger you hold against my companions."

"Time will tell on that," Cassie sniped at him. "Where are the rest of the Douglasville Pack? Parke will want to offer condolences when he gets here."

"They're under that stand of trees behind us; I've shielded them," Will replied. "They have to take stock and consider their dead."

"There shouldn't be any dead," Cassie hissed. "If I were in charge, the idiot who sent Shakkor Agdah in this direction should lose his position at the very least."

"Werewolf or demon?" I asked.

"Hmmph. Why would I tell you?"

Not Parke—she mentioned him offering condolences. Can't be Cliff—he's smarter than that, I informed Will.

That leaves a certain Packmaster, then.

That's my guess. If I know Cliff at all, that Packmaster's ass will be out of a job before lunch tomorrow.

"Question," Yosuke turned toward Cassie. "Who was the information given to? Who actually lied to the one carrying the news to Black Myth?"

"The new Prince of Alabama, who else?" Cassie's words were hissed, with smoke accompanying them.

I've never seen that happen. Will sounded half amazed and half terrified.

"It's like the old stories—about dragons," Yosuke's voice held reverence. "You are indeed special, lady demon." He had the nerve to bow to her again.

"What the hell?" I turned to stare at the huge motorhome making its way across the field. It stopped roughly a hundred yards from us. That's when I noticed the huge rip in the side of it, because the metal screamed in anguish as it was shoved away from the rest of the vehicle.

Three rock demons stepped out of the enormous gash, while a vampire rose from the driver's seat.

Trey, Parke and two rock demons had found a way to get here. I imagined the interior of the motor home reflected the abuse it suffered from its passengers riding inside it.

The last one to get out I certainly recognized, even in wolf form.

Cliff, Grand Master of all werewolves, had come with them.

CHAPTER 6

*B*lackWing X
    Zarigar

Travis, William Winkler and I watched the recorded images again. "You had nothing to do with this?" Winkler asked as we watched the fire demon killing swaths of murderous humanoids who called themselves Shakkor Agdah.

"I watched it happen when she arrived. Her method of teleportation is new to her, but extremely effective. No interference occurred on my part."

"That's outstanding. The hole she put in that one black cloak was as small as a bullet," Travis observed as he reviewed that section for the third time. "Where do you suppose the black robes got those ranos pistols?"

"I do not know," I said. "But this concerns me a great deal. That technology should not be anywhere near this planet."

"Somebody had to import them, then," Winkler said. "I say we do some research and then investigate those black robes."

"I concur," I told him. "We should certainly observe them—and anyone they've had dealings with. Someone sold or provided those weapons; they did not come from any world connected to this one."

~

Near Douglasville, Georgia

Cassie

"I don't care what you have to do—take him into custody. I want a conversation with him, first." Parke was angry as he spoke into his phone. I had no idea who he'd called, and at this point, I didn't care. Weariness hit me shortly after sunrise, and I only wanted to crawl into a bed somewhere and sleep.

I did know he was talking about the Prince of Alabama, though. If I knew Parke, and if Greenville had actually told Shakkor Agdah anything, he was a dead demon.

I didn't have a problem with that. "I hear you're responsible for turning our attackers into crispy critters," a werewolf in human form held out his hand to me. "Benjamin Stokes," he introduced himself.

"I met your sister-in-law, Beverly," I told him, mustering up a tired smile. "She's awesome, by the way."

"Hell, get her and my wife together, you get the best Thanksgiving and Christmas dinners you've ever had," he pumped my hand several times before letting go. "I'm sorry, I didn't get your name," he added.

"Cassie," I said.

"Well, Cassie, we've got food coming in, thanks to a handful of human wives, mine included. You're welcome to join us. I have to say, I'd never seen one of your kind before last night."

"And you probably don't want to see another," I said.

"I think I'd be grateful as long as a fire demon was on our side," he assured me. "Come on," he motioned for me to follow him. "They'll be here any minute."

"How many of your packmates died last night?" I asked him as we crunched over charred grass.

"We lost nine. Almost half the pack. If the sprite and the wizard hadn't shown up, we'd all be dead. Would have been dead anyway, if you hadn't come along."

"I'm sorry I didn't get here sooner, but I didn't get the information until it was almost too late."

"I hear a Prince's head is gonna be on the chopping block over this."

"You heard right. They'll have to move quickly to take him into custody before the enemy kills him."

"You think that could happen?" Benjamin stopped walking for a moment and turned his eyes on me, searching my face for the truth. If anything, he'd paled beneath his dark skin—Benjamin Stokes belonged to a rare strain of black werewolves, and they were powerful and effective when they turned.

"Yeah. Did you happen to see the two ice demons who were here until things turned against them?"

"I did." Benjamin continued walking, so I followed.

"That was Dalton and Morton King. If they get to the Prince in question before we do, then he's a dead demon and we won't get our questions answered."

"I want to watch him die—the one who sold us out, so I'd prefer the Kings don't get there before our side does."

"Well, I want to watch Morton and Dalton die, so I understand where you're coming from."

"Right on." He held his fist out—I bumped it with mine.

"Solidarity, all the way," I told him.

"Benny?" I heard a woman's voice calling.

"That's my wife," he said. "Come meet her." We didn't get far before Beverly's sister, Faith, came running toward Benjamin. He took off and met her halfway, picking her up and hugging her, in the middle of that charred field. She wiped tears away when he set her down.

"Baby, I want you to meet Cassie," he turned and motioned me forward. "She helped save us last night."

"Oh, my goodness," Faith opened her arms and hugged me hard.

"I met your sister," I gave her a watery smile when she let me go. "We love her already. I wish I'd gotten here sooner, but we did what we could to help."

"Come on, then. We have food, water and coffee," she pulled Benjamin and me toward a table being set up not far away. I could smell the coffee already and went willingly.

"Oh, my goodness, she's barefoot," another woman exclaimed as I accepted a paper cup of coffee from her.

"It's okay," I attempted to wave off her concern. "I've gone through worse than this." Landing naked in a tree outside the burning courthouse in Tuscaloosa came to mind; that had been much more painful than this.

"I have some flip-flops in the car," she said and took off before I could stop her. Soon enough, I had a pair of gold-studded flip-flops on my feet, and assured her that I'd return the shoes, even though she said I could keep them.

At least her husband, like Benjamin, had survived the attack the night before. Several other women were gathered beneath a tree nearby, while Parke, Cliff and one of the local werewolves consoled them.

"I know you're not feeling charitable toward me right now, but I want to thank you for what you did—and to extend Averill's gratitude as well," Rob came to stand next to me. Someone placed a coffee cup in his hand; he nodded his thanks.

"Rob, you have no idea how much I'd like to wipe the last three months out of my life and take up where we were before, but that won't happen, will it?" I turned toward him then and looked him straight in the eye. He broke contact first, lowering his head in a slight nod.

"I know. That debt will never be paid, Cassie. We both know that. It squeezes my heart to know I contributed to the pain you feel. All my life, I've considered myself a good sprite—one who's never caused an innocent's death. Turns out, I was fooling myself all along."

"He's right," Will came forward, then, with Yosuke beside him. "All this time, we were sacrificing the wrong ones."

"This isn't helping you in the forgiveness column," I snapped.

"He knows that," Yosuke said quietly. "He will survive without forgiveness. None of us may survive if we fail to work together to eliminate the threat of Black Myth."

There it was—truth in a single sentence.

"I will never trust you again," I told Will. "But I will agree to a truce, if the Chancellor also agrees."

"I do have one question," Rob said.

"What's that?"

"How did you get here last night?"

"I have no idea," I replied.

"Trey had to smooth things over with Georgia Highway Patrol on the motor home before he had to leave—probably got singed before getting to a safe place for the day. As for the motorhome, we had to promise to replace it with a newer model and pay for the loss of personal belongings and the unexpected rental of the ah, vehicle," Parke explained as we drove away from the field two hours later.

I hadn't really paid attention to what he, Pete, Jerry and Cliff had dressed in at dawn, but it looked like hunting and fishing outfits to me. Parke sipped on a fourth cup of coffee he'd gotten before we left. Cliff stayed behind with the pack to help them sort things out—they had unexplained deaths to make sense of.

As for Rob, Will and Yosuke, they took up the back portion of the damaged motor home; Parke agreed to the truce, so they decided to ride back with us. If we kept the motor home, I wondered if Will had a spell to fix the enormous gash in the side of it. For now, the faster Jerry drove, the louder the wind whistled around the torn metal. If I weren't so tired, I'd have become fire again just to seal the damn thing shut.

That could wait; I wanted a shower and a bed, in that order.

The door squawked when we opened it after our arrival at the house; Beverly waited at the front door for us when we reached it. Parke and Pete walked in first, followed by Jerry and me.

Beverly didn't do more than nod at the others. I was pulled into a hug so tight I almost couldn't breathe. "Faith told me what you did," she whispered against my ear. "Thank you."

"Beverly, I would do it again if I had to," I said. "Let's hope it won't be necessary."

"I see we have some new ones," she said, stepping back to let Rob and Will walk in ahead of Yosuke. "I may have to find room in a closet somewhere."

"Yeah, they may have to sleep in the stolen motorhome," I joked. "After I fix it."

"What's wrong with it? Is it really stolen?"

"Not now," I patted her shoulder. "We're paying for it, and then some. As for what's wrong with it, well, the door wasn't big enough for a rock demon to climb in, so they ah, made some adjustments."

"With Cassie's help, I believe we can heal the gash," Yosuke told Beverly. "If you need me for anything, I'll be in my room."

"I need a shower," I said. "And some sleep. But if you need anything, like Yosuke said, let me know."

"I can call the police," Beverly said as I walked toward the hallway and the suite waiting there—and a shower and a bed.

"Beverly," I turned back toward her, "if this enemy shows up, the police are the last folks to call."

Parke

Daniel and I couldn't go to bed; that meant Pete and Jerry were with us when the word came that Ralph Greenville had been found and taken to a safe place. The fool had stayed the night near a lake, where his van was parked. His full moon had been peaceful and uneventful. Ours was anything but. The former Prince of Alabama now waited for my arrival—and his judgment.

He should have skipped town the second he gave information to Shakkor Agdah. *Wrong* information, as it turned out. As yet, I hadn't spoken with Cliff about Mac, who'd given false information to

Greenville—he was also responsible for deaths in Douglasville, and that was untenable.

Perhaps Cliff should allow the Douglasville Pack to decide his punishment. Granted, the lie had saved us from being attacked directly by Shakkor Agdah and the Kings, but an unsuspecting pack had paid the price for it.

"I have Cliff's key to the Escalade—he had it built with bulletproof glass," Daniel informed me. "Pete and Jerry are already waiting for us in the garage."

"If you don't mind, Will and I would like to go with you," Rob walked into my makeshift office.

"Good enough, just don't piss us off and don't interfere with our questioning."

"No intention to do that," Rob held up a hand. "What he says could be more than important to all sprites, as well as the demon and shifter communities."

"I want to know what he knows about the Kings," I growled at Rob. "Since he's in the area, I figure he gave them a ride to Douglasville."

"That is what Will and I have determined. And, as we have been tracking those two ice demons, we also want to hear what Greenville has to say about them."

"Let's go, then. The sooner we get this taken care of, the sooner we can get some sleep."

Rob

Will and I sat in the back row, with two rock demon guards sitting in the middle. Parke rode up front, while Daniel drove. I'd learned that Ralph Greenville was being held at a vampire safe house outside Athens, Georgia. It took more than an hour to get there.

A small, frame house stood atop a hidden, underground bunker, which would be light-proof and bomb-proof, if I knew vampires at all.

We trooped down two flights of steps located inside the house before coming to the locked door of the bunker. Parke knocked; we were let in by one of the rock demons acting as guards. Greenville sat on the cold floor of the bunker in the far corner, while an ice demon watched him closely.

Ice freezes water. Greenville worried for his life.

As he should. I doubted he'd walk out of this place, and his water would evaporate soon enough, leaving nothing to mark his grave.

His eyes grew round when he saw Parke; I believe he knew his death was coming then, if he hadn't figured it out before. For the life of me, I couldn't figure out why he'd been placed in the Prince's position in the first place. Averill and I knew he was too weak to be effective.

Except to get half the Douglasville Pack killed.

"Start talking, Greenville," Parke hissed at him. "The more useful your words are, the longer I let you live."

"They threatened me," he began, his voice little more than a whine.

"In what way?" Parke crossed arms over his chest. "And why didn't you tell me about it?"

Because they paid him, Will's voice sounded in my head.

Bribed, I sent to Parke.

"How much?" Parke shouted at Greenville. "How much did they give you to sell us out?"

"F-fifty thousand," Greenville attempted to make himself smaller. Parke was already looking down on him. This confession and subsequent cowering didn't improve my already dismal opinion of the former Prince of Alabama.

"Did you not consider that I'd have paid five times that much for the knowledge of where to find Morton and Dalton King? That reward is posted on every Prince and Princess' website."

"They threatened me," he whined again.

"With what?"

"They said they'd make sure I lost my position."

"And what are the odds of that happening now?" Parke snapped. "Damn, Greenville, you're dumber than mud."

"Who threatened you?" I spoke out of turn, but I couldn't help myself. All along, I'd assumed it was Shakkor Agdah, but something in his voice this time warned me it could be someone else.

Couldn't be the Kings; they're broke, Will informed me.

He was right.

"Parke," Daniel warned as Parke's prelim began to manifest.

"Who?" Parke hissed between growing fangs.

"Gorham and Franks," Greenville's words trembled on his lips. He'd named two prominent ice demons, who'd moved to Alabama recently after spending most of their lives in Mississippi. They had multiple businesses in Mississippi and I'd wondered why they moved.

"Looks like Shakkor Agdah likes ice demons," I snorted.

"That means we have four to hunt instead of two, and I'm not surprised that Gorham and Franks knew Dalton and Morton. I figure they're calling in more favors from ah, old friends," Daniel surmised. "Not just for Shakkor Agdah, but to put this fool in the Prince's position."

"You think Morton and Dalton have done some things for Gorham and Franks that required less than legal solutions?" Parke turned toward Daniel.

"Sounds about right," Daniel drawled.

"What do you know about that?" Parke snapped at Greenville, and the second round of questioning began.

Cassie

My stomach growled so loudly it woke me. Turning toward the bedside table, I checked the time; four-fifteen in the afternoon. With a groan, I rolled off the bed and padded toward the bathroom.

I'd gone to bed with my hair still damp from a quick shower earlier, and now I paid the price for that as I studied my image in the bathroom mirror. A hurricane might have had less impact on it, I decided, before digging through drawers to find my curling iron.

After twenty minutes of mostly fruitless effort to get my hair in some sort of recognizable formation, I pulled it back in a bun and headed for the kitchen. I hoped the werewolves hadn't cleaned out the fridge and pantry while I slept.

What I found was Cliff and Kent, sitting at the kitchen island eating fried chicken. Cliff didn't try talking with his mouth full, but he pulled out the chair next to his. I grabbed a plate from a stack beside a covered pan of fried chicken and helped myself.

There was potato salad in a separate covered dish, plus asparagus in another. All of it was wonderful. I tore into a chicken leg while Cliff got another thigh to wolf down. I owed Beverly a hug for this—it was all homemade.

"Is there any left for us," Parke walked into the kitchen, followed by Daniel, Pete, Jerry, Will and Rob.

They were only now coming back from their visit with Ralph Greenville, who was now a former everything, including among the living, I assumed. All of them looked as if they could sleep standing up.

"I take it there's a vacancy for Prince of Alabama?" Cliff asked as Parke and the others took empty chairs around the island.

"Yep." Parke pulled the stack of plates toward him, then handed them out in both directions so everyone could eat.

I pushed the flatware caddy toward him, followed by the stack of napkins. At least Beverly knew how to cook for supernaturals—there was enough of everything for all of us.

"Find out anything useful?" Cliff went on.

"Found out the Kings have been thick with Gorham and Franks, and that Gorham and Franks have been thick with Black Myth," Parke bit into a chicken breast.

"Fucking hell," Cliff swore softly. "That means we have four ice demons to hunt instead of two."

"Just what I said," Daniel acknowledged.

"Let me guess—dear old Dud and Grand-dud have been doing shady crap for Gorham and Franks," I snorted.

Parke was chewing, so he tapped his nose and nodded at my words.

"I demoted Mac for his part in all this—he should have alerted us the moment that call came in instead of waiting until the last minute, when we were helpless to do anything about it. Some present company excepted," Cliff bumped his shoulder against mine.

"How did he take that?" I asked, lifting the napkin over the fried chicken and searching for another leg.

"I think he's happy to still be alive," Cliff growled. "He better be—I thought about letting the Douglasville Pack hand out justice."

"They lost a lot," Kent agreed. "If I were Mac Harbour, I'd be looking for another pack—out of state."

"He has a brother in the Savannah Pack—he may go there," Cliff said. "In fact, I suggested it. He said he'd consider it."

"He may not go, because everybody there will know what happened," I pointed out.

"True. He needs to tuck his tail between his legs and go wherever he can after that stunt. Getting your brothers killed isn't looked upon kindly by any pack."

"Parke?" I turned toward him.

"Hmmm?" He was still eating.

"Did Greenville hear from the Kings after they deserted last night?"

"He didn't," Rob answered for Parke. "They left him to twist in the wind. No doubt they're holed up somewhere, waiting this out. I doubt Shakkor Agdah is very pleased with them right now."

"Do Franks and Gorham have any property here in Georgia—except for their overly-expensive homes?" I turned to Cliff.

"We can get that information easily enough," Cliff wiped his fingers on a napkin before tugging his cell phone out of a jeans pocket. Seconds later, he had someone on the line.

"Hey, Zach," he said. "Cliff here. How hard is it to check for property ownership by a couple of folks who used to live in Alabama?" He listened for a bit, the said, "Great. I'll get that information to you tomorrow, then. Thanks."

Cliff ended the call, turned to me and said, "He's at his cabin today, but he'll be back in his office tomorrow. He'll call and get the information from me, then. I can go for a quick visit while you're talking to Kirk Chalmers tomorrow."

He'd given me Doctor Chalmers' full name. I didn't feel comfortable calling him anything other than Doctor Chalmers. Or my shrink. Outside his werewolf hearing, of course.

"I'll feel better if someone is there at the office, waiting for Cassie's appointment to end," Rob spoke up.

"You offering?" Cliff frowned at Rob.

"If she'll have me."

"Fine. You ride in the back," Cliff grumped.

I wanted to argue that I could take care of myself, but there was too much testosterone sitting around the island at the moment. If Rob wanted to be bored for an hour, then he could sit there and twiddle his thumbs while I had a tell-all session with my werewolf shrink.

Dalton King

"At least it's a double-wide," Morton grumbled as he dropped his duffle in the center of the living room floor. Our new accommodations turned out to be double-wide, pre-fab housing that Gorham arranged for us on property he'd recently acquired. That heavily wooded property lay between Hickory Flat and Alpharetta, and the closest neighbors were more than a mile away.

I wondered if our seclusion was worth the fact that we had a propane stove, a solar generator and bottled drinking water. If we wanted a bath, we had to go to a nearby creek for that, or drive twenty miles to the nearest truck stop with facilities.

Franks had arranged for someone to pick us up after we called the night before, and he and Gorham promised to meet with us after we settled in here. I didn't want to tell them that the Chancellor had found a new fire demon, because they'd pass that information along to Vaalenn, with confirmation that the army she'd sent to take him down had not only failed, they were all dead.

The fact that Morton and I survived would tell her we'd cut our losses shortly after the fire demon arrived. It probably wouldn't matter when we told her it was the biggest fire demon we'd ever seen or heard of; we'd be branded cowards and given shit work from now on.

Unless she wanted to kill us by sending us after the fucking fire demon.

Gorham didn't bother to knock; he let himself in, with Franks right behind him. I'd been so lost in thought, I didn't hear them drive up.

"I suppose I don't have to tell you that Vaalenn is furious about last night," Gorham snapped at me. Morton was in one of the bedrooms stomping around and didn't know we had guests yet. Trust him to let me take all the heat for what happened.

"We got bad information," I griped at Gorham. "That's on you and your source. The Chancellor wasn't there when we arrived—only the local pack. We did what we could, fighting off sprites and a warlock, until that fucking fire demon showed up. I'm telling you now, you do not want to meet up with that bastard. He filled half that field with fire, he was so big."

"Vaalenn says there are only two fire demons left, and they're both still in Europe."

"That's not what we saw last night," Morton walked in and decided to join the conversation. "I don't know if they've had this guy under wraps or what, but that's not something I want to see again. We'd have taken all of them down last night if that monster hadn't shown up."

"Instead, Vaalenn's entire army is killed," Franks' forehead wrinkled in a deep frown. "She's pissed, as you may imagine. Last I heard, she sent somebody looking for the source of the faulty information. I doubt he'll survive long."

"Go ahead and say it's Greenville—that's the only thing that makes sense in any of this," Morton stabbed a finger toward Franks.

"He may already be dead; I tried calling him earlier," Franks admitted. "Don't worry," he held up a hand when Gorham whirled to face him. "I used a burner phone and didn't leave a message. They won't know who tried to call."

"You think the Chancellor caught up with him this fast?" Morton barked a laugh. "There's nothing to lead them in that direction."

"Hmmph," Gorham coughed into his hand.

"What did you do?" I narrowed my eyes at Gorham. "How did Greenville get the information to begin with—the wrong information, as it turns out."

"He called a Packmaster in the Atlanta area that he'd met once or twice," Gorham stated flatly. "It's possible he may have eventually sniffed the wind and wondered why Greenville wanted to know the Chancellor's whereabouts."

"Then you better pray the Chancellor didn't get to Greenville before Vaalenn did, or we could all be screwed," I said.

"You think we don't know that?" Gorham whined. "That's why we're leaving the state. We have friends in Oklahoma, and we're gonna hole up in their cabin for a while. If you two want to go with us, you'd better grab your gear and toss it in the back of my truck. We're getting out of here this afternoon."

"Get your shit," I snapped at Morton. "I hope that cabin in Oklahoma has running water, at least."

Cassie

I found Destiny in Kate's room—they were watching a popular game show and trying to guess the answers.

"Come sit with me," Destiny patted the carpet beside her. Kate sat on a chair in a corner; Destiny chose the floor.

"If I get down here, I may need a hand to get back up," I told her as I settled on the floor.

"Were you injured last night?" Kate asked. Destiny, who held the remote, muted a commercial so Kate and I could talk.

"No, but I am a little stiff—I haven't exerted myself that much in a while," I confessed. "I think I'll soak in a hot bath before bed tonight."

"There's a hot tub by the pool," Destiny breathed, looking at me with wide, hopeful eyes. "Kate says I can't get into it by myself."

"Did you bring your swimsuit?"

"I did."

"Then I have to check and see if I have one, too," I told her. "If so, we'll get in the hot tub after dark."

"Goody," Destiny clapped her hands in excitement.

Parke

The sun was going down when I woke, after getting five hours' sleep. I felt like crap warmed in a microwave and figured Daniel and the rock demon guards felt the same way.

I didn't care if Rob and Will suffered for their lengthy night and day. Hell, I didn't care whether they'd found a decent bed to sleep on. We had a truce going, nothing more. They could see to their own comfort.

I needed to talk to Trey and Grim, who'd be up and around shortly. The information I'd gotten from Greenville before Daniel killed him ought to be passed on, and we needed to start looking for four ice demons, rather than two.

If we were lucky, they'd be together. If we weren't, they could have scattered to the four winds by now. We desperately needed the information Cliff wouldn't get until the following day, plus any help Trey's division could get us on tracking credit card usage for Gorham and Franks.

We still had the problem of tracking the female Shakkor Agdah, who could be infecting anyone and everyone in her path.

"Parke?" Cassie knocked gently on the bedroom door.

"What is it, baby?" I asked.

"Trey and Grim want to meet with you when you're up and around."

"I'm up. Let me get dressed. See if Daniel and the others are awake, yet. We need to have a discussion about our newest set of problems."

"All right."

I heard her footsteps as she walked away—she was wearing the flip-flops someone had given her in Douglasville. I couldn't decide whether the sound was comforting or irritating.

Maybe both, I decided and slouched toward the bathroom.

~

Cassie

"I'll get in the hot tub with Destiny," Kate said. "Go to the meeting with Parke. They need your input, just like any of the others."

"Tell Des I'm sorry—we'll get in together another time," I told her.

"Not a problem. My bones are achy after last night anyway. Tension and worry tend to do that."

"Thanks, Kate. I owe you," I said, before heading toward the living area that Parke had claimed as his office.

"You don't owe me anything," she said as I walked away. "We owe you, and you ought to know that."

I didn't have time to turn back and argue with her. Most days, I felt like a fraud; people had a tendency to claim heroism, when it was mostly a frantic preservation of ourselves and those we loved.

With a bit of interference from Will, the asshole wizard.

Cassie?

I stopped still. Yosuke was calling me.

What is it? Something in his voice told me that I was needed, and it wasn't in Parke's office.

We have someone watching the house, he replied. *I doubt they're innocent in their motivations, either. I need a small fireball from you, if you wouldn't mind.*

Where are you?

On the east end of the house, near the garages. Here, he sent a mental image.

Be right there. I had the image in my mind, and the knowledge that I'd gotten from point A to point B in a hurry the night before.

Yosuke didn't even blink when I appeared next to him. *See the car?* He jerked his head toward the road. *He's recording the house and any movement around it with an infrared camera.*

Do you know who he is?

An enemy spy. That's all I need to know.

Fireball coming up, I said.

I'll enclose it in a shield, and when he drives away, I'll send it after him. He should be at least a mile away before it detonates.

Will it kill him?

I'm counting on it.

I formed a small fireball and left it hanging in midair. Yosuke enclosed it in a shield before sending a fearful feeling toward the car. How I felt what he'd done, I had no idea. Maybe I should ask him to teach me that—if I could learn it, that is.

The car immediately went into gear and drove away. The fireball followed.

"Now, we wait," Yosuke spoke aloud. Less than five minutes later, we heard the detonation and saw a plume of smoke rise in the distance.

"Good enough," Yosuke held out a hand. An expensive camera landed in it. He grunted his satisfaction before turning and walking toward the open garage door. I followed him; he was going to the meeting with me, it appeared.

CHAPTER 7

*C*assie

"Where the hell did that come from?" Parke asked when Yosuke set a camera on the table in front of him.

"It came from the person who was staking out the house," I explained. "Yosuke and I took care of the situation."

"What did you do?" Daniel growled.

"We waited until his vehicle was more than a mile away before we caused his gas tank to explode," Yosuke replied, his words frosty. "I pulled his camera away before he and the car were toasted."

"Why weren't we informed?" Daniel demanded.

"Because it required immediate action." Yosuke retained his cool, while I became more agitated by Daniel's treatment. "We didn't have time to call a committee meeting," Yosuke added.

Be calm, he spoke into my mind. *The ice demon is only frustrated because he failed to discover the threat.*

You're a better wizard than I, Gunga Din, I replied.

If I ever carry water, I'll remember that, he said.

"May we be included?" Rob and Will stepped inside the room. Daniel deflated somewhat, Parke motioned for everyone to sit, and the meeting began.

~

"I'll pass this information along to my superiors in the department, and to those in the Council," Trey said after we'd discussed Gorham and Franks' involvement in the Douglasville massacre. "Every vampire in the surrounding states will be placed on high alert, and we'll be contacted if any of those four are seen."

"I've done the same with the Packmasters already," Cliff agreed. "Parke can get the word out to the Princes and Princesses."

"We still have to find a replacement for Greenville," Parke grumped. "We can't leave that spot vacant long, and we sure as hell need somebody in there who's on our side."

"If it wouldn't expose her to the enemy, I'd put Cassie back in that spot in half a second," Cliff said.

"I believe the sprite kingdoms would support that decision, too, but it is understood about placing her in danger," Rob nodded.

"What if she wore a disguise and was introduced as a rock demon or some such? We need someone with more clout than a water demon, this time," Yosuke suggested.

"Can you do that? Disguise her?" Parke's question was sharp as he stared at Yosuke.

"I can, or Zedarius can, although I believe you'd prefer that I do it. She will still look like herself to those who know her; she'll only appear to be different to those who don't. Her name, of course, will also have to be changed for the time being."

"I'm not sure I want anything to do with this," I said. "I don't want to be railroaded into the position, like I was last time. Most of you know what happened shortly after that."

"With a different name, that won't be a problem," Rob said. "Plus, it could help keep the myth of your death going—if Parke is seen showing a bit of interest in a rock demon Princess."

"I can be seen dating—just not marrying, so to speak," Parke insisted.

"Aaaannnd we're back to railroading," I said.

"Cassie," Cliff said quietly. "I think this may be a good idea. Our closest allies will know it's you. Our enemies won't have a clue—as long as we're vigilant about your identity change."

"What he isn't saying is that every sprite kingdom will be behind you, one hundred percent," Rob stated. "You're the miracle we never expected, Cassie. Sprite armies will line up behind you to fight the enemy."

"Then this is what you have to do, Parke," I turned to him. "You have to let everyone know that you now have a male fire demon at your beck and call—one your father kept hidden for decades. I don't care what story you make up, but he needs a name and a biography that will convince the enemy. Let them go chase a phantom. Maybe that will keep them out of my hair while we figure out how to deal with Lady Poison-Pants."

"I fully support that proposal," Yosuke said. "I, for one, would like to act as one of Cassie's assistants. She should have at least one other, and perhaps two, to handle the everyday work of a Princess while she deals exclusively with the others in this room. The enemy is a grave danger at this point, and we could lose many lives if we do not stand together."

"I'm all for that," Parke agreed. "Cassie, we'll have to find a suitable name—one that other rock demons won't question. I'll check the rolls after the meeting and get back with you."

"I may have a suggestion," Daniel offered.

"What's that?"

"The Mountain Clan in Northern Canada."

"Now there's a thought." A slow smile formed on Parke's lips.

I had no idea what they were talking about, but I'd find out soon enough.

Rob

Will and Yosuke took me to a nearby restaurant that stayed open late, so I could meet with Averill. He and three guards sat around a large, corner booth, waiting on their order of burgers and sodas to arrive.

"Just coffee for us," Will told the waitress who arrived at our table quickly.

"Is she really going to accept the position?" Averill asked the moment the waitress left.

"It appears that way. She'll be disguised and carry an alias, but it will be her."

"Good. I've heard from the other kingdoms—they're all willing to send guards or assistants."

"You mean to have someone representing each kingdom beside her —to ferry information," Will observed.

"That's the basic desire, yes, but only our best will be sent to protect and assist."

"The home near Tuscaloosa has been compromised," I pointed out. "We'll need somewhere else to stay if she returns to Alabama."

"I can have people searching for the best locations beginning tonight," Averill tapped his water glass.

He meant plenty of open ground, water access, and something easy to defend. Ground and water would provide access by Earth and Water sprites; Air would have access anyway and Fire could certainly help defend it.

"There's only the problem of having the doctor available," Yosuke said softly.

"Let me work on that," Will offered. "Perhaps we can find a solution to satisfy everyone."

"Has the home in Atlanta been compromised?"

"We believe so; Cassie and I took care of a spy who'd parked near the home and recorded images of the activity around it. I wished to take care of it before the vampires became involved. This way, the vehicle was more than a mile away when it was destroyed."

"Good thinking," Averill nodded.

The waitress was back with a tray of food; she set plates in front of Averill and his guards, then set three empty cups and a carafe of coffee next to Will.

After the waitress left, and while Will and I poured coffee for ourselves, Yosuke spoke. "The home in Alabama must remain secret," he warned. "Neither the Chancellor's name, nor any others the enemy could recognize should be on the lease or sale agreement."

"I think we can work that out," Averill nodded before taking a huge bite from his double cheeseburger.

"He'll have something for us in two days or less," I turned to Yosuke. Nobody was better at locating appropriate real estate than an Earth sprite.

"Should we keep the house in Atlanta occupied?" Will asked Yosuke.

"Perhaps. Let me consider that. I doubt the Chancellor will approve any of us staying behind, once we solve the doctor conundrum."

"You could take her back and forth," Averill told Will.

"I'll take that assignment," Yosuke agreed. "I doubt she'll trust Will enough to buy pizza for her."

"Understood," Averill said after considering that for several seconds.

"It may take some work to convince her to accept assistance from the sprites," I pointed out. "Perhaps Yosuke can help with that, too."

"I'll do what I can," he said. "But trust may be something each assistant has to build with her."

"I have a question for you," Averill told Yosuke. "With two wizards awake, now, how much trouble do you think we're in?"

Cassie

"Your appointment is tomorrow," Parke said. "You should get as much rest as you can."

Everyone else had left his office except Daniel and Trey. "I'll do that, but first, you're going to tell me about the Mountain Clan from Northern Canada."

"They hold citizenship in every state," Daniel began.

"Why is that?"

"It was granted in perpetuity by Parke's grandfather, for saving his family and the lives of the Princes and Princesses across the country. That was back when we still had yearly conclaves, and everyone was required to attend."

"The Canadian Mountain Clan are a close-knit community," Parke took over the tale. "Quite a few came south that year to see the sights with their Prince. They protected the conclave when a faction of rebellious demons attempted to blow up the building where the meeting was held. Some of the Canadian Clan died defending those inside the hall. The vote was unanimous to grant them citizenship in every state across the country, for their acts of bravery."

"So someone from Canada can just walk into a position as Prince or Princess? In any state?" I asked.

"From that clan, yes, if they're approved. And I'll see to it that you're approved. I need to advise them of what's happening, first, and get their permission to impersonate a member of their clan."

"Are they still trustworthy?"

"Yes. We communicate at least once a month; I send information on the events in the lower forty-eight. They send information from their region. They don't see nearly as much action as we do, and there were few human deaths from the disease there."

"I hope they understand how lucky they were," I sighed. "Let me know what they say. I'm going to bed, now."

I left the room, only to find Rob and Yosuke waiting in the hallway for me. "We will accompany you to your appointment tomorrow," Yosuke told me. "You will have more guards and assistants, soon, but until then, we will protect you as well as we can."

I didn't know whether to protest or thank him. I settled for the latter and wished them a good-night.

Lilith Sloane

I was out ten thousand with nothing to show for it but a crispy murderer-for-hire, his toasted vehicle, and no sign of his camera. Probably melted to the rest of the wreck somewhere, with no way to salvage any part of it.

I was more determined than ever to get Gemma the bitch, but my funds had taken a big hit from the half-payment to a now-dead assassin. It was in cash, too, so no way to get any of it back without telling the police the whole story.

Nope—that wouldn't work.

Maybe I ought to tail the bitch myself. Wouldn't hurt to do it for a few days, anyway, before finding someone with more reliable transportation than the last guy. Cops figured the gas tank had a leak, and that had led to the explosion and burning of the car. There was no evidence anywhere that it could be anything other than an accident.

Therefore, I pointed my car toward the ritzy neighborhood, hoping to catch a glimpse of her. I wasn't good with a gun but there were others who could be hired, all of whom had steadier hands and a better aim.

Cassie

I found Rob and Yosuke in the kitchen, waiting for me. Rob had a mug of coffee in his hands; Yosuke drank a fragrant, hot tea. It smelled good and I wondered what kind it was.

"Ready?" Rob slid off his barstool and took a final sip from his mug.

"I suppose. Where's Cliff?"

"Went out to put gas in the Escalade," Rob answered. "He should be back any minute."

"Did he go out alone?" I frowned at Rob.

"Kent was with him. He'll probably stay with him, too, while he goes to his friend's office to collect information on certain ice demons."

"All right," I said, while the knot forming between my shoulders loosened a little.

"I feel it too—a touch of tension and worry where the Grand Master is concerned," Yosuke nodded. "A guard will certainly help, although it may require more than that."

"Who else can we pull in to help Cliff, then?" I asked.

"I can go," Jerry sauntered into the kitchen, looking freshly showered and clean.

"Problem solved," I allowed all tension to leave my shoulders. "Thanks, Jerry. Do you have to tell Parke you're going?"

"He suggested I ask to come along."

"Good. You're with the Grand Master, then." Yosuke dipped his head to Jerry, as a sign of appreciation.

Jerry grinned in reply, before leading us toward the garage where Cliff's vehicle was usually parked. Cliff was pulling in when we walked through the door into the garage. Kent rode shotgun, and I felt he ought to stay there.

"I can get in the third row," I said.

"Ride with me in the middle," Yosuke suggested. "Jerry and Rob will ride in the back."

"Are you sure?" I asked Jerry. "It's kinda cramped back there."

"We'll fit," he reassured me.

"It's not a long drive, Cassie," Cliff had gotten out of the Escalade to join our discussion.

"Fine, but Jerry and Kent stay with you," I pointed a finger at him.

"Wouldn't have it any other way," he grinned. "Come on, or we'll be late. Atlanta traffic is a bitch."

"Says the guy who just told me it wasn't a long drive."

Cliff grinned again before climbing into the driver's seat and shutting the door. Yosuke and I waited for Jerry and Rob to get into the back row and get comfortable before sliding into the middle seats. I went in first; he settled in last and closed the door while I pulled my seatbelt on.

If anything happens, burn through your seatbelt and get away, Yosuke sent.

You're expecting trouble?

I don't feel anything now, but things can change quickly, as I'm sure you know.

Yeah. Things had certainly changed quickly on the full moon.

I stiffened when I realized why Yosuke was worried. Parke hadn't told me anything at breakfast, but there was a new rumor to put out that he'd employed a new guard—a male fire demon. Somewhere, somehow, Shakkor Agdah would get that news, and a new target would be painted on Parke and anyone else around him. Shakkor Agdah wouldn't be parked on the roadway waiting for us; they could hide themselves far better than that.

Breathing a heavy sigh, I leaned back in my seat and crossed my fingers that this new worry wouldn't make me a blubbering mess in front of my new shrink.

~

Lilith Sloane

"They're heading your way," I told Jinx over the phone. "Black Escalade—a new one. I watched it go out earlier, then it came back, then left again in five minutes. Get the tag number if you can—I was too far back in the neighbor's driveway to see it."

Jinx, Doyle's brother, was helping me out today for free—he didn't like his brother in a prison cell any better than I did.

"They just passed me," Jinx replied. "Alabama plates on the car," he reported. "It's a personal plate. GM-119," he said. "We'll have to have help in Alabama for that one, I think."

"We'll get it, even if we have to pay for it," I said. "Keep your eye on the Escalade for a while, then turn off someplace. We don't want them to know they're being followed. At least not until we find out who we're dealing with."

"You got it."

~

Cassie

"Good to see you, Cliff," Doctor Chalmers shook Cliff's hand when we walked into the doctor's office. Yosuke and Rob had taken seats in the waiting room, although I couldn't picture either of them idly flipping through old magazines while they waited.

"Thank you for taking care of this one," Cliff said, patting my shoulder.

"Hidden records?" Doctor Chalmers asked softly before releasing Cliff's hand.

"Extremely well-hidden," Cliff agreed. "As in this is life-or-death private."

"Understood. We'll be done in an hour."

"Thanks again, Doc," Cliff said and shut the door behind him when he left.

"I hear you're a special case," Doctor Chalmers motioned me toward a comfortable chair. He took a seat opposite me while I made myself as comfortable as I could. "Can you explain that to me?" he went on.

"I hardly know where to begin," I told him, with a shake of my head.

"How about the beginning?" he said.

"Well, I suppose that would be when my mother disappeared, and my first suspect in her disappearance was my own father."

Cliff

"Zach's office is close to downtown," I told my passengers as I put the Escalade in gear and pulled out of the clinic's parking lot.

Traffic was heavy enough where we were; it would get worse the closer we got to downtown. If it snarled much more, we could be late coming back to pick up Cassie.

I wanted to have lunch while we were out—the Buckhead Diner was calling my name. I figured Cassie would love it, too, provided she wasn't too upset to enjoy good food.

After twenty minutes of long traffic lights and sketchy driving around us, I pulled into the parking lot where Zach's PI agency was housed. "I should only take one inside, any volunteers?" I asked.

"Let Jerry go—in case somebody needs smashing," Kent suggested. "I'll stay with the car."

"Good enough. Let's go," I motioned for Jerry to follow me. He followed me into the building, which housed two other businesses, both of which took up more space than Zach's agency.

"He's expecting you," Kira, Zach's assistant gave me a nice smile. "Go on in." Jerry nodded to Kira as we passed her desk and walked through Zach's open door.

"Cliff," Zach stood and held out a hand. "Good to see you, man."

"Good to see you, too," I replied.

"Sit down," Zach pointed toward his guest chairs. "Want coffee?"

"I'd take water if you have it," I said. Jerry accepted the same offer, and soon enough, Kira brought two bottles of water to us before closing the door to Zach's office and returning to her desk.

"Who are we looking for?" Zach asked, lifting a thermal mug of coffee to his lips.

"You're probably going to like half of this assignment," I offered him a grin. "We're tailing Gorham and Franks, in addition to Dalton and Morton King. There's a good chance they could be together for the moment."

"Partners in crime?" Zach's left eyebrow elevated, and there was a glint of speculation in his eye.

"Got it in one," I said. "I guess you heard about the Douglasville Pack?"

"Yeah. Knew a couple of them, too. These four involved in that?"

"Up to their eyebrows. As was the former Prince of Alabama. But you didn't hear that from me."

"Already gone, eh? As in permanently?"

"Yep."

"Somebody didn't waste any time, then."

"That somebody was the Chancellor. I wasn't there, but I got a firsthand report after."

"I'll dig into the records right away, then," Zach promised. "I'll have property records for you first, and then vehicle registrations after."

"We've got someone else on that already," I said. "They're also tracking credit card usage. If there's a recent real estate purchase made by Gorham or Franks, that's the information we'll want from you, first thing. If you can talk to anybody who may have been involved in those purchases, including former owners, I'd like all the info you can get for me."

"Got it. You gonna be in the state for a while?"

"Maybe for another day or so. I'll let you know when I head home."

"All right. I'll have something for you in three days at the latest."

"Thanks, Zach." I stood and offered my hand. We shook on the deal; I pulled a check from my pocket and handed it over. "I'm good for anything over that, too," I said.

"I never worry about the bill if I'm working for you, Cliff."

"Makes for good business all around." I nodded to him and then walked toward the door, with Jerry right behind me.

"That didn't take long," Kent said as Jerry and I climbed into the car.

"That means we get lunch sooner," I teased and shut my door.

Cassie

Doctor Chalmers didn't say a word about what I did to get away from Ross Diablo. I was worried he'd tell me I should have gone to the police or the Chancellor or somebody else. Instead, he listened carefully while I told him about that particular episode.

I wasn't asked to explain anything regarding how many people Ross had under his thumb, or that my main objective was getting Destiny to safety. I was afraid Ross would use her against me, and he'd ended up doing just that.

That confession would wait for another visit, because my hour was up.

"Are you having anxiety or depression now?" Doctor Chalmers asked as he set down his notepad.

"I don't think so; I'm just having major trust issues."

"That's understandable. Cliff knows how to get in touch with me personally, so let him know if there's anything you need between now and our next appointment. I also think keeping a journal of your thoughts, feelings and memories may be a good idea. You can share those with me or not, but it often helps just putting them down on paper."

"I'll consider that," I agreed. After all, what would it hurt?

"Good. I'll see you next week, then," he said.

"Thank you for seeing me, Doctor Chalmers."

"No problem. I'm here if you need me."

"Cliff is about five minutes away, and wants to take us to lunch," Rob reported when I walked back to the waiting area.

"Lunch sounds good," I said. "I was afraid to eat much at breakfast —I didn't think the doctor would like me nervous-barfing in his office."

"Always a downer," Rob drawled.

I wanted to snicker. A small one may have escaped anyway, but there was still a wide gulf between Rob and me, as much as he wanted it to be smaller.

Cliff pulled into the parking lot in less than five minutes; Rob and Yosuke followed me out the door. Yosuke gripped my arm the moment I felt an uncomfortable tingle tighten my shoulders.

Someone is watching, Yosuke informed me. *Into the vehicle. Quickly, now.*

Ducking my head, I allowed Rob to step in front of me. Yosuke took the position behind. We may have broken a record for getting into the Escalade and shutting the door.

"Problem?" Cliff frowned as he backed up.

"Someone is watching us," Yosuke explained. "I cannot determine who without staying longer, and we should not stay longer."

"Yeah," I agreed. "I feel—itchy and worried at the same time." It was the closest description to the uncomfortable feeling I had. Yosuke's eyes may have narrowed slightly at me, but he didn't remark on my statement.

"Let me know if they follow us to the restaurant. I'll fight somebody over that," Cliff declared and slid out of the parking lot into traffic.

The uncomfortable feeling faded the farther from Doctor Chalmers' office we drove, and Yosuke gave the go-ahead to Cliff when we stopped at the Buckhead Diner. Outside, it looked like a classic fifties-style diner, with a chrome exterior. Inside, it held a nice, fully-stocked bar and waitstaff who wore white gloves.

"The food is amazing," Cliff said after checking in with the front desk.

"I second that," Rob said softly. That meant they'd been here together in the past. "Matthews Cafeteria is awesome, too, but that's farther away," Rob added.

"Matthews Cafeteria is just a small building next to train tracks in Tucker," Cliff explained. "Everything is down-home southern and amazing."

"Then maybe we could go, sometime," I said. Talking about food made me hungrier by the second, and my stomach growled in response.

"Right this way," a smiling waiter arrived to take us to our table. We were led to a round table near the back windows, with enough chairs to accommodate us. Water was poured and menus were distributed.

"The mac and cheese tots are good as an appetizer," Rob grinned over his menu.

"Want to share?" I asked him.

"Oh, yeah."

"We'll get three orders for the table," Cliff agreed. "That'll keep us busy until the rest of our food comes out."

"These are addictive," I said, stuffing another mac and cheese tot in my mouth. "If the rest of the food is this good, this is a keeper, for sure."

When I tasted the meatloaf not long after, I knew I'd want to come back. Cliff grinned when I made my *yum* sound; he'd ordered the same thing.

Rob wouldn't let Cliff pay at the end; he pulled out his wallet and plunked down cash, including a generous tip.

I suspected he didn't want to leave a credit card trail, in case whoever was watching earlier went looking for that information. I wanted to shiver as that thought crossed my mind. I didn't appreciate anyone knowing anything about us being here.

Are you on your way back? Parke sent as we loaded into the Escalade.

Just now. Is there something you need?

Just to talk. I've gotten permission from the Mountain Clan to go ahead with our plan, with a couple of adjustments.

What kind of adjustments?

I'll explain when you and Cliff get here. It's nothing you won't want, so don't worry about it.

All right. We'll be there soon.

How was lunch?

Parke, I really want to bring you to this restaurant. You'll love it.

Then we'll go sometime.

With Destiny and your mom.

Even better.

"I have a name for you to use, and they're sending two rock demons to guard you, so it'll appear more authentic," Parke informed Cliff and me. "They're scheduled to arrive at the Birmingham Airport in two days, so we can pick them up on our way back. We don't have a new location, yet, but I figure we'll have something soon enough."

"Will it be in the Tuscaloosa area, or somewhere else?" Cliff asked.

"I don't care where it is," Parke said. "As long as our requirements are met."

"Averill may have found something," Rob tapped on the open door.

"We were just talking about that. What do you have?" Parke asked.

"There's new construction on Sandpiper Lagoon in Gulf Tides. It's comparable to the house outside Tuscaloosa. The owner had it built just before his tech stocks tanked, so he's looking to sell quick. Averill and the other sprite kingdoms have offered to buy the property if you find it suitable."

"Easily defensible?" Cliff demanded.

"Yes. The property is enclosed in an eight-foot wall on three sides, with an electronic gate just off the street. The back side is open to the water, of course, and has a private dock. Ten bedrooms, plus a separate guest cottage with four bedrooms and a kitchen," Rob described the property. "Nearly twenty-thousand square feet, total."

"How much?"

"The price isn't a problem; we only have to approve the property. If it isn't suitable, we'll find something else."

"Do you have pictures?" I asked.

"I have pictures," Rob said, grinning. "Want to see?" he held up his phone.

"Yes," I said, feeling more excited than I probably should. "Gimme." I held out my hand for his phone. He walked in and handed it to me. There, already pulled up on the screen, was the exterior image of a neo-Victorian beauty, with pointed-roof turrets on each front corner.

Built in a creamy stone, with gold and brown accents, it was any princess' dream.

"Did Averill go looking for a castle on purpose?" Parke blinked at Rob after studying the photo.

"I believe he went looking for what fit your requirements," Rob said dryly. "This is the closest he could get."

I swiped the screen to get to the next image, which was a grand entryway beyond a wide, double front door. "Do you know how nice this would look decorated for Christmas?" It was my turn to look up at Rob.

"That's your holiday, not mine, but I have been known to participate from time to time." His eyes held a gleam of mischief as he told me that.

"He likes eggnog and pumpkin pie," Cliff snorted.

"Spiked eggnog," Rob amended.

"I'll raise a glass with you at Christmas if this house is still standing," I breathed as the next photo showed a massive kitchen. "This is a cook's dream."

"He didn't cut any corners, that's for sure," Rob agreed. "Princess Cassie of Alabama, does this house meet with your approval?"

"It has my approval, but Cliff and Parke have the final say."

"I say we take it," Cliff nodded as I kept swiping through pictures. "Being built of stone is a big plus in my book. A high wall is another plus. We may have room for everybody there, too," he breathed as I reached the photos of the wine cellar. It wasn't really in a cellar, I learned, but in an interior room with locks and safeguards all around it.

"People don't build basements in Alabama as a general rule," Cliff explained as he studied the wine cellar closely. "The soil is generally too wet, or has too much clay in it, or both. This close to the gulf, it will definitely be wet soil."

"As long as Trey and the others can lock themselves in, they'll be okay with this," Parke said, peering over my shoulder. "They made a good choice, building the walls of the wine cellar in stone."

"Parke?" I looked up at him.

"What?"

"I have a feeling we ought to take Beverly and Gemma with us. I don't think anybody is safe here after Yosuke and I got rid of that spy yesterday."

Parke frowned as he considered my request. "You may be right," he agreed. "We've already paid the lease on this place for six months; I doubt the owners will grumble, as long as we arrange for a grounds crew that lives off the property to maintain the outside and clean up the inside before we officially vacate in six months. We've already paid everybody's salary anyway—it's included in the lease price."

"I think I can find a reliable service to tend the lawns and flowerbeds, and there's already a contract with the pool cleaners," Cliff said.

"I'll get to work on the sale, and convince the owner that we need immediate occupancy, since this is a cash sale," Rob said, taking his phone back. "I'll keep you updated, Princess." He strode out of Parke's temporary office, looking happier than when he walked in.

"Rob will be one of my assistants—I don't think anybody else would be better at the job," I sighed.

"But forgiveness is still a way off," Cliff nodded.

"Yeah."

CHAPTER 8

"The Escalade drove up to the building. Five people went in, but one stayed with the car. Two walked back out. I figured they'd be back after a while, so I waited at a coffee shop across the street," Jinx told me over pizza.

We'd chosen a Mellow Mushroom not far from my apartment to talk about everything he'd seen. "So how long was the Escalade gone?" I asked.

"More than an hour, and three people walked out and got in the car in a hurry." Jinx lifted a fresh slice of pepperoni and took a big bite of it.

"All men?" I asked.

Jinx shook his head and held up five fingers.

"Five men and one woman?"

He nodded, still chewing.

"Did you get a good look at any of them?"

A slight shake of his head. He didn't want them to know he was there, so he hadn't gotten closer than the coffee shop.

"Was the woman Gemma?"

Another shake of his head.

"What business did they go into, do you know?"

A shrug, this time.

Well, there were only three businesses in the building. Had to be one of those. That meant they were either visiting the realtor, the shrink or the accountant. Drumming my fingers on the tabletop, I struggled to come up with a way to find out where they'd gone and who to put pressure on to get information.

Maybe running down the tag would help, and somebody was already working on that for me. I'd told Jinx not to follow the Escalade, but was glad he'd ignored my instructions. He had information we didn't have before, and I wondered whether I ought to drive by the house again on my way home or ask Jinx to do it.

"You want to run by the house on Alys Drive on your way home tonight?" I asked Jinx.

"Sure, but I'm stopping by Pit's house, first." He took another bite of pizza.

"Good. Call me when you get home. Let me know if you saw anything."

Parke

"They didn't take any flights, public or private. There are no hits on credit cards, either, so our quarry's using cash, wherever they're going," Trey told me after sundown. "We've got the FBI looking, along with state police all around us, but so far, nothing's come up."

"They didn't hitch a ride on a crop duster, even?" I asked.

"Unless it's an unregistered plane, they're on the ground somewhere. May even be taking back roads when possible, because they know we're after them by now."

"What about friends, neighbors or other connections? Chances are they know somebody who knows somebody who can hide them for a while."

"We're looking into that, along with any movements in the past— vacation spots, whatever and wherever. It's a no-brainer that they'll want to be as comfortable as possible while they're hiding. These aren't your normal, camping-in-a-tent-in-the-backwoods kind of guys."

"Our profilers say the same thing. The general opinion is that if the Kings are with them, they'll be used as a shield by Gorham and Franks."

"I wonder if the Kings have figured that out, yet."

"Want to know what I think?"

"Yeah."

"I think it'll be a toss up on which pair survives. Dalton and Morton don't have a merciful bone in their bodies, and Gorham and Franks are all about the money. Too bad nobody will be filming any of this for our review later."

"What do you have on the car Cassie and Yosuke destroyed—along with the man inside it?"

"Private Investigator who lost his license for less than legal practices," Trey said. "I sent the images from the camera to the experts; he was certainly interested in this house and what was going on around it."

"Cliff says that Yosuke felt someone watching them when they left the doctor's office earlier today. You think the PI had some help on this case?"

"It's possible—that camera was brand new and worth a lot. To me, that spells a big retainer off the books."

"I can't imagine anyone staking out this house except to spy on us," I began.

"That's the logical supposition," Trey agreed. "What we really need is to see who comes to claim the body, and then start tracking backward."

"You think we'll find Shakkor Agdah at the end of that path?"

"I don't know. It would make sense, but why hire a human? Why not send their own? They can certainly hide themselves better than the one we caught."

"You think he was a decoy?"

"Grim and the others are out there now, sniffing around with a couple of wolves. If they find the slightest scent of the enemy, we'll know soon enough."

"And if it's not connected to Black Myth?"

"Then we have another mystery on our hands. Just as well we're relocating, I'd say. The new location is more than three hundred fifty miles away from here."

"Too many questions and not enough answers," I growled.

"I will say this—the old tag is still on that motor home. How much trouble would it be to drive it out of here and rendezvous with the other vehicles elsewhere?"

"You know—that's a good idea," I pointed a finger at Trey. "Maybe the best idea I've heard in a while. Since the sprites are footing the bill for our next home, we can afford to lease a few cars and trucks."

"I can arrange to have them listed under false identities," Trey nodded. "Grim is good with that sort of thing."

"Cliff will have to leave his Escalade here, but it should be safe enough, unless the Kings find it, of course."

"Or Shakkor Agdah decides to reveal themselves and torch the place, but they're not that fond of fire. Or so I've heard."

"Enough reason to take everyone who's staying here away with us, don't you think?"

"We'll hide our tracks as well as we can."

"Good enough. Let's get the ball rolling, shall we?"

"Right behind you all the way, Chancellor."

Cassie

"Well, at least I only have to pack a few extras," I sighed, staring at the pile of clothes I'd laid on the bed.

"Parke wants Gramma Kate and me to go back to Seattle," Destiny sat in a chair near the bed and grumbled.

"Honey, things may not be so safe around here," I said. The feeling of eyes on us when I walked out of Doctor Chalmers' building still haunted me. I didn't want any of that to touch Destiny, Kate or anyone else for that matter.

Destiny had enough trauma from Ross and his bunch trying to kill her. She didn't need to see the horror that Shakkor Agdah could create.

"You think you can really fix the motor home?"

"With Yosuke's help, maybe. I can seal the gash so it won't leak air all the time, anyway. It won't be pretty, but it'll do."

"What if you die for real?" Destiny asked the question that troubled both of us.

"Honey, nobody knows what tomorrow will bring. Just remember that I'll do everything I can to stay alive—and keep the others alive, too."

Cassie! Yosuke's mental shout made me jump and shriek. *Come quickly*, he added.

With barely a thought in his direction, I relocated next to him, just as another grenade was tossed onto the grounds from across the road.

I knew what Yosuke wanted before he said anything else; he transported us across the road where the fool tossing grenades stood beside a car, pulling the pin on another one.

The fireball I tossed at him exploded as the heat set off the bomb in his hand. A neighbor had already called the police; in the distance, a siren sounded.

We must go, Yosuke reminded me as I glared angrily at the furiously burning vehicle and the blasted remains next to it. He transported us to the garages at the side of the house.

"What the hell?" Parke stomped out of the house, already going prelim. Two vamps, with Cliff and Kent helping, were putting out a blaze around the small crater a grenade created in the front yard. Somehow, this didn't sound like Shakkor Agdah. The fool who did this had no idea what he could be facing by doing something so stupid.

Parke, you and Cliff need to talk to the police. That means you have to be human, I reminded him.

Sirens were coming closer, and three neighbors were already surrounding the burning car—from a safe distance, of course.

Come, Yosuke gripped my arm. *We should go inside and let the Chancellor and Grand Master handle this.*

Parke

Cliff presented his ID to the police officer asking questions, while a firetruck and other emergency vehicles parked alongside the road and eventually doused the burning vehicle.

"He was lobbing small bombs or Molotov cocktails from across the road," Cliff explained while the officer took notes. "We were already out here, trying to put the fire out when the perp exploded."

"A device may have detonated in his hand," the officer snorted. "Any idea why he would target this house?"

"None," Cliff replied. "We rented this house for six months, and only moved in five days ago."

"Any enemies who'd do this sort of thing?"

"None to speak of."

I wanted to laugh but didn't.

"Did you get a good look at the car or the attacker?"

"We were too focused on putting out the fire he'd caused, and it was too far away to see anything clearly."

"Officer ah, Santos," Trey approached and addressed the policeman. "If you need more information, contact my superior at this number." He handed Santos a card. The officer's eyes widened, while his mouth opened to say something.

"We're investigating the death of the Lieutenant Governor from Alabama. The trail led us here, but I doubt we'll stay. You'll keep that last part to yourself," he laid compulsion.

"Damn," Santos swore, staring at the card.

"You'll keep us informed on the case and give us the identity of this attacker when you have it," Trey placed more compulsion.

"Yes. Of course."

"That will be all," Trey finished.

"Yessir."

Officer Santos walked toward his colleagues across the road. They'd be here for a while, picking up pieces of the body to haul away, taking photographs and removing the vehicle for forensics to examine.

"Well, we'll have to hire somebody to fix the lawn and the damaged sprinklers," I sighed.

"I'll have somebody on that tomorrow. We need to get out of here soon," Trey said. "First, the attack in Douglasville. Then the spy, and now this. I don't like where this is going, Chancellor."

"I don't like it, either. How quickly can we put things in place and get out of here?"

"I say it's time to put our wizards to work and bypass normal travel."

"Where to? I doubt we can take over the Gulf Tides house, yet."

"Why not? It's empty. I think I can smooth things over if there are complaints."

"What about furniture?"

"Leave that to me."

"Damn, you really can move mountains when you have to," I shook my head at Trey.

"When I have to, I can call in help through the Council. I can have furniture delivered tonight as long as they can get into the house, and I'll see they get in. Do you know where the sprite is right now?"

"In the house, I suppose."

"Let's have a conversation with him, then."

"The money was wired shortly after you agreed to accept the location," Rob told us. "We technically own it; there's only paperwork to sign and keys to collect from the realtor."

"Money talks, and cash yells loudest," Trey nodded. "We need to ask the wizards to transport us out of here by tomorrow morning."

"I'm sure they'll agree. I'll go ask," Rob said and turned to leave my makeshift office.

"Do you think I ought to send Jon back with Destiny and my mother?" I asked Trey.

"Up to you," Trey shrugged.

"I'll think about that for a couple of hours, then. Right now, I need to talk to Cassie."

"I'd say that right now, she and Yosuke have been our best protectors here," Trey pointed out. "Without their help, things could be a lot worse."

"As wizards go, so far I don't hate him," I said. "Cassie is getting along with him, too, and that's a big plus. He has also pledged not to harm any of us."

"Good to know. What about Will?"

"He says he'll never consider harming Cassie again. He'd better be telling the truth."

"Since we're not that familiar with wizards and their ways, I can't predict one way or another. I will say that I have been and intend to continue watching him closely."

"Same here."

Zedarius

I cannot explain it, Yosuke admitted. *No other demon, in my long memory, has been able to do what Cassie has done since her near-death. None can relocate. None can make themselves larger than they previously were in their full-demon form. As for releasing fireballs with this much accuracy, it astounds me.*

Humans have tales of a few of their kind recovering from near-death experiences with extraordinary abilities. Do you suppose this could be similar?

No fire demon has ever survived the spell we've laid to destroy Shakkor Agdah. There are no records to read and discuss, as this is an anomaly—a singularity in all of demon history.

"The Chancellor wants to leave by morning, and has asked that you provide transport," Rob found Yosuke and me having our silent discussion in the kitchen.

"To the new location?" I asked.

"Yes."

"I suggest we take people first, then bags and belongings," Yosuke said.

"Fine with me, as long as we get away from this place. Something is going on here—do you feel it?"

"I feel uncomfortable, but it has a lesser quality to it than Shakkor Agdah," I replied. "I have no idea what that means at the moment—perhaps we'll know more when we learn the latest one's identity."

"When will the first ones be ready to evacuate?" Yosuke asked.

"I'd say in an hour or so, but Parke and Trey will decide the order of relocation."

"We will be ready," Yosuke told him.

"Good. I'll inform the others." Rob walked out of the kitchen.

Should we discuss these new events with Cassie? Yosuke asked.

You can discuss them with her; I doubt she'll talk to me about it.

I think I'll wait a few days; perhaps she'll come to me instead.

I hope you're right, I said. *This is a puzzle, and I dislike something I cannot explain.*

Patience, Zedarius.

Sure.

Cassie

Kate insisted, so she and Destiny were going with us to Gulf Tides for a week, unless things became dangerous there. If that happened, Parke was prepared to send them to Seattle.

Gemma and Beverly packed; Beverly called her sister, who asked if she and her husband could come along to help us.

Parke took less than five minutes to hire Beverly's brother-in-law away from his security position with the Metropolitan Atlanta Rapid

Transit Authority, or MARTA. Parke offered more money, better benefits, and the likelihood of more danger, but that didn't deter Benjamin Stokes, werewolf, from jumping at a chance to work for the Chancellor.

Faith, who'd worked as a legal assistant in the past, was hired on to help me with Princess duties. She'd be assisting Rob, but it wouldn't hurt to have a woman supporting me in this.

Will and Yosuke took Parke to collect them after they'd packed.

Things were happening almost too fast, in my estimation, but Parke and Trey had their minds made up already, so we were leaving. At least I hadn't had time to settle in too well, so it wasn't a wrench to let this house go.

I was hopeful that we'd like the next one better; from what I'd seen so far, it was a fairy tale come to life. We were relying on Trey's vampire contacts to provide furniture and bedding. If beds weren't in place when we arrived, it could be a very long night.

"I have the identity of the grenade bomber," Trey announced as he walked into the kitchen.

"Who?" Parke, who'd come in to get a cup of coffee, turned toward the vampire.

"Norville Pittman, age thirty-two. Has a record—arrests made for making bomb threats a time or two and possessing destructive devices."

"Well, he didn't make threats this time—he just went ahead and did it," Parke grumbled. "You think he was paid—like the PI? And how did he get his hands on grenades?"

"I imagine somebody sold some to him—from who knows where. With his record, it's apparent that he has a fetish for explosives. Don't worry, the FBI is now involved in the crime, along with the Georgia Bureau and the ATF. We'll get updates as the investigation progresses."

"Good. I want to get to the bottom of this, and soon."

"I worry that the next outbreak of the disease will follow our exit," Trey said quietly. "We killed a large army sent against us, then foiled two other attempts. It's only a matter of time, I think."

"I've considered the same thing," I agreed. "Damn, we need to find the Kings, Gorham and Franks. They have contact information, and possibly a location, too. I want to know who we're fighting and where the hell they are this time. We didn't figure it out last time until it was almost too late."

"I've sent information to my superiors that a woman may spread the disease this time, but if she can change her image like the sprite says, nobody may be safe."

"I know we're sitting on top of a pressure cooker—stop making it worse," I said.

Lilith

"Pit's dead." Jinx's voice was flat. "He offered to check on the house and let me know if he saw anything afterward. His mom just called—police told her he threw a few bombs on the lawn, but the last one exploded in his hand."

"Jinx," I hissed into my phone, "I thought you knew better than to get somebody else involved in this. The cops will investigate, and they'll be questioning his friends. That's you, you ignorant dope. If they find out who you are, and who your brother is, you can bet they'll be looking at everybody in that house, trying to figure out who the target was."

"I'm leaving town, then. Let's see 'em find me." The call ended. I tried calling him back, but he didn't answer.

Fuck. "Jinx, if I find you before the police do, I'll kill your ass myself," I breathed while searching for the television remote. Maybe the destruction Pit caused was on the news. Maybe I'd get a look at the real enemy in this.

Gemma—this was all her fault, and I wanted her dead—now more than ever.

There was breaking news on the television, but I stopped short before switching the channel, since it wasn't about the house in Atlanta.

Deadly disease infects several truck drivers, the chyron announced.

"Authorities in South Carolina, Louisiana, Texas and Tennessee are reporting evidence of a new outbreak. This same disease is responsible for thousands of deaths earlier in the year," the talking head reported. "The CDC warns everyone to take precautions and approach strangers with caution. Call authorities immediately if you see anyone with symptoms. Do not touch anyone suspected of having the disease, as it is so contagious it will infect another quickly."

"Damn," I swore. If I could get my hands on a sample of that stuff, I'd risk my life just to hand it to Gemma myself.

"In other news, a bombing outside a house in Temperance Acres has police baffled," the man continued. "Damage was done to the front lawn before the bomber accidentally killed himself with one of his own devices."

"Pit graduated in the bottom third of his terrorist bombing class," I quipped. "Nothing to be done about it now. Jinx, you're a fucking idiot."

Cassie

I helped Beverly, Gemma and Faith put food from the refrigerator into a cooler, while bags, both plastic and paper, contained everything we'd placed in the pantry recently. If we didn't take it, some of it would go bad. I didn't want to throw it out and announce to the garbage collectors that we'd left town.

The fewer people who knew that, the better off we'd be. The owners better have good insurance on the property; there was a decent chance it wouldn't survive.

There was also the question in my mind as to why the man throwing bombs at us hadn't tossed them farther than the first ten feet of lawn. He was a poor bomber, in my opinion—Destiny could have hit the house from that distance with her eyes shut.

I'd save that question for Rob or Yosuke, later. In the past, I'd have asked Will, but that would be my last option from now on.

"Parke wants the ladies transported first, with a couple of guards,"

Yosuke entered the kitchen and studied the cooler and bags of groceries.

"Who's coming with us?" I asked.

"Jerry and Benjamin volunteered. I believe Will and I together can transport all of you at once."

As he spoke, Jerry herded Kate and Destiny into the kitchen, followed by Benjamin Stokes, Faith's werewolf husband.

"Are we ready?" I turned toward Beverly.

"I suspect we are," she smiled. Just as I thought—Beverly ought to be nominated for sainthood. She'd taken all this in stride, as if it were any other day.

"We're ready," I turned back to Yosuke. Will walked into the kitchen, then, giving me a nod without speaking.

In moments, we found ourselves in the kitchen of the Gulf Tides house, which was larger than the one we'd just left.

"This is nice," Faith touched the massive island at the center. "I don't suppose we'll ever know how they just moved us?" She blinked at Yosuke as she asked her question.

"It's something we can do," he shrugged. "We have to go back for the others, now." We watched as he and Will disappeared.

"Don't that beat all," Beverly's right fist was on her hip as she shook her head. I had no idea I'd find humor in her statement, but I did.

Parke

Trey insisted that Will and Yosuke take our bags and belongings before he and I left the house in Atlanta. Trey was on the phone most of the time while we waited, as vampires hauled in two trucks with beds and bedding, plus other furniture and supplies.

"We have connections to a furniture store in Pensacola. It's an hour drive, plus loading time," he told me. "At least the kitchen appliances were already here, plus the ones in the laundry room."

Once the bags of groceries and the cooler of food had been transported, Beverly, Cassie and the others were busy putting things away until the trucks arrived. Then, they'd started putting sheets on beds and towels in bathrooms.

"Thank you for mobilizing the vamps for us. Moving furniture is so much easier with their help."

"It's no trouble. Call it payback for what you and Cassie did for us last time."

Trey's phone rang again, only this time, the news was different. Our female enemy had managed to infect several truck drivers with the disease, and now we had a new outbreak to deal with. In addition to that news, Trey's department had backtracked on the drivers' activity, and all of it led to a truck stop in Birmingham.

Agents had already taken steps to shut the place down and quarantine anyone working there, in addition to tracking everyone who'd been there in the past three days. Truckers were in isolation wards in hospitals in at least four states, and we had questions to ask before they died.

CHAPTER 9

Gulf Tides, Alabama
Cassie

I stood behind a set of French doors at the back of the house, sipping a cup of coffee after a short night of bad sleep. The sun sparkled on water ripples in the lagoon behind us, and I watched as two kayakers paddled by.

"Princess, the Chancellor has called a meeting," Rob stepped up beside me, a large mug of coffee in his hand.

I knew about the outbreak that started at a truck stop on the western edge of Birmingham. Even exhaustion couldn't give me good sleep after that news the night before. We still didn't have cable hooked up to the house, so we couldn't watch the latest news that way. Parke had likely been awake and talking to dozens of people before dawn, when Trey and the other vamps had to find shelter and a bed for the day.

"Do they have security images, yet?" I turned to Rob.

"Yeah. Parke has them on his laptop," Rob replied. "She's taunting us by using the same disguise she used last time."

"And when we release a photo, that will change, no doubt." I sipped more of my coffee, trying to clear the cobwebs of no sleep and deep anxiety away.

"No doubt," Rob agreed dryly. "Come on; Cliff and the other werewolves are already in there, with the rock demons and the ice demon."

"So. They're waiting on the fire demon. Huh."

I turned and followed Rob, because I had no idea where Parke had set up his new office. Jon stood outside the upper-story room, looking as if a sneeze would make him jump through the roof.

Parke really ought to send him home, I thought.

Yosuke and Will had come to the meeting, too, and both looked tired from the night before. If Shakkor Agdah attacked us now, they'd have an easier time killing us, we were so weary.

Once we were all in the room, Jon came in and closed the door. "All Princes and Princesses have been alerted to this new attack," Parke announced without bothering with a greeting. "All of them will be on high alert, as will the shifter communities."

"Werewolves have been asked to report immediately if they sniff even the slightest evidence of Shakkor Agdah or the disease," Cliff took up the announcement. "Other shifter communities are coming on board quickly. We can't have an outbreak like the one before, especially since the carriers will now be much harder to identify."

"Human authorities have started calling the woman Viroid Mary, because she carries the disease without dying from it," Parke took up the thread again.

"Because they have no idea she isn't human," Rob sniffed.

"True. The CDC has been alerted, but the story is the same—a possible vaccine could be years away, and everybody could be dead by then."

"So we're back to trying to contain it," I sighed. "Which we can't do until we find the one spreading it."

"This is the first time any Shakkor Agdah has stepped from the shadows to make themselves a visible target," Will said.

"The disguise she wears is quite good, as there is no visible evidence of the poison sacs on her skin," Yosuke pointed out. "All

Shakkor Agdah carry those, in an attempt to kill anyone attacking them, and to spread the disease if they are so instructed."

"Hence the need for the cleansing fire of a fire demon," Rob agreed.

"Yes."

"We've destroyed roughly two thousand of them," Will reported. "Those last spring, and the army killed recently in Douglasville. This means they will also be keen to replace those lost in battle, which is somewhat tricky. Their females do not come into season as often as human females, and new warriors will have to mature before they are trained and given their own poison sacs."

"But we have no idea how many there are of them, do we?" Parke argued.

"No, we don't," Will admitted.

"Two thousand could be nothing to them," Parke said. "Given the amount of time between their last destruction and now."

"That could be true," Yosuke nodded. "We do not know their numbers, but I do know that the recent deaths have angered them. That is why there are new victims of the disease."

"Let's call it what it is—a plague," Rob suggested.

"I second that," I said.

Parke

"There's an ongoing effort to arrest every truck stop hooker in every state, to test them for the plague," Cliff told me after the meeting ended.

"Time, effort and money will be wasted on human women, when they don't stand a chance against the real culprit," I countered.

"I have no authority where human government is concerned, or what they're willing to release to the general public on actual non-human causes. Granted, it could paint a target on any supernatural, but we're the only ones immune to this crap and therefore, the best chance they have to destroy it."

"Just like last time," I assented.

"And we bought them a reprieve—one that almost cost us too much," Cliff said.

"Any word on the Kings, et al?"

"A couple of reported sightings, but neither panned out," Cliff sounded frustrated.

"Where were those?"

"One in Memphis, another east of Little Rock."

"No credit card purchases?"

"None."

"I think I'll ask Trey to get us into that truck stop tonight," I said.

"To do some sniffing?"

"And maybe the wizards can help with that."

"Maybe they can. Is Cassie coming?"

"I think we should ask her to come."

"When are the demons arriving from Canada?"

"In two days or so. I'll make the announcement then that we have a new Princess of Alabama."

"Do you think we'll get blowback fast when you leak information on your new male fire demon?"

"It could happen. We have to be ready for it. If Gorham and Franks are still checking the website, they'll pass that information straight to the enemy."

"And it will match up with what they've already experienced in Douglasville."

"Yeah. I'm sending Jon back to Seattle when Mom and Destiny go."

"Probably a good idea. I thought he was gonna jump out of his own skin this morning. Who will you put in his place?"

"I'm thinking about asking Faith to fill in temporarily. If she wants to, that is."

"Not a bad idea. And here, she can wear shorts or jeans to work."

"A selling point, for sure."

"Cassie should have enough help with Rob and the other sprites the kingdoms are sending."

"When?"

"Could be any time. I'm sure Rob will get a message before they get here."

"Excuse me, but the sprites are scheduled to arrive this afternoon," Rob poked his head inside my study door.

"You'll be taking point on herding them around and getting them updated on what needs to be done for Cassie?"

"I've already had several conversations with them," Rob tapped his temple. "They'll be up to speed by tomorrow."

"Are any of them trained to fight—in case we're attacked?" Cliff drawled.

"All of them," Rob sniffed, as if the question weren't necessary. "They sent their best soldiers who are also equipped to handle office duties."

"Does Cassie know?"

"She does; I told her first—she sent me to tell you. She says she wants to visit the truck stop when the rest of you go."

I was just about to ask Cliff to ask her, but the sprite had saved us the effort. "We'll be leaving shortly after sundown—when the vamps are awake," I told Rob. "Trey is pulling strings with his connections to get us in."

"She'll be ready to go," Rob said. He turned to leave. "Beverly says lunch will be ready in half an hour." He lifted a hand in a sketchy wave and left my office.

"I have some calls to make before lunch," Cliff walked toward the door. "Let me know if anything changes before then."

I was alone in my new office for the first time since I'd arrived. The furniture-moving vamps had done a good job picking a desk and other furniture. Any other time, I'd have settled on the comfortable leather chair and taken stock of my new surroundings, complete with an excellent view of the lagoon behind the house.

Instead, I had a list of worries that threatened to grow like wildfire if we didn't get a handle on them soon. Cassie and I needed to talk about how we should proceed; in the past, she'd come up with the best ideas to minimize the damage from Black Myth.

I hoped she had some ideas left because I was stumped. When my cell phone rang, I wasn't surprised to hear from the Prince of Georgia, who told me three men in Douglasville had now been diagnosed with the disease and were in quarantine until they died.

Shakkor Agdah was certainly punching back for the killing of their army and doing it in the ugliest way possible.

~

Cliff

"I have information on a recent land purchase made by Gorham," Zach told me over the phone. "Out in a rural area, and a second-hand mobile home was set on it shortly after he signed the papers. I have photos I'll send to you. There may be some evidence that the Kings were there, along with Gorham and Franks."

"No indication where they went afterward?"

"None. There were tire tracks in the grass outside the place—I took pictures of those, too, in case it might help, along with the ones I took inside the mobile home. They didn't even bother locking it when they left, like they knew they weren't coming back."

"Probably got wind of Greenville being removed from office," I growled.

"Could be. Left in a hurry, from the looks of things. Dropped a few things while packing up; I can ship a copy of the deed and the bag of evidence to you or somebody else, for research and testing if you want."

"I may drop in to pick it up tomorrow, if I can get away," I hedged. I didn't want anyone knowing my new address for any reason. Trey could have the deed and the other evidence examined by his department easily enough.

"It's locked up in my safe," Zach said. "Just come in during business hours."

"Good work, Zach," I said. "Let me know if you find anything else."

"Will do, boss."

~

Lilith

I wasn't the only one rubbernecking on Alys Drive the day after Pit's death. The charred grass across the street from the house, where he and his car died a fiery death, was the main attraction.

Of lesser interest were the burned craters on the lawn of the mansion. Nobody was out on the grounds, either, although yellow crime scene tape was still looped on stakes around the shallow pits.

I revised my opinion of Pit's skills—he was in the bottom ten percent of his terrorist bombing class. On a bad day, I could have lobbed a grenade a lot farther than he had. The line of cars ahead of me rolled to a stop, then crept forward a few feet before stopping again.

Soon enough, I realized why. Police had set up a roadblock at the end of Alys Drive and were checking drivers' licenses to see who belonged in the neighborhood and who didn't.

Fuck.

My cell phone rang while I waited and fumed to get past the checkpoint. Lanny, my contact in the Atlanta PD was calling. I answered.

"Lanny, did you get a hit on that license plate?"

"Sure did. Not sure why you'd ask me to look him up, though."

"Who?"

"Former Public Defender in Tuscaloosa County, Alabama," Lanny reported. "Cliff Young. Sources say he's on a special assignment of some kind."

I felt cold in the Georgia heat. *Public Defender. Special assignment. Had Gemma somehow come to his attention? Did an Alabama Public Defender even have authority in Georgia?* "Anything else?" I asked, feeling as if my throat had constricted too much to allow normal breathing.

"That's it, and I had to call in a favor for some of it."

"Thanks, Lanny. I owe you," I told him. "Gotta go, now. Mwah."

I hung up before he could ask for a dinner date or a quick screw. Lanny figured I was a free woman while Doyle was in jail. I let him think that because it got me favors I wouldn't normally get from the police.

Lanny would never know how much I despised the police—for arresting my Doyle on false charges and then putting him in jail after a fake trial.

"License and registration, please," the cop told me as I pulled up next to him and rolled down my window. I'd already pulled those things out, so I handed them over without saying anything.

"You have friends in the area?" The cop squinted at me after frowning at my license.

"Just curious, officer. I'm sorry I came, actually."

"You and a bunch of others, all of whom have tied up traffic and left the neighborhood in gridlock today," he handed my license and paperwork back. "It's a nice day; enjoy it somewhere else." He waved me through the line, so I got the hell out of there as fast as the speed limit would allow.

Vaalenn

"Of course they'll show up at this—truck stop. We only have to watch and wait for their arrival," I snapped at Werlekk.

"I dislike this—what you are doing to spread the disease," he whined. Werlekk wished to become my consort—and the father of my future children. In his opinion, cavorting with humans was beneath the dignity of any of our kind.

"It. Is. Necessary," I hissed at him. "Ruudann is dead. I am his chosen heir. I decide how to attack humans. Do you have better ideas?" I glared at him, making him cower.

"What if the sprites form an alliance again?" he whimpered.

"They will not," I shouted, making him cower more. "The one who formed that alliance is dead—she died killing Ruudann and those he kept close beside him. While the demons appear to have a new fire demon champion, this one cannot perform the same miracle; I'd bet my life on it. Besides, according to our ice demon slaves who saw the fire demon firsthand, this one is a male. No female could make herself so large or cause so much destruction."

"You don't think the sprites will band together again?" Werlekk's voice was barely a whisper.

"By the time they understand that it's necessary, it will be too late. Go, now. Make sure we have enough watchers on the truck stop. When the Chancellor and his servants appear, we will move in."

"And if our efforts fail?"

"They will not fail. You will not fail me, Werlekk, do you hear? If we cannot take them, then we follow if we can. If we cannot follow, then we recall our demon slaves to continue the search. Is that clear?"

"Yes, your Malignance."

"Madame Vaalenn?" One of my trusted guard approached as Werlekk turned to leave.

"Come forward, Braxxenn," I gestured for him to approach.

"I have news, your Malignance," he bowed to me.

"What news is that?"

"It appears that the pyramid fragments have finally dissolved in the acid," Braxxenn reported.

"Even the largest fragment? I saw it only two days ago," I frowned.

"Nevertheless, it is so," he said. "All the fragments have finally disappeared."

"This is a portent for the best outcome when we meet the enemy," I smiled at my guard. "Good news is always welcome, Braxxcnn. Thank you."

Cassie

The unease I felt started shortly after lunch and grew steadily worse throughout the day. If I went to Parke and told him I was beginning to think a visit to the truck stop was a bad idea, would he listen?

Or, would it be the usual male version of *You're imagining things, Cassie?*

I needed an ally in this—somebody who'd listen without thinking I was an idiot—or worse—a scared idiot.

In the middle of my dilemma, three sprite assistants arrived. Rob brought them promptly to me and introduced them. I shook hands with Zephyr Seabreeze, from the air sprites and the only female, Blaze Fireglow from the fire sprites, and Ebb Tidewater, from the water sprites.

"I've already gone over quite a bit with them already, so they should be up and running in no time," Rob sounded proud of himself.

"Thank you for coming," I told them. "I appreciate all efforts on my behalf, and on the behalf of my associates and the state of Alabama."

"We volunteered for this assignment, as did many others," Zephyr informed me. She stood straight and tall, as a warrior should, and I wouldn't want to challenge her to a swordfight or a filing contest.

"They went through rigorous testing before they were chosen to represent the sprite kingdoms," Rob said. "You have the best available standing before you."

"I don't feel worthy," I told them truthfully.

"Songs are already being composed of the battle of Georgia, Princess," Blaze grinned.

"The battle of Georgia?" I frowned deeply at Rob, who shrugged.

"I can't stop the telling of those events by the sprites who came to help us," he said.

"Are you sure it isn't the tall tale version?"

"Very sure. Averill speaks to each individually—a debriefing of sorts, before any sprite bard can begin writing a song."

"Please say it won't be played on Sprite Radio," I sighed.

"Princess, we do not have Sprite Radio," Ebb began.

"Ebb—may I call you Ebb?" I asked.

"Of course."

"Ebb, I was joking. Sort of. I just feel embarrassed that anyone would go to that kind of effort. Rob, I have a question," I told him.

"What question is that?"

"Are you having second thoughts about the trip to the truck stop tonight?"

"I hadn't really thought about it," he replied. "Are you feeling something?"

"Yes. I think I'd like to speak with Yosuke before this goes any further. I just feel uncomfortable about it, suddenly."

"I'll go fetch the wizards—no doubt Will should hear this, too," Rob said, his words dry.

"Yes—all right. Bring them in so we can discuss this."

Zedarius

Yosuke didn't even glance my way when Cassie explained the uneasy feeling she'd developed regarding the planned truck stop visit. The trouble was, Yosuke and I had discussed that very thing not an hour before.

"Can you describe it?" Yosuke asked her. For now, only he, Rob and I were meeting with Cassie. We needed to pull the Chancellor and the Grand Master into this meeting eventually, but for now, Yosuke was carefully navigating through Cassie's wariness, attempting to find a name or a reason for it.

"You remember the day I went to Doctor Chalmers and we felt as if someone were watching when we left the building?"

"I do."

"It's similar, but more a feeling of—dread, I suppose. Like I know something will happen if we go."

"Do you feel personal danger?"

"Not really. I just—worry that someone could get hurt."

I have the same feeling, I communicated silently to Yosuke.

As do I. Not personal endangerment—but danger all the same.

Then I have a suggestion, I told him.

You want the three of us to go first, don't you?

Yes. If there is something there, perhaps we can pick up on it, without having to argue our case with the Chancellor.

"Are you interested in a scouting trip, then?" Yosuke asked her aloud.

"Maybe," she drew out the word as if thinking it over while she said it.

"You won't go anywhere without your sprite escorts," Rob cautioned.

"I don't feel their danger, either," Yosuke turned to look at me.

"Nothing here," I confirmed.

"I say we go ahead, and tell Parke later," Cassie nodded. She fully expected one of us to argue the point with her. Instead, we agreed.

"I'll call the sprites in here," Rob said. "If we're not gone long, nobody will ever know we left."

～

Cassie

Yosuke transported us; it was just as well, because we all felt the wrongness the moment we were set down amid trees behind the truck stop. On the highway that ran past, trucks and passenger vehicles swept past, disturbing the air and the unnatural quiet permeating the now-closed truck stop.

Can you feel them? Rob's feet were bare, his toes digging into the soil beneath a pine tree.

Zephyr looked as angry as I could imagine was possible. *They are here*, her voice hissed in my mind.

The moisture in the air reeks of their poison, Ebb agreed.

I feel the heat of their breaths, although they are well-hidden, Blaze reported.

I feel their presence, but not specific locations, I admitted.

I can give you locations, Rob sniffed. I stared at his bare feet; they were half-buried in Alabama loam.

I can verify the Earth sprite's information, Zephyr said. *There are nine surrounding the area.*

Touch both Air and Earth, Yosuke suggested. *They will show you where each black cloak is hiding. Zedarius and I will continue to hold the invisibility spell around us. Create a fireball and send it in nine directions. I think you can do this, Cassie.*

～

Parke

Cliff read what I'd written for the website, announcing the new Princess of Alabama, Beatrice Chaumont of the North Canadian Mountain Clan. I'd also made note of the newest addition to my staff —fire demon Verity Beaufort, a distant grandson of the famed Honoré Beaufort, who'd once saved a walled city in Europe from a siege by setting the nearby river water afire and driving back attackers.

It didn't hurt that the city emptied its sewers into the river, and dumped oil into the water before Honoré set it on fire.

The result was the stuff of legends, since the sewage also burned. Human records only reported that the sewer gases were lit and the fire poured out of the depths of the castle, igniting the oil poured on the water. Only the demons, sprites and other supernaturals knew the real history.

Honoré did have two sons, but eventually his line faded into history. I doubted Shakkor Agdah would be able to trace any part of that bloodline or be inclined to do so.

"I figure they'll be out for blood the minute Dalton and Morton pass on this fire demon information," Cliff said. "If they haven't done so already. Are you prepared for that?"

"I have to be," I said. "Don't I?"

"I reckon you do."

"Then I'll hit send." I tapped the key on my laptop. The message was distributed in two blinks.

"If they find out where you are, they'll hit this place like a hurricane," Cliff's dark eyes locked on my face.

"Are you saying I shouldn't be here?"

"I think I'm saying you may not be safe anywhere—right along with the rest of us."

Cassie

I didn't have fancy electronics like they did in movies to lock onto my targets. What I had were two sprites, who had vague images of feet and bodies for me to aim at.

Then, I had to hold all the images in my mind at once and pray that none of my targets decided to move or chase a squirrel. *Build your fireball, Cassie,* Yosuke's silent word carried calm reassurance. *I see it,* he went on. *A little hotter—that's it.*

Now!

Parke

"What the holy hell?" I stared at the live news video on my laptop shortly after Cliff got a call from his investigator in Georgia.

Nobody was allowed close enough to the inferno that once was a truck stop outside Birmingham to show more than the massive, uncontrolled firestorm—the same truck stop where the enemy infected several truck drivers with their plague days earlier.

"No word on how it happened," Cliff said, watching the image over my shoulder. "Security cameras from a restaurant down the street just show it blowing up—like something triggered a bomb," he added.

"Is it just the building?"

"And the gas pumps," Cliff replied. "Maybe I'm wrong, but this looks like a trap to me. One that didn't go as planned."

"How so?"

"Chancellor, it may be a good thing that it didn't go as planned. I have the feeling that trap was set for us."

"In what way? Who'd know we'd show up? Is there a leak in our ranks?"

"The enemy hasn't survived this long by being stupid."

"What's that supposed to mean?"

"It means we don't know what they're capable of—not really. Maybe the sprites have an idea—maybe the wizards do, too. None of the rest of us have been alive that long or have much in the way of records on the subject. If I were in their place, I'd figure we'd show up sometime to look into the matter."

"Why didn't you say that before?"

"Because I didn't have Zach's help coming to that conclusion before."

"Your PI?"

"Yep." Cliff rapped his knuckles on my desk, as if that put a period at the end of this twist of fate. "He used to work in the intelligence field—for a government agency to be named later. He pointed out that they could have been watching the place for us to show up. No idea what set it off early like this, but that could be a good thing."

"Where's Cassie?" I turned my head to blink at Cliff.

"Don't you have the mind thing? Ask her yourself," Cliff tapped the side of his head.

Cassie? I called out to her. *Where the hell are you, and did you have anything to do with the explosion at that truck stop?*

BlackWing X

Zarigar

"That's—it takes my breath away," Denevik Lith, the only High Demon aboard ship breathed his admiration as we watched images of how the fire demon had sprung a trap meant for others and not only rendered it useless, but caught the Shakkor Agdah guarding it unaware. They were now dead, whereas the fire demon and her companions were still very much alive and unharmed.

"I feel the same," I told Denevik. "Nine directions at once—on the first try. I feel—pleased."

"I feel proud," Denevik shook his head. "I would love to meet this woman."

"I would also welcome the opportunity," I agreed with him.

*P*arke

"Start talking."

Cassie refused to sit, choosing to stand instead, her arms crossed tightly around herself in a defensive stance. Rob and her sprite assistants stood with her, as did Will and Yosuke.

"It was a trap," Cassie snapped.

"How do you know?"

"I knew the second I killed nine Shakkor Agdah surrounding the place. They were watching for you, Parke. You, Cliff and your new fire demon, whoever that may be."

"Since when do you know so much about any of this?" I flung at her. "No demon would understand any part of this."

"A wizard would, and did," Will intervened. "Yosuke and I knew it the moment those black cloaks died. The spell set by Shakkor Agdah was designed to detonate the moment a fire demon released his—or her—power. This would serve two purposes, Chancellor. First, it would kill or seriously injure anyone inside the building, including you and the Grand Master. Two, it would immediately reveal the presence of the fire demon they want revenge against. We left the area before more Shakkor Agdah arrived. The authorities can't get close enough to the building while there is fuel burning. Neither can Shakkor Agdah, but they didn't understand that part of their plan until now."

"You're saying they can't get close to it, either?"

"Exactly. They outsmarted themselves, and almost outsmarted us, too."

"And now all the evidence is gone," I complained. I wanted to yell at Cassie, the sprites and the wizards.

Which would be a dumb thing to do. They may have saved many lives by doing what they'd done. "Tell me," I said, still feeling angry, "What sent you on this mission in the first place?"

"A bad feeling," Yosuke said. "The later it got, the stronger it felt. We've relied on these subliminal messages for millennia. They tend to keep us alive."

"So you decided to take Cassie and the sprites with you?" I turned my wrath on the wizards.

"No, I asked them to come with me," Cassie glared in my direction.

"Because you had a bad feeling, too?"

"I did. There. Let your truth demon sort that out. We're tired and thirsty." She stalked out of my office, the sprites and wizards right behind her.

"You have a strange way of saying thank you, Chancellor." Cliff strode toward the door and shut it behind him.

"Damn," I muttered and dropped my head in my hands. My truth demon had sorted it out. Cassie wasn't lying about any of this.

Cassie

"Cable's getting hooked up tomorrow," Beverly set a glass of wine in front of me before pouring for the others.

"So Parke can get his bad news the old-fashioned way, from any room in this house. I adore you, by the way," I lifted the wineglass in a toast to her before gulping the liquid.

"I'll make sure the installer has our best interests at heart," Will said.

"And if he doesn't?"

"We'll detain him until Trey or Grim wake."

"When is he supposed to be here?" I turned back to Beverly.

"Appointment is at three. You know what that means."

"He'll be here at six, maybe," I nodded.

"If we're lucky. I'm putting another grocery list together; with this many people, we're running out of everything fast. Might ought to consider getting another fridge and a freezer for the pantry."

"I can place an order for those things online," Rob offered. "They can be delivered pretty quick."

"I'll look for a grocery delivery, if you want," Zephyr said.

"Do we want somebody coming to the house?" I asked, leaning in so I could see her where she sat beside Rob.

"It may be safer than going out to get it ourselves—we have no idea what sort of network the enemy has built to hunt for us," Blaze said.

"True," I agreed. "After what we found at that truck stop, I'm suspicious of everything, now."

"They wanted us dead—there's no doubt about that," Rob sipped more of his wine.

"I triggered their spell, just by using my fire," I said. "This doesn't bode well for the future, does it?"

"Princess," Ebb spoke for the first time since we'd taken seats at the kitchen island. "If there are enemy to kill, you are the one capable of doing that easily. The rest of us have to come much closer to be effective. Now that we are warned of what the dangers are, we can get out of the way while you take them down."

"It wouldn't hurt to practice evacuations," Blaze observed.

"Blaze is correct," Zephyr said. "Any of us could be harmed if we fail to evacuate quickly." I watched as she and Blaze fist-bumped. Somehow, such a human action displayed by immortal sprite warriors made me smile.

The wine may have helped a little with that, so I lifted my glass and emptied it.

~

Sallisaw, Oklahoma

Dalton King

The plan was to get off I-40 in Sallisaw, then take Highway 59 South until it became Highway 259, which would take us into Idabel. That's where the hunting cabin was located, according to Gorham.

I'd already done some research on my own—there was a casino in Idabel. That meant plenty of cash on the premises. A plan was forming for an ice demon heist, and nobody would be the wiser if Morton and I played our cards right.

"Pull over at that truck stop." Franks, who rode shotgun while I drove, directed me to an exit on the outskirts of Sallisaw. "We can stretch our legs and get something to eat."

"You sure that's safe?" I asked.

"Safe enough. Besides, I'm hungry, and we're leaving I-40 here anyway."

"Suit yourself." I signaled to get off; now wasn't the time to disobey traffic laws. "How long is the drive to Idabel?"

"It'll take about three hours."

"Mind if I let Morton drive?"

"If he wakes up."

Morton and Gorham were asleep in the back seat of the truck cab. Both snored, too. Gorham woke the moment I pulled into a parking space and shut off the engine. Morton kept sleeping until I reached over the seat and backhanded him awake.

"Fuck you," he growled, his skin turning to frost. I'd pissed him off, all right.

"You're driving the next leg," I informed him. Gorham and Franks paid no attention to our familial spat—they wanted food and were used to getting regular meals. Maybe they should have considered that before sending all of us to bum-fuck nowhere.

Besides, if we got into the sandwich restaurant fast enough, maybe Franks would pay for our food. "Come on, lout. Sandwiches are waiting," I said, opening the door to let myself out. Morton grumbled the whole time, but he got out with me. Empty stomachs were always good motivators.

Birmingham, Alabama

Werlekk

Even if the fire demon managed to escape somehow, those with him should have died in the detonation spell.

"There's nothing there," a third psychic body-scenter informed me.

"Not even a rat carcass?"

"No, Commander. Not even that much. We do not search for insect bodies, as that can take too much time."

"I'm not interested in the human-befouling, fucking descendants of crustaceans," I cursed at the body-scenter before me. "Vaalenn doesn't give a fornicating fuck about them, either. Somebody set off that pox-spreading spell. Don't try to tell me he came alone and then disappeared before you could tap his essence. Something—residue or whatever—has to be there."

"If it's there, it's cloaked so heavily we can't get past the shield, and that's impossible," the chief body-scenter pushed his underling aside and leveled his gaze directly upon me. "We have destroyed two pyramids; our power has increased sufficiently that we should certainly scent it."

"Then send the lore-bearer to me. Someone has to explain this debacle, and it's obviously not you."

He bridled at my intended insult, then turned, his cloak whirling dramatically about him. I watched in satisfaction as the fool stalked away. Vaalenn demanded answers, and I'd find them if it killed me.

Cassie

"The groceries can be delivered to the guest house; I don't want them coming all the way to the main house," Parke insisted when he was presented with the option of a delivery service.

"That sounds reasonable and won't raise as many suspicions as meeting them at the front gate," Cliff said.

"Just remember that you'll need a pickup or something to bring them on to the main house," I said.

"We have enough people here to handle that," Parke frowned at me.

"Not if you lay in enough supplies for a siege," I said.

"We need to plan for a siege?"

"What will it hurt?"

"I guess it wouldn't," Cliff drawled. "Besides, Beverly says we're out of milk and the way we're going through food, we probably ought to buy six gallons and ten loaves of bread. Gina's writing out the list while Beverly dictates."

"Gina and your mother are helping with the cooking, but you're sending Kate and Destiny back to Seattle," I told Parke. "That leaves us short on help. Gemma may not be able to keep up with the laundry and cleaning by herself in this behemoth. Destiny's been helping her with laundry and stuff."

"Do you want Mom and Destiny to stay?" Parke's shoulders sagged.

"I can protect them here. Not so easy to do in Seattle."

"Then they can stay as long as there's no real danger," Parke sounded defeated. "What about Jon?"

"Let me talk to him first. I'll let you know."

"We'll talk after you let me know."

Parke hadn't forgotten about my leaving without telling him; he'd only tabled the conversation. I wasn't looking forward to anything he had to say.

"Jon, what does your husband do?" I asked him. I found him downstairs, standing on the wide, covered back patio. The sun would be setting soon on the gulf coast, but there was still enough light to see Sandpiper Lagoon. We didn't have patio furniture yet—I considered asking Rob to order that for us, too.

"He's an administrator for a nursing facility," Jon answered my question. "The company he works for sold the facility three weeks ago, and the new owners may be bringing in replacements for the management staff." Jon turned toward me, looking as vulnerable as I'd ever seen him.

"Administrator, huh?"

"A good one. His previous employers never had a problem with his work."

"You're saying he could run a good-sized place, then?"

"And make arrangements for everything, including medical staff, down to food service and linens."

"How much does he make at his job?"

"Around one-fifty, plus benefits and a bonus if everything runs smoothly and the place passes inspections."

"What's his temperament? Does he get rattled easily?"

"Are you kidding? If a hurricane blew in, it would avoid Richard Lester because he would tell it to clean up after itself."

"You're saying the breakroom fridge is kept tidy?"

"He sneaks in at night sometimes to do spot checks," Jon laughed for the first time in days. "Keeps the staff on their toes every day."

"You like the benefits you get working for Parke?"

"Rich is jealous of my insurance," Jon said. "And he works in the medical field."

"I have sprites who are refusing a paycheck, which means I have money in the Princess budget to hire an experienced administrator. We've got a bunch of people here, Jon, and they all need to be fed, have schedules, get their personal supplies ordered, food delivered, bills paid and the Chancellor kept happy. Do you think he'd be interested?"

"If he took the job, he'd know the same things I do, now?"

"Yes—it would be helpful if he did."

"I'll ask. Who should he interview with?"

"Let me ask you something, first," I said. "Are you afraid to be here?"

"Well, ah," Jon studied his shoes, which were sturdy flip-flops, I noticed.

"Be honest. You don't have to make something up to spare my feelings."

"I uh, had a talk with Pete and Jerry."

"And?"

"They gave me the inside scoop on Black Myth—that's easier to say than the other name you have for them, by the way. There weren't many deaths from the plague in the Seattle area."

"I know. All the prisons they emptied were in the Southern U.S., and they really didn't have time to migrate that far before they started dying."

"Yeah. Pete said that."

"What else did Pete say?"

"That nobody was safe—no human was safe—anywhere. They told me I was better off here—behind the walls of protection they were forming around the Chancellor than I'd be anywhere unless I wanted to travel to the Arctic."

"You want to travel to the Arctic?"

"Not really."

"Want to call the hubs and see if he's available for an interview?"

"I would love to."

"Set it up for your favorite restaurant in Seattle tomorrow, if he's interested. I'll get Yosuke to give us a lift. I figure you'll need to reserve two tables; I doubt Rob and the others will allow me to go unsupervised."

"I think somebody needs to explain about sprites," he sighed.

"First of all, they're immortal unless somebody manages to murder them," I said. "Rob's never told me his age, but it could be in the thousands."

"You're kidding?" Jon's eyes widened in surprise.

"Hey. Remember those times before—when you didn't know about any of this?"

"Yeah."

"All of us existed before you were told, and it didn't impact your life one bit. Did it?"

"I guess not."

"Your life hasn't changed because of us, Jon. All lives have changed because of Shakkor Agdah—Black Myth. The last time they caused trouble, the sprites and wizards thought they'd wiped them out. They'd just gone underground so they could build up their numbers and come back stronger, with more technology at their disposal. Pete is right—the safest place to be is near the Chancellor."

"Jerry actually said that the safest place to be is near the Chancellor's wife."

"Did he, now?"

"He did, and Pete nodded after he said it."

"Well, that's different, I guess."

"I have a question," Jon said.

"What's that?"

"I know Parke talked to Faith about working as his assistant if I went back to Seattle. He said that he'd originally hired her to help you, but she had training as a legal assistant, and that's what he needed. Here's my question—can Faith go ahead and work for Parke?"

"I suppose so. Why?"

"Because I want to work for you."

"If Jon wants to switch, that's fine with me. However," Parke leaned against the front of his desk, his legs and arms crossed as he considered the other item on my agenda.

"However what?"

"I will be going to Seattle with you for the interview."

Jon had called Richard while we were still on the back patio. Richard had gotten news hours earlier that he was being replaced by an administrator hired by the new company. He'd get a severance package which included insurance for six months, but officially, he was unemployed.

I hoped the interview went well; we needed somebody to run the compound so we wouldn't have to worry about groceries, burned-out lightbulbs or dirty bathtubs. If we needed another housekeeper or two, then he could handle that as well. Trey would make sure they didn't talk outside work.

"I don't mind if you go," I told Parke. "I hope the food's good. We haven't eaten out in a while." I waggled a finger between the two of us.

"What I want to avoid," he began, "is another incident like Birmingham, in which I learn about it after the fact."

"Do other Princes and Princesses have autonomy, or do you demand they report their every move to you, too?"

"While that is a fair point in most cases," he uncrossed his legs and stood straight, giving me a hard look, "We are married, or have you forgotten?"

"I haven't forgotten, although at times I think you have."

"Cassie, married couples communicate, or so I've heard. Especially if one or the other is going into a potentially dangerous situation."

"Generally that's true, although I didn't have the best role model in my father, you know."

"Which brings me to my main question—why didn't you tell me?"

"Because I didn't want to have an argument about it. I knew I had to go; Yosuke and Will felt the same. Rob and the sprites went to guard me; what could you have done that they didn't?"

"I would have known, dammit, rather than getting blindsided by it later, and showing everybody that you don't trust me."

"Parke, the person I don't trust the most in this house is Will. He knew and he went. Trust has nothing to do with this. Most of the time, I feel like I need your permission to sneeze. I hate that. You make decisions every day that I don't know about. If you told me right now you were going to Birmingham anyway, would I argue with you about it?"

"Probably not." He walked around his desk and flopped onto the chair before looking at me again.

"The only point we might differ on is whether I went with you as added protection," I said. "I was going with you anyway—before the bad feeling started. Things have changed since I died, Parke. Some of those things are expected. Others certainly aren't. I still don't know how I got to Douglasville to destroy Shakkor Agdah, but it's a damn good thing I did."

Parke lowered his eyes to stare at his hands, which were clasped together atop his desk. "I can't explain it, either," he sighed. "Look, I promise to try—because it's in my DNA to argue cases, you know—but I'll do my best to understand that these feelings you're getting should be heeded."

"That's all I'm asking for, Parke—for you to listen rather than argue."

"Are you hungry?"

"Yeah. I sent Jon to eat before I came looking for you. There may not be anything left by now."

"Come on, let's see if they saved anything for us while we meet with the vamps and get them up to speed."

The sun had set while Parke and I talked; he was right—Trey needed information on Birmingham.

Dinner was pot roast; Kate and Beverly made sure there was enough left for Parke and me while we discussed Birmingham with Trey, Grim, Wallis and Jackson. Cliff and Kent were patrolling the grounds outside until the vamps could take over.

"How the hell did they get in there to set a spell in the first place?" Trey asked. His government-issued phone lay on the kitchen island in front of him—he toyed with it while Parke and I explained what we knew.

I figured he was wondering what to tell his superiors regarding the truck stop explosion.

Rob? I think we need your help—and maybe Yosuke's too. Trey needs to know how Shakkor Agdah got close enough to set a spell without anybody knowing.

Rob and Yosuke joined us moments later. "They got in

underground—I asked Averill to double check and it's true," Rob reported.

"Their power to remain hidden is legendary, and has been enhanced recently, no doubt, by the destruction of a second pyramid," Yosuke took up the explanation.

"Pyramid? What the hell does that have to do with anything?" Parke frowned at the wizard.

"There were four, hidden around the globe to hold Shakkor Agdah's power at bay. All along, they have searched for them. The enemy has found and destroyed two. Only two remain to do the work of all four. As you may imagine, Shakkor Agdah is now testing the limits of those two, in addition to searching for them diligently. If they are destroyed, this world is lost."

"Like Cassie's pyramid?" Parke's frown deepened. I froze. If they asked me to bring it out, they'd see it had magically healed itself and for some reason, I didn't want it known.

"It is safe enough with her," Will strode into the room.

"Is it safe?" Parke turned an accusing frown on me.

"It's as safe as I can make it," I replied, struggling to keep my voice from trembling.

"We sprites will guard her and the pyramid," Rob said, standing and bowing to Parke.

"Good. You're going to Seattle with us tomorrow, then, so Cassie can interview a prospective employee. We're having dinner at La Cocina del Gato."

"Please say that's a Mexican restaurant," Rob perked up.

"It is, with great food," I told him.

"We would have gone to protect you anyway; tamales will make it a joyful task."

"You know, I'm full now, but I'd still eat a tamale," I teased Rob. I blinked after I said those words—I was slipping back into my old ways with him, and I swore I wouldn't do that.

"Either Yosuke or I will take you there," Will said. "And act as additional protection."

"I think we should check your house while we're in the neighborhood," I turned to Parke.

It took him a moment to understand why. "You think they've laid other spells, don't you?"

"Anywhere the two of us may show up together. Make sure your insurance policy is up to date."

"Fucking hell. I'll call the staff and ask them to leave now." Parke rose and stomped out of the kitchen.

"Wise move," Will sighed. "Perhaps it's a good thing he didn't send his mother and your sister back."

Southeastern Oklahoma

Dalton King

"When is the last time anybody came here?" Morton's temper was short as another tree limb slapped the windshield. The road was nothing more than two parallel ruts with grass and weeds growing in the middle. Night had fallen, making it harder to follow the makeshift road, and overgrown trees weren't helping.

"They only use it during deer hunting season, and that's in November," Franks answered.

"Is it air conditioned?" I asked.

"I think it has window units—no idea when they were used last." Gorham's temper was fraying, too. We were cool enough in the truck, but outside—even at night—it was hot and muggy. Mosquitoes would be a problem for humans, I figured, but ice demons could freeze the little bastards to death on our skin.

I was looking forward to killing something, and anything that got close enough would die. My fingers itched to get to my laptop, too, so I could scope out the nearby casino. With Gorham's truck and a duffel of cash, Morton and I could head back to Mexico and parts south of the border.

Especially if we left bodies behind instead of live conspirators. The only thing standing in our way was Vaalenn—if she decided to call us back.

Too many times I cursed the sigil Ruudann tattooed on our shoulders —Franks and Gorham wore them, too. Black Myth could find us anywhere and force us to do their bidding.

Money and promises—that's what we were given. Only recently had I begun to question that choice. Ross Diablo was supposed to win the war against the Chancellor, and then, with all demons working with Black Myth, the world would be ours.

Ross and his cronies failed because my own fucking granddaughter decided to get in the way. At least the bitch was dead, just like her mother and that miserable water demon she called her aunt.

"Here it is," Franks announced as Morton pulled the truck to a lurching stop.

I blinked at the cabin, which was larger than I imagined. If the electricity was working, I could charge my phone and get my research done.

Half an hour later, we were inside the cabin with everything from the truck unloaded. Gorham and Franks took the two bedrooms with only one bed inside; Morton and I got the third room, lined on two sides with bunk beds.

I took the lower bunk on one side; he got the other. "We should have stopped for groceries somewhere," Morton grumbled as he sorted through his duffel. "There's nothing to eat or drink in this house except water." He found what he was looking for; his cell phone. He sat on his bunk to read through it—most likely to check Demonnet regarding Ralph Greenville's demise and the incident in Douglasville.

"We'll get groceries in the morning," I told him. "Around here, they roll up the sidewalks at eight or nine, and you'll be lucky to find a gas station or convenience store open after that." I pulled out my cell phone before digging around in my own bag for the cord to charge it.

Morton's drawn-in breath told me he'd found something important. "What is it?" I growled at him.

"Greenville's replacement is set to arrive tomorrow. It's a princess—a rock demon from the Mountain Clan in Canada. That's not all," he turned the phone toward me.

"I can't read that tiny screen from here," I said.

"The Chancellor announced his new fire demon," Morton hissed at me. "Somebody his father had hidden away for years."

"He's only now bringing this guy out?" I was on my feet and snatching the phone from Morton's hand.

"Didn't need to—he married your daughter, remember? Now that she's dead, he pulls out the big guns. We saw just how big he was, too, remember?"

"I remember. Damn, Verity Beaufort—a distant grandson of Honoré Beaufort. We need to get out of here, before Vaalenn puts us on his trail."

"She won't know about this unless we tell her," Morton pointed out.

"Or if Franks or Gorham told her already," I hissed, shoving the phone back at Morton. "Come on, we have work to do."

Morton blinked at me for a moment before realizing what I meant—Gorham and Franks would only stand in our way. He was halfway to his feet when Franks burst through the door, informing us that Vaalenn was calling for our services, and that we'd be leaving here in two hours.

"Unnnh," Morton gripped his left shoulder just as mine began to burn.

Damn. Damn it all to hell and back.

assie

Breakfast was over; the morning was fine and hot on the gulf coast and Faith was on her first official day as Parke's assistant. Jon was taking her through the steps on what he did for Parke and the list of things needing to be done.

"Cassie?" Rob drew me away from the window, where I found myself staring at the lagoon behind the house.

"Sorry, I was miles away," I told him.

"I only had to call once," he grinned.

"Good. Great. What's up?"

"Well, we figure that Shakkor Agdah has the information Parke released yesterday, if they didn't have it before. That means they'll be searching even harder for us and the fictional Verity Beaufort. We have to be prepared for more attacks by them. According to the news, the truck drivers infected by the woman we're hunting are beginning to die. It's only a matter of time, now."

"Do you think it would do any good to talk to them—the ones still alive?"

"We'd have to sneak in; they're guarded better than the President."

"You think Yosuke can get us there? I know he and Will can hide us once we're in."

"Trey's people have already questioned them. Do you think we can learn anything they haven't?"

"I don't know, but isn't it worth a try? If something slipped past the others, maybe we'll understand better. Do we know which one was the last infected?"

"I think we can get that information," Rob appeared thoughtful. "By the way, your disguise is now in place; anybody who doesn't know you or isn't someone you trust will see rock demon Princess Beatrice Chaumont, from the Canadian Mountain Clan. Beatrice was real—she died when she was ten in a skiing accident before she learned how to transform properly. As you may imagine, her parents were devastated, and were brave enough to offer their daughter's name for your disguise."

"Remind me to send them a gift for their generosity," I sighed.

"Try not to die again—I think they would appreciate that. Now. Shall I call for the wizards and the other sprites, Princess?"

"Please. We'll be sure to inform his lordship before we go, too, but he's not stopping us."

"As is proper, my lady." Rob bowed elaborately and left my office. I sighed and allowed my shoulders to sag. I expected Parke to attempt to argue anyway. Something—a feeling, perhaps, told me that more information could be had before it was too late and the last victim died.

"Will and I have discussed this, but were waiting to ask your permission," Yosuke said after Rob and I told him what I wanted to do.

The other sprites nodded their agreement; Rob had already communicated with them, I think, as they were dressed in their armor and ready to go.

"You have to be back for the interview and dinner tonight," Parke stalked in. Cliff followed him, but he wasn't radiating displeasure like Parke was.

"Do you want to come?" I asked as calmly as I could.

"I have work to do," he complained, as if what I intended to do wasn't considered real work. "Besides, I've read the reports Trey got—I doubt there's anything else to be learned, here."

There it was—his opinion and resulting disgust for the decision to ask more questions. "I'll try to make it a short trip," I said. "Besides, the poor man we're going to see will die soon anyway, so we can't stay longer than that."

Parke deflated; he knew just as I did that the man had less than a day left, at most. While Black Myth considered human lives worthless, those of us in my office did not. We'd lost human friends, demons, vampires and shifters to Shakkor Agdah, and we all considered their lives worth avenging.

"Let me know when you get back," Parke demanded, before turning and striding out of the room.

"I'll go with you," Cliff offered.

"Thank you," I told him. "I appreciate that."

Saint Agnes Medical Center

Charleston, South Carolina

Cliff

We had to wait ten minutes until the doctor and two nurses left the isolated room where Michael Southern lay dying.

"We'll have to hurry," Yosuke whispered to me. I was the only one present who didn't hear the telepathic messages between the others, but I'd catch the softest whisper the wizard could utter. I nodded, letting him know I understood.

He transported us inside the isolated room, where the patient lay, his eyes fixed on the ceiling while an IV dripped in his hand and other monitors constantly measured his heart rate, blood pressure and anything else known to the medical community.

"We don't want to alarm you," Zephyr, the air sprite, stepped forward and smiled down at Michael.

"Are you an angel?" He stared at her face, framed by blonde hair.

"No, it is not yet time for that," she said. "We are here to ask you questions—perhaps there is something you can tell us that will help find your attacker."

"I hope you do find her," he squirmed into a more comfortable position on the bed. "She needs to be stopped."

"And that is what we intend to do," Cassie moved to stand next to Zephyr. "I know you've already answered questions for others. Is there anything else that they didn't ask—that you remember from that night?"

"She knocked on my cab door—nothing different in that," he closed his eyes as if in pain. "I rolled down the window. She said she'd take forty if I was interested. Should have known better—my wife hasn't even been here to see me since I came down with this shit."

"What about her—did you notice anything different about her?" Cassie went on.

"Had a weird tattoo on her neck," Michael said.

"What did that look like?" Yosuke was now very interested.

"Got paper and a pencil? I can sorta draw it for you."

"Here." I lifted the small notepad I carried in my suit coat, plus a pen from my pocket.

"They won't give me anything like this," Michael groused as I handed both items to him. "They don't want to touch any part of me. Can't even get my kids in here to give me a hug good-bye."

"This disease is so contagious, it could kill them, too," Zephyr reminded him gently.

"I know. Please tell me you'll make her pay for this."

"If we find her, she'll certainly pay," Cassie promised.

With a nod, Michael began to draw the tattoo from memory. I hope it was clear enough that the sprites or wizards could make sense of it. I doubted I'd have the least idea what, if anything, it meant.

Michael finished his drawing and handed the notebook to Zephyr. She studied the page he'd written on before tearing it out and handing the notebook back to Michael. "Write your good-byes," she said. "This is your opportunity to tell your loved ones how you feel."

"Thank you," he breathed.

Zephyr handed the paper to Cassie, who drew in a breath at the image.

"She knows what it means," Will said softly. "As do Yosuke and I."

"We need to go," Cassie turned toward me. "Michael, thank you."

I have no idea which wizard transported us back to Gulf Tides, and I didn't care. Obviously, Cassie had come away with important information, and that was a good exchange for my favorite pen and a small notepad.

Cassie

"Shakkor Agdah royalty?" Parke paced as Will, Yosuke and I faced him in his office.

"It's likely that she is now in charge, after the deaths last time," Will said. "It is very likely that her predecessor carried a similar rune."

"What the hell is she doing spreading the disease around, then? Why not send a flunky to do it?"

"She wants us to pay for those other deaths—personally, I think," Yosuke replied. "Besides, I am beginning to believe that she doesn't have the poison sacs on her face and arms like the others—in all the images we have of her, the face and arms are not covered, but the rest of her is. Only royalty would have the power to decide that for themselves. All others are required to carry the poison sacs everywhere."

"Did Trey's information include the tattoo?" I asked.

"I don't recall seeing it in the report."

"Suppression," Will said curtly.

"Suppression?" Parke stopped pacing and settled a puzzled glance on Will.

"Was there a decent description of the woman anywhere in the report?"

"We had camera images, so they probably didn't ask," Parke admitted.

"Was the tattoo visible in any of the images?"

"I don't know. I'll have to ask." Parke sounded frustrated, which echoed my own situation. We were likely dealing with the Queen of Shakkor Agdah, and she was a vengeful bitch.

"Remember that her sort must hide from the sprite kingdoms, so they will not be found. Somewhere, there is another concrete bunker or reinforced underground space, where the Earth sprites cannot detect them," Yosuke pointed out. "I imagine that this will not be a recent construction, as that led to their discovery last time."

"So they've got more than one hiding place, then?" Parke frowned at Yosuke.

"It makes sense to divide their numbers. It also makes sense that they would settle only one or two of their royalty in each place, to protect the race from being killed in a single attack."

"Great. They've learned military strategy, then?"

"They learn and read the current languages, just as humans do," Will said. "Know your enemy, remember?"

Parke stiffened as if he'd been insulted. In a way, he had. He didn't believe me when I first told him about Black Myth's reappearance months ago. It wasn't until we had physical evidence—as in bodies— before he was convinced.

Zedarius and I wish to speak with you after this, Yosuke's words filled my mind.

All right. I have some questions for you, too.

Perhaps they are the same questions.

Maybe.

Maybe they were just as curious as I was regarding my recognition of the symbol for Shakkor Agdah royalty, as I had no explanation for it.

"Look, we haven't had lunch," I told Parke. "If you have other questions, save them for later. I have to figure out how to interview Jon's husband, tonight."

"Fine. Go eat. We'll talk later."

We found Rob and the other sprites in the kitchen, having hot roast-beef sandwiches. Plates were set in front of us quickly, so we began to eat. Rob was the one to ask the pertinent question first, however.

"How were you able to read that rune?" He asked as I stuffed a huge bite of roast beef, bread and gravy in my mouth.

I don't know, I told him. *I just knew what it was the second I saw it.*

You have not seen this sigil before? Yosuke, who was eating just as I was, asked the next question.

Not that I can remember. Its meaning just popped into my head when I saw it.

He and Will exchanged glances. *Can you now read the pyramid you have?* he asked.

I haven't tried, exactly. Why?

Only the wizards can read everything written on the pyramids, Will replied. *If you can now read the pyramid, we have no idea what that would mean, as we've never heard of such an event before.*

I'll look at it when I get back from Seattle tonight, I said.

Will you tell us if you can decipher it?

I imagine that I can't, but sure. I'll let you know, I answered Yosuke's question.

"Maybe dying has its perks," I spoke aloud before cutting another bite of sandwich and stuffing it in my mouth.

"I've heard of stranger things," Rob sighed and lifted his wineglass to drink.

La Cocina del Gato
Seattle, Washington
Parke

Jon introduced his husband, Richard, shortly after we arrived at the restaurant. Jon had called ahead to make sure we didn't have a wait ahead of us, so we were led to two tables set side-by-side to accommodate us, the wizards and the sprites.

"We're looking for someone to manage an estate, I suppose," Cassie told Richard after our drink orders were taken.

"What is it you're looking for?" Richard dropped his napkin in his lap.

"Somebody to oversee the day-to-day operations—hiring and managing a lawn service, making sure repairs are done, groceries and cleaning supplies are ordered, hiring and supervising the cleaning staff, that sort of thing," Cassie told him.

"You should see the house, it's huge," Jon said. "It needs somebody to look after it."

"There is a separate guest house, too, so that's included in the job description," Cassie nodded. "We have a lot of people staying there, some of whom are official government employees, and you'll be briefed on who and what everybody is if you're hired."

"Jon hinted at an element of danger?" Richard made it a question rather than a statement.

"There is an element of danger," Cassie agreed. "But if you can't be protected by those around you at the property, then there's no saving you anywhere."

Richard considered that for a moment as drinks were set in front of us. He and Jon had ordered red wine, so he lifted his glass for a sip before he said anything else.

"Jon said something similar. And, as there are government employees involved, I assume that there's a high level of secrecy involved in this job?"

"Yes. You'll be informed if you're hired. Are you still interested?"

"Not just interested. Intrigued, too," he said.

"I read your resume earlier—Jon handed it to me," I broke in. "You served in the military?"

"Army—for six years—until I was outed under don't ask don't tell."

"That's a shame. I imagine you were good at your job," Cassie said.

"I was promoted to second lieutenant before getting my discharge," he didn't sound happy about that. "I met Jon afterward, so there was a silver lining."

I'd sifted his words for truth from the beginning—so far, he hadn't lied to either of us. He was taller than Jon, and sat with his back straight, as if he were being grilled by a superior officer.

"Jon told me that you often went in to check on the night staff at your current place of employment—sounds like you kept the staff on their toes," Cassie said.

"That's right—just because my hours were usually during the day didn't mean I'd allow the night staff to slack off. All nursing facilities are subject to state regulations and surprise audits. It was my intention to never be caught off-guard."

"I have a question about that," Cassie said.

"Go ahead."

"We're a bit more relaxed than what you're used to, I think. If we hire you, you'll have complete control over the grounds crew, cleaning crew and anyone else hired to do maintenance and upkeep, but the kitchen belongs to Beverly. Whatever she says goes."

I blinked at Cassie—she'd already taken the measure of this man and knew he might clash with the best cook I'd ever hired. She was right, too. The kitchen would be ruled by Beverly, no matter how good the property manager was.

"Will you be hiring cook's helpers for her?"

"Maybe one or two. You can ask questions during those interviews, but the final decision will be Beverly's."

"I can deal with that," Richard agreed.

"Beverly is the best cook, ever," Jon said. "I had no idea how much I'd love southern cuisine."

"People will forgive you for almost anything if your biscuits are made southern style," Cassie grinned at Jon.

"With gravy, at breakfast," Jon agreed.

"Now wait a minute," Richard held up a hand. "Biscuits with gravy doesn't sound that tempting to me."

"Says the man who's never tried it," Jon elbowed Richard lightly. "Just wait. It's heaven on a plate."

"If Beverly can't convince you otherwise, then nobody can," Cassie said. "Do you think you can handle the job?"

"I think so."

"When can you start?"

"I'm officially unemployed now. I can start tomorrow."

"Perfect. Pack your bags. You'll be going back with us tonight."

"You already have a plane ticket for me?" Richard frowned.

"We don't need a plane," Jon teased. "Wait and see."

"Are you ready to order?" Our server appeared from nowhere. It's a good thing I knew the menu; I ordered chicken enchiladas with a taco on the side.

Cassie

Yosuke, Rob and the other sprites went with me to Jon and Richard's apartment after telling them we'd meet them there. Richard had driven to the restaurant and had to drive the vehicle home.

We gave them a half-hour head start and still made it to their apartment before they did. After following them inside, we waited for the inevitable discussion of what to take and what to leave behind.

Will took Parke to his house in Seattle, before returning to Gulf Tides—Parke's patience would have been stretched during the two hours it took for Jon and Richard to get things packed.

Then there was *the cat*.

The relatively *new* cat, that a neighbor had given Richard when she moved to another apartment that didn't allow pets.

That meant a scramble to gather the litter pan, litter, cat food, scratching post and cat toys.

"His name is Cheddar, but I've been calling him Chet," Richard explained. Chet stood at my feet, gazing up at me as if I were his lifeline in an apartment suddenly gone crazy. A ginger tabby, he had to weigh at least fifteen pounds.

In other words, he was a large housecat. Chet meowed softly at me. "You want me to pick you up? Is that it?" I asked, bending down to give him a scratch around the ears.

He purred.

I was lost.

"I think you have a cat, now. He only yowls at me," Richard said as he carried a box into the kitchen.

"Do I need a cat? Do I?" I massaged around Chet's face. He loved that. "All right, but I can't carry you around all day, you know. I have Princess things to do." I hefted him into my arms, where he appeared perfectly comfortable.

"Princess?" Richard was back, a look of disbelief on his face.

"Princess of Alabama," Rob explained. "Is this everything? If not, we can always come back later."

"It's enough for now." Jon brought one more bag to the kitchen and dropped it on the floor.

"Yosuke, can you take all this in one trip?" I turned toward him.

"If I can bother you for a bit of extra energy," he said.

"As long as it's not painful," I said.

"It won't be. You may feel a little tired after, but that's it."

"What do I need to do?"

"Take my hand." He held his out. Drawing in a deep breath and settling Chet against me with one hand, I gripped Yosuke's fingers with the other.

In moments, we—and all of Jon and Richard's bags and boxes—were transported to Gulf Tides, Alabama.

Yosuke

"I doubt she felt the slightest pull on her power," I informed Zedarius.

"That's good for us, isn't it?" he asked.

"It is—but it's also a good thing we've promised not to sacrifice her again."

"Why?"

"I doubt we'd be able to fight her if she turned what she has against us."

"Where is she now?"

"Showing the cat where his litter box is—in the laundry room."

"The cat didn't come to you, first?"

"It went straight to her."

"Interesting."

"Yes."

"Should we wait until tomorrow to ask about the pyramid again?"

"Yes. It is late and we can be patient in this."

"You're better at being patient than I am."

"You should learn to be better at it."

"Thanks for the advice. I'm going to bed."

Cassie

"We'll have a meeting first thing in the morning," I told Richard. "You'll hear all about what's going on then. After that, I have a list of things on your to-do list, and one of those things is getting a couple of cat beds for Chet. That tiny thing he has doesn't fit his ginger magnificence."

Jon, who stood beside Richard, smothered a laugh. Richard almost grinned. "Thank you for taking his ginger tabbiness; he and I didn't always see things the same way. It's just that DeAnna was such a good neighbor, I couldn't tell her no."

"That's fine—Chet and I are good. I always wanted a cat, but, well, my life hasn't been settled enough before. I hope Chet and I found each other at the right time."

"As long as you feed him, he'll be friends for life—or that's what DeAnna told me," Richard said.

"First thing in the morning," Jon promised, pulling Richard away.

"Good-night," I told them and headed toward the suite I shared with Parke. When I got there, Parke was absent. Chet, on the other hand, had not only found where I sleep, he'd settled himself on my side of the bed. He slow-blinked clear, amber eyes at me, as if we'd known one another forever.

"I see how this is going," I scolded unconvincingly, and went to pet him again.

~

Parke

"None of the videos show the tattoo, but they're all at night and grainy," Trey narrowed his eyes at the clearest of the images. "You say the tattoo denotes Black Myth royalty, according to the wizards and the sprites?"

"And Cassie," I said, my voice rougher than intended. I'd spent most of the day wondering how the hell she'd recognized that rune from a crappy drawing—done by a dying man. Trey told me the man died earlier in the evening, which left me feeling angry and confused.

I didn't go with Cassie and the others and I should have. They found information nobody else had gotten, and I wanted to kick myself for it.

"The family is refusing to claim the body," Trey sighed.

"I'll pay for his funeral," I said. "He gave us valuable information, so a decent burial is the least I can do."

"I'll send a message for someone to make arrangements and send the final bill to you. Is there a limit on the cost?"

"Try not to go over fifteen thousand, and that includes flowers and a decent memorial service."

"I think we can do that," Trey agreed. "Anything else?"

"Cassie just hired Jon's husband to run the estate. If you want to lay your requirements out, then do it tonight."

"I'll have Grim take care of it. Now, tell me how Cassie recognized the tattoo."

"I have no idea, and every time I ask her about it, it only upsets both of us. I keep digging, and she doesn't have answers. The only reason she can give is because she died."

"Can it not be that? Remember, you're talking to a vampire, now, who has also died and gone through a change."

I must have stared at Trey for seconds before my brain actually switched gears to work again. "I—ah, admit I never considered that," I conceded.

"It's something we vamps are reminded of every morning, when the sun rises."

"So far, I haven't seen limitations in Cassie. Not like that."

"You haven't seen a twenty-foot fire demon before, either, but that's what Ben says arrived to save the rest of the Douglasville Pack."

"I heard that, but figured there was some exaggeration to the story."

"Not under compulsion, there isn't. I have to be thorough for the unofficial report, you understand."

"Trey?" Grim tapped on my office door, which was open.

"What do you have?" Trey asked, swiveling in the guest chair he occupied.

"We just got a hit on Gorham's bank card—cash was pulled from an ATM near Broken Bow, Oklahoma."

"What the hell?" I was on my feet in seconds.

"Did the ATM have a camera?"

"Sure did. It was Gorham, all right. And we have images from the parking lot of the convenience store, too. Three others were in the truck Gorham got out of. I don't need to tell you who those other three are, now do I?"

"Any idea which way they're headed?"

"None," Grim walked into the room and shut the door behind him. "We've got a BOLO out to all police departments in the area, with the FBI hotline number to contact and a *do not approach* warning. We've asked for patrols on all roads out of Broken Bow, so we'll see if they show up again or go to ground."

"You think they're heading south or west?" I asked.

"I would assume the Kings would head south. As for the other two, who knows? Unless their Black Myth Queen is drawing them back this way, after we managed to thwart her attempts at the truck stop in Birmingham."

"Then maybe we ought to send Daniel and a couple of others in that direction—to watch for their arrival," I suggested.

"If they drove straight back to Birmingham on the fastest route, it would take at least nine hours," Grim observed. "I doubt they'll take the fastest route, as that includes interstates, where they're more likely to be seen."

"True. At least we've gotten a hit on them—purely by accident, I believe," I said. "We may need to brainstorm as to what their move will be if Black Myth did call them back to Alabama."

"We need to be in that meeting," Trey pointed out.

"Agreed. Want to do it now, or before dawn?"

"Best time is now," Grim said. "They won't appreciate getting out of bed for this, but if new information comes, we can deal with that as it's reported."

"Fine. I'll get Cassie and her guards up. Also, her rock demon guards from Canada are set to arrive tomorrow morning. They're already in the states, but wanted to spend a day in Michigan, to visit a relative there."

"Then it's up to you to read them in on the latest," Trey said. "Come on, Grim. We have to get people out of bed in the guest house."

Cassie

I showed up to the meeting in pajamas and a robe. I had no desire to get back into something less comfortable, only to hear uncomfortable news.

Rob, Zephyr and the other sprites took it in stride; Will and Yosuke likewise. Chet didn't like being shut out of the meeting, so I discreetly allowed him in when nobody else was looking. He ended up asleep on my lap.

The last two to arrive were Jon and Richard; Richard was about to get his baptism by fire, as the saying went.

"Gorham used his bank card to get cash at a convenience store in Broken Bow, Oklahoma," Trey began when everyone was settled inside Parke's office. "We have security camera images of him, plus the other three in the truck outside the store. Dalton King is driving, with Morton in the front passenger seat. Franks and Gorham were in the back when the truck left the store."

Jon placed a hand on Richard's shoulder; he wanted to ask questions, that was quite clear.

"Where are they headed?" Cliff asked.

"No idea, but we've got local police notified in Oklahoma, Arkansas and Texas."

"They may be headed back this way, if our Poison Penelope wants to stir up trouble after the truck stop incident," Cliff said.

"That's what Trey and Grim discussed with me earlier," Parke said. "We know she's big on revenge, and that means she's not willing to let us get away with this. We managed to kill some of her own, so why not send in demons to deal with other demons?"

"I'm surprised Dalton and Morton haven't killed Gorham and Franks, yet," I said. "I know they're thinking it—it's what they do."

"What we don't know, lady demon," Blaze dipped his head to me, "is how much of a hold Black Myth has on all four. I imagine that their leader will not look kindly on the killing of her other servants, unless she orders it herself."

"Point taken, however," Ebb nodded to me. "You are correct—if they will kill their own friends and family for some kind of gain, there is nothing to stop them from killing two wealthy demons who've chosen the same dark side as they, unless their mistress prevents it in some way."

"Gorham and Franks will be limited in the amount of cash they can pull from any ATM, and each time they risk being recorded," Parke took up the conversation again.

"He is an ice demon—he could have easily frozen the camera and broken it," Will said. "Do you suppose that he wishes to be captured, rather than remaining under his mistresses' thumb?"

"Or it could be a trap, to pull us in again," Ben Stokes suggested.

"Yes," Trey pointed at Ben. "Exactly my thought. They've eluded us for days, only to flagrantly expose themselves now? It doesn't make sense otherwise."

"We've issued a *do not approach* warning, asking those who see them to contact the FBI hotline," Grim said. "If we can track their movements, perhaps we can discover the kind of trap they're laying."

"We will send out information to the sprite kingdoms," Rob offered. "If any movement of Shakkor Agdah is detected, we'll report it."

"Same with the wolves," Cliff agreed. "They'll hear from me right after this meeting."

"Word has already gone to the Council," Trey said. "All will be on alert."

"I'm asking Daniel, Benjamin and Wallis to go to Birmingham in case the ice demons show up. They'll get the information to us quickly, so we can formulate a plan. I do not want them confronting any of these four, in case it is a trap," Parke went on. "Are there any questions? If not, go to bed. We'll have a full day tomorrow, and it starts early."

CHAPTER 12

*C*assie

"I suspect an explanation is warranted," I said after seeing Richard's expression. He and Jon had followed me out of Parke's office, after Richard heard the words demons and wolves tossed around.

"If you don't, I may not be able to sleep. Ever again."

"You may not anyway, after I answer your questions. Come to my office; I hope Chet doesn't mind." The cat was still sleeping in my arms as if nothing of import had just been revealed in a secretive meeting.

"Want tea or coffee?" Rob poked his head in the door after we arrived. Chet was happy to get on my desk and lie on my list of things to do the following day.

"Sure—coffee, please. Would you mind sitting in?" I said.

"Not at all. I'll grab Yosuke, too, if he's available." Rob took off to get coffee. Grim walked in shortly after he left.

"Thought you might need some help," he grinned.

"Absolutely—have a seat. I'd ask if you wanted coffee, but I know better."

"You're right—used to drink it, though. Kept me awake during night shifts. Now, being awake at night is *de rigueur.*"

"What did you do in your coffee drinking days?" I asked.

"ER doctor."

"Seriously? I think I want to know more of that story," I said.

"Not a problem—when we have ten minutes to spare, I'd be happy to tell the Princess of Alabama."

Rob arrived with a large carafe of coffee, followed by Gemma, who carried a tray of coffee cups. Yosuke was the last one through the door. Gemma poured coffee for those of us who wanted it, then left, shutting the door behind her.

I wondered what it was that kept her in heavy makeup mode, as it troubled me. In this hot, muggy climate, it would bother the hell out of me to be so covered up.

"We'll get right down to business," Rob told Richard. "If you decide that you don't want to take the job after all, then we'll send you back home tonight."

"I'd like to hear what I'm dealing with, first," Richard said, sounding stiff and uncomfortable.

"What you're dealing with," I said, while Chet rubbed his head on my shoulder, "are werewolves, elemental demons, all four sprite kingdoms, shapeshifters, vampires and an enemy known as Shakkor Agdah, or Black Myth. Black Myth is behind that horrible disease that keeps breaking out, and there's no known cure for it. Their goal is to eliminate all humans, so they can have the Earth to themselves."

"Without humans, we vampires will die," Grim stated bluntly. "My government agency, as well as the Vampire Council, agree that Black Myth wants to eliminate anyone who isn't Black Myth."

"Are we in trouble, here?" Richard's eyes were wide as he stared at Grim.

"Not from vampires," Grim waved off Richard's concern. "We drink bagged blood. There is no direct human contact unless it's a dire emergency."

"But what about the others—the werewolves? What if we're bitten?"

"You won't become a werewolf, and any decent werewolf knows not to bite a human unless they're threatening the werewolf's life or those of the pack. Here, that pack includes sprites, vampires, humans and demons," Rob replied. "Everyone on this estate, except the human employees, are dedicated to one purpose, and that is finding and eliminating Black Myth and their servants."

"I take it the servants are the ice demons mentioned in the meeting?" Jon asked.

"Yes. Unfortunately, I'm related to two of them," I said. "That doesn't mean I won't kill them without a second thought," I added. "They murdered my mother and my aunt Shelby, and who knows how many others. I won't even stop to ask questions, and neither should anyone else. Kill first, contemplate later, where Morton and Dalton King are concerned."

"Should I be armed?" Richard asked, surprising me. Yes, he was military trained, but I hadn't considered arming him. Generally, bullets had little effect against a demon. I had no idea whether a normal gun could harm Black Myth, although I doubted it.

"A gun will only be effective against human intruders," Rob explained. "As long as we're in the house, you should be safe enough, although if there is an attack and a subsequent fire, get out as quickly as you can."

"You expect them to set fire to the estate?" Richard didn't understand.

"No, but Cassie's fire is the one guaranteed way we have of killing Black Myth."

"I'm a fire demon, Richard," I sighed, while Chet arched his back beneath my chin to solicit more petting. "If I set the place on fire, then that is the last option available on the estate. Anywhere else, they'll be blasted to death before they can blink."

"Look up the report on a recent fire outside Douglasville, Georgia. They're still trying to pin down the reason for such a scorching, localized blaze," Grim said.

"I wondered about that," I turned to Grim.

"Just what's in the official report—my agency has the full details, of course. And Richard?" Grim went on.

"What?" Richard's eyes met Grim's.

"You won't be able to repeat anything you've heard in either meeting tonight. That's all."

"Get some sleep," I told Jon and Richard. "We'll be back here soon enough in the morning."

~

Tuscaloosa, Alabama

Lilith Sloane

"You sure this is where Cliff Young lives?" I turned to Jinx. I had to track him down; he was serious about getting out of town. He was also serious about making Cliff Young pay for his association with Gemma the bitch and any part he had in Pit's death.

"Yeah."

I'd parked my car on the side of the road, where we could see a house in the distance, past a hay field and backed by a heavily wooded area. "Likes the remote life," I said.

"Makes it easier to torch it, don't you think? We've been here for ten minutes and not a single car has gone past."

"I want to dig around inside, first, unless we set off an alarm."

"What do you think you're gonna find?"

"I have no idea, but there could be valuables inside, or addresses or something."

"Fine. If we don't find an alarm, or can cut the power, we'll go in first and look around. Then we burn the motherfucker down."

"Agreed. He'll learn not to mess with us."

"Let's do it at midnight," Jinx nodded, as if talking to himself. "Yeah. That'll work."

~

Cassie

"I need a triple shot latte," I moaned, sliding onto a kitchen barstool and closing my eyes. As expected, the morning after the late night had come much too early.

"Do you want me to order a cappuccino machine?" Richard and Jon walked into the kitchen, although Jon asked the question.

"Would you? Do you know how to use one? Where's a barista when you need 'em?"

"It's not that hard, once you learn how to steam and froth the milk," Jon said, sounding far too perky for this kind of morning.

"Good. You are in charge of frothing from now on."

"Plain old coffee," Beverly set a cup in front of me. "I don't do espresso."

"I still love you," I sighed and lifted the cup to drink. Beverly chuckled and went to fill breakfast plates with Kate and Destiny helping her.

I'm sorry your summer sucks, I sent to Destiny, knowing she wouldn't hear. Instead, she bobbled the plate in her hands and almost dropped it, before turning to stare at me.

"You heard me?" I set my coffee cup down with a thump, splashing hot, brown liquid on my hand.

"Here," Jon covered my hand with a napkin. "Are you burned?"

Destiny laughed; it was a very welcome sound. "Nothing hot can burn Cassie. Trust me." She set the plate of food in front of Richard. "I hope you like ham. Since you're the newest, you get food first."

I would like to go swimming, Destiny explored her new-found talent. *But the pool is empty and filled with leaves and dirt.*

"Richard, after you hire some help for Beverly and Gemma, look for a pool service. Destiny needs a swim."

"I'll get on it right after breakfast," Richard pulled out his phone and began making a list.

"Yay," Destiny bounced and clapped. "Thank you."

"The water may be cold at first," Jon warned.

"Ice demon," I pointed at Destiny. "Nothing cold can hurt her."

"Seriously? Fire and Ice in the same family?" Jon blinked. "I've had a few conversations with Jerry and Pete."

"I had a great-something-or-other-grandfather fire demon," I shrugged. "Our mother and ah, our biological father were both ice demons. I got the recessive gene," I explained, before feeling a shiver go up my spine. As if what I'd just said was a *lie*.

Suddenly I was questioning my heritage, and I had no idea why. I'd never felt this before—as if someone were trying to tell me something. I shuddered, hoping to dispel the feeling.

Cliff didn't have to announce bad news when he walked into the kitchen—I could read it plainly in his expression. "What happened?" I scooted my barstool back to stand.

"My farmhouse was burned down last night," he said. "I need Rob's help to see if Shakkor Agdah had anything to do with it."

"Only human scent, and nothing I recognize," Kent told Cliff after making the change from wolf to humanoid. He'd gone sniffing down the road leading to the house, while Cliff had sniffed around the house.

I wasn't sure if he could get anything other than the scent of smoke and burning from the place, but he was determined to try.

At least the local authorities had stopped their investigation long enough to let Cliff in to survey the damage; he promised not to disturb anything in the rubble, and since he was still officially on the county payroll as their Public Defender, they allowed him to take us through.

Rob, on the other hand, had already stuck his bare toes in the earth, searching for signs of Black Myth.

And found nothing.

"Does this mean Black Myth has new human slaves working for them? That's unusual, isn't it?" Parke walked up to Cliff's side.

"I suppose it's possible. I'll get my insurance agent on the phone and get the ball rolling on that stuff, but why attack this place now, and send in humans to do the job? They've known all along where this place was, and also knew I haven't been here in a while. Pretty stupid, actually, not to show up themselves. I figured it was another trap, for sure."

"They remember the beating they got last time in a direct confrontation," I said. "I doubt they were looking to tangle with the new fire demon again. If they had any part in this, it was out of petty revenge, and that would be a stupid move. We've seen the type of revenge they prefer, and that's spreading their disease around."

"Plus, it was way too early for the Kings to get here and torch the place," Cliff nodded agreement. "Doesn't make a damn bit of sense."

"Was there anything in the house worth taking?" Parke asked.

"An old shotgun and a fire safe that didn't have anything important in it. I moved everything else when we got the other place."

"Can you ask the investigators to search for both?" I asked. "Maybe the motive was robbery, and then covering up the break-in."

"Alarm should have gone off, and it didn't," Cliff raked fingers through his hair. "Unless they managed to cut it off."

"Did you have an older system that sent signals through the phone line?" Kent was acting as the police officer he was.

"I did," Cliff said, hunching his shoulders. "Never thought I'd need to change it to wireless. That means the alarm went off, but no signal went to the police or fire department."

"That matches the report," Kent said. "Somebody drove by and saw the fire. Called it in. By the time the fire department got here, it was too late to save anything."

"I'll tell them to look for the gun and fire safe. There's nothing else to be done here. If I smell either of those two humans again, though," he didn't finish. Instead, he turned away and stalked toward Will, who'd waited outside the perimeter to take us back to Gulf Tides.

"You get any vibes from this?" Rob asked. He'd put his shoes back on and now stood beside me, while Parke moved to follow Cliff. Cliff was upset—I knew that feeling. This was his home, and somebody had maliciously destroyed it.

"I get an itchy feeling about it," I confessed, as he and I began walking toward Will. "Like it's something to pay attention to, but not a top priority right now."

"It bothers me in some way, too, but I'm not a sensitive. I'll ask Will if he got anything."

"Let me know, all right?"

"I will."

~

Rob

"Revenge was certainly a motive, but given the werewolf's occupation, the humans involved could be anyone connected to past cases, I suppose," Will answered my question once we were back at the estate. "Revenge has a certain—bitterness about it, that takes long practice to detect. What I can tell you is this—one of the humans was male, the other female, and not connected by blood."

"You got that much? Damn, you're good."

"I wish I were better," he said. "But in every case, specific names elude my kind, else I'd have drawn attention to the Kings long ago."

"Where and when?" I demanded.

"They were sitting in a car not far from Cassie's aunt's property, after they burned it down. They were sent to watch for Cassie's appearance, by Shakkor Agdah, no doubt. I fogged their windows so effectively, we'd come and gone before they could see through them again."

"Talk about missed opportunities," I complained.

"I know. Consider it yet another failing."

"No—I consider that a success, because they never saw any of us. Do you know what sort of accelerant they used on Cliff's house?"

"Gasoline, although they removed most of the evidence. I imagine that the authorities will reach that conclusion soon enough."

"What about Cliff's property—he said the only things there of any importance were an old shotgun and a fire safe."

"The firearm was certainly not there—I sense-searched for

181

weapons of any kind. If they found the gun, no doubt they took the safe as well."

"I was afraid you'd say that."

"You asked, I answered."

"Right. I'll let Cassie know."

Cassie

"I've contacted a temp agency for the help we need; since I didn't know how long we'll need them, I promised two months salary, and have the right of refusal on anyone they send," Richard reported as I sank into my office chair.

"When will they be here?" I asked, while wishing I had more coffee.

"Tomorrow morning. That means we should put a list of duties together, while I scope out the house; I don't want to look like a fool while showing them around. I've already asked for a list of supplies and food to order, and I have a call in to two pool services. They'll be here this afternoon to give us an estimate."

"Coffee," Jon walked in and set a fresh cup on my desk.

"You are awesome," I told him and lifted the cup to my lips.

"I asked to have the hot tub included in the pool maintenance, even if it's in the nineties outside," Richard went on.

"Good idea," I said after consuming a heavenly mouthful of dark brew. Chet, who'd walked in so quietly none of us noticed, jumped onto my desk and came to give me a headbutt.

"I cannot believe he took to you so fast; at best, we had an uneasy truce." Richard shook his head at the cat, who purred while trying to rub himself all over my face. "I was hoping he'd have a connection with Jon. Instead, he seems to have taken you as his human. Er—demon."

"I've heard of witches having familiars, but not this," Jon teased.

"Right. Where's my phone?" Chet's tail waved in my face as I searched through desk drawers for my purse. I had to spit out cat hair twice before I pulled the phone from my handbag in a bottom drawer.

"I love you, but I don't want to sniff your butt, Chetward," I told the cat. "Go find Kent—he'll probably oblige."

Instead, Chet sat on the desk as if he were in charge. After dialing Beverly's cell phone, I waited for her to answer.

"Richard has a couple of people coming in to interview as kitchen and cooking help," I told her. "You can ask questions and have the final say whether they stay or not."

"That'll be nice. Does this mean I get a day off?"

"I think we may arrange for two, if things work out. If nothing else, Kate, Gina and I can cook one night, and let the new staff do the other. Does that sound fair?"

"Sure does. Is it possible that Faith, Ben and I can have weekends off together?"

"I don't see why not. It's only right. You've put up with us so far. I will say this, though. If you go out, take a guard with you—Pete, Jerry or one of the vamps. Just to be safe, you know."

"Not a problem. Thanks."

"What's next on the agenda?" I asked after ending the call with Beverly.

"There's a shower head in the guest house that needs to be replaced, some cracked tile in the same bathroom, and one of the burners on the stove in their kitchenette doesn't work," Richard replied.

"Contractor problems," I said. "I don't know what kind of deal the sprites worked out with the seller. I'll get with Rob to see if it's something covered by a buyer's warranty, or if we're stuck with the repair bills."

"Let me know; I'll take it from there."

"All right."

"Did you find out what happened to Cliff's house?"

"Arson. Somebody out for revenge, but we found evidence of humans instead of Black Myth."

"You haven't really told me anything about them, other than they're evil."

"They cover their skin with sacs containing the disease—if you shake hands with them, you'll have it. The woman who's been spreading it lately, though, she didn't cover her face or hands with the poison sacs. She wears street clothes; the rest generally cover themselves up in dark cloaks. In fact, that's what they're called occasionally—black cloaks."

"I've heard some people refer to the disease as a plague."

"It's similar. According to Rob, they had their fingerprints all over the Black Death, back in the day."

"You think this is a variation of that disease?"

"If it is, the CDC has never reported it as such."

"They don't talk much about it on the news."

"Most of them have no idea where it came from. Only a few—like Grim's department, know everything."

"Does Grim's department know what he is?"

"The entire department is made up of supernaturals, so I guess they do."

"Do they have any like you?"

I had to draw in a deep breath, close my eyes for a moment and then let it out slowly before I answered. "Richard, on the entire planet, there are only three fire demons left. The other two are in Europe, somewhere. Most of them have been killed by Black Myth because they present a unique danger to their race."

"How? If you're so deadly to them, how can they kill you?"

"Some of us died with a little help—sacrificed by the group that Will and Yosuke belong to, to kill many Shakkor Agdah at once."

"What she isn't telling you is that she was chosen as a sacrifice too," Will strode into my office. "I made a grave mistake then, and one that will not be repeated. Through the years, Black Myth has targeted fire demons when they are humanoid, because they are easier to kill in that guise."

"That's why you have guards around you," Richard said.

"Yes. That's why I have guards around me when I'm like this."

"So you weren't sacrificed," Richard sorted out what we were telling him.

"No. She was sacrificed. She came back from that. I cannot say how," Will admitted. "It has never happened before."

"I died. I remember dying. And then I woke up," I gesture with my hands. "It's not the best of memories. Can you save your other questions for later? I think I need to take a walk or something."

I barely glanced at Will as I scrambled out the door; he looked as if he wanted to say something but didn't. Just as well—I wasn't in the mood for a conversation with him.

Somebody had bought fabric-covered camp chairs for the back patio. Cliff sat on one of them, staring at the lagoon. I took the chair next to his.

"Been a crummy day," he said. A beer bottle dangled in one of his hands—he lifted it to take a long drink.

"Yeah," I agreed. "I'm sorry about your house, Cliff. I still remember the first time I went there."

"Bad and good memories then, too."

"I know."

"Shotgun belonged to my dad."

"Oh, no. Is there a way to identify it if it ends up in a pawn shop?"

"I got people on that. I worry that somebody will do murder with it, instead."

"Was there anything important in the safe?"

"Old papers. Maybe an address book from years ago. Probably no good to anybody, but you never know."

"Sometimes people are scum," I sighed.

"Right there with you, Princess." Cliff emptied his beer bottle.

"Need another one?" I asked as he set that one on the flagstones beside his chair.

"Nah. What brings you out here?"

"Richard's questions, and Will's answers."

"They got to that part, huh?"

"Yeah. It's unsettling every time. Cliff, I have a question," I turned to look at him. His eyes were still straight ahead, staring at the lagoon, or something beyond that in his mind.

His jaw worked for a second; I noticed he had scruff from not shaving earlier. I didn't know how old he was, but he still had dark, thick hair, a strong jaw and eyes so dark they looked black most of the time. I wondered why he wasn't married, but that wasn't my question.

"What's the question?" he turned toward me.

"Is it possible, you think, to check DNA or whatever on demon siblings?"

"Maybe, but we'd have to get one of our doctors to run the tests and destroy the samples. Why do you ask?"

"I just got a shivery feeling when I talked about my father—like I wasn't really connected to him, you know?"

"I've kinda wondered how he was able to father two such good girls myself," Cliff sighed. "I just didn't want to bring it up before. Neither you nor Destiny look anything like him, to be honest. If you want me to check into this, we can do it when we're in Atlanta for your next appointment."

"Yeah. I think I'd like to check—just to know whether I'm wishful thinking or what."

"What would you do if you found out that he's not your father?"

"A happy dance."

"We'll get the test run. I'll find out what the doctor needs to do it. Just remember those results will take a little longer than they show on TV."

"I know. Thanks, Cliff. I didn't want to talk to anybody else about this."

"Can I ask why that is?"

"Because I have trust issues."

"Understood. Look, are you hungry? Have you had lunch yet?"

"No lunch yet," I said.

"Good. Let's find one of those new rock demon guards of yours and go find a restaurant somewhere."

"They're here?" I squeaked.

"Yep. Parke has been giving them the low-down, I think, but that doesn't mean we have to see this place as a prison."

"Thanks, Cliff."

"Anytime, Cassie."

"They have shrimp po'boys on the menu," Rob said. We waited to be seated at a popular seafood joint about a mile away from the estate. I found I couldn't leave the house without my sprites and both rock demon guards from the Canadian Mountain Clan.

"I hope you like seafood," I blinked up at Landon and Liam Belanger, who appeared more than happy to be where they were.

At least my disguise was in place, according to Rob and the mirror I passed on the way into the restaurant. Blonde hair wasn't my preference, but if it hid me, all the better.

"We like seafood fine," Landon grinned. "Haven't been here before; it's a bit hot, isn't it?"

"Welcome to summertime in the south," I told him.

"We have your table ready," a waitress approached with a stack of menus in her hands. No surprise—there were eight of us to seat.

My cell phone rang just as we were seated; it was Parke calling.

"If they have clam chowder, get six orders to go. Got enough cash?"

"Uh," I floundered, digging through my purse. Eventually I opened a little-used zipper compartment and found three hundred dollars inside. "Yeah, I think it's covered," I told him. *Why didn't you use telepathy?* I asked.

Because I'm in the guesthouse, and there's a repairman looking at the showerhead. "Kent, Gina and Jerry wanted clam chowder, if they have it," he continued aloud.

"It's on the menu," I told him, opening it to check. "Anything else?"

"Pete wants gumbo."

"Right. Let me write this down," I said, digging in my purse for a pen and paper.

"Hushpuppies, too."

"Got it."

"I think that's it. Oh, and one more thing."

"What?"

"I've been grumpy, and I'm sorry. And, in case you've forgotten, I love you."

"Wow. Way to go, Worth, telling me now."

"Why? What's wrong?"

"You haven't kissed me in three days."

"Seriously?"

"Yep. I get more attention from Chet."

"Great. I'm competing with the cat. Look, I'll see you when you get back, and we'll fix a few things."

"Fine."

"Bye."

"Bye."

Cliff snickered when I ended the call. He could hear both sides, unlike the others, and found the conversation funny. I wasn't about to call him out about it—not after the morning he'd had.

I ordered the flounder with red beans and rice plus coleslaw. Cliff ordered peel-and-eat shrimp for an appetizer, then ahi tuna and shrimp for the meal. The rock demons followed Cliff's example; the sprites ordered either fish and chips or shrimp po'boys. I guess they didn't get much fried foods back home.

"We used to get shrimp pizza in Tuscaloosa, but they stopped making it," I sighed as Cliff offered me a peel-and-eat shrimp off his plate.

"Was it good?" he asked.

"It was amazing. I loved it." I peeled the shrimp, dipped it in the red sauce he'd ordered and popped it in my mouth. "Mmmm," I said.

"Just the right amount of horse radish in the sauce," he smiled. "This is really good."

"Yeah. That stuff can clear your sinuses if they get too heavy with it."

Cliff's phone rang as his entrée was set in front of him. He looked at the caller ID before rising and answering as he walked away.

"What?" I heard him say as he headed for the door. He didn't sound happy when he said it, either.

Cassie, Parke broke into my thoughts. *Your shrink was shot half an hour ago—he's in the hospital and they don't know whether he'll make it or not. His receptionist is dead. Both shot with a shotgun, according to preliminary reports.*

Fuck.

Exactly.

CHAPTER 13

*D*ecatur, Georgia
Lilith Sloane

Jinx shot the receptionist before I had time to ask questions; the shrink came rushing out of his office with a pistol and shot at Jinx before Jinx unloaded the second barrel into his chest. Jinx had fucked this up from the get-go, and now we had no idea what the connection between the shrink and Cliff Young was.

Jinx had a bullet in his right shoulder, now, and I couldn't take him to a hospital; they'd know what was up.

"Damn, it's still bleeding," he whined from the passenger seat of my car.

"Yeah—you're getting blood all over everything, you asshole. What the hell did you think you were doing, shooting first? Now you've got a murder charge against you, I'm an accessory and we still don't know a damn thing."

"I thought if we shot somebody with his shotgun," Jinx whined.

"Where the hell did you get your brains? At a discount store? That gun will be reported stolen, you moron."

"I'm not a moron. I'm bleeding."

"Right. And there's nothing we can do about it, unless you know a doctor who can keep his mouth shut."

"I have a friend who flunked out of vet school."

"You want him working on you?"

"It's all I got, and this won't stop hurting. What if I bleed to death?"

"I'd say you deserve to bleed to death for being an idiot."

"Somebody had to pay for Pit."

"Stop talking, or I'll kill you myself."

"Where are we going?" He craned his neck to look through the windshield.

"My cousin has a trailer outside Duluth. We're going there. Shut up."

Cassie

"His business address was in my address book—the one inside the fire safe," Cliff's words were barely discernible around the constant growling as he paced.

"Somebody was watching us that day—when we went," I said. Parke frowned at me, but nodded his understanding.

"Probably got Cliff's tag number off his Escalade, and found his name from that," Parke said. He, Cliff, Kent and Jerry were inside Parke's office, discussing the shootings in Atlanta.

"That, in turn, led them to Cliff's residence on record," Kent agreed. "They cut the phone line so the alarm wouldn't go off, ransacked the place, took the gun and the safe, then burned the place down. Do we have any security images from the shooting?"

"I'm sure there's something, but we haven't been able to get around the red tape to be included, yet," Parke replied. "Damn, I wish Trey was awake."

"I've already talked to the PD back home, telling them that the stolen shotgun may have been used in this crime," Kent said. "If they get any feedback after contacting the authorities in Atlanta, they'll let me know."

"Call Trey's superior, Director Logan," I said. "Maybe he can loop us in."

"I'll do that." Parke pulled his cell phone off his desk and strode into the hallway to make the call.

I huddled in one of Parke's guest chairs, feeling small—this was my fault. I'd needed Doctor Chalmers' help, and that had exposed him and Cliff to this horror.

"We have information," Parke rushed in. "He's sending it to my laptop. They may have ID on the perps, too."

"More than one?"

"Probably the two Kent and I detected at the house," Cliff sounded feral, and his eyes held a strange light in their depths.

Parke tapped on his laptop after sitting at his desk. It only took a moment to load up the video sent to him. All of us crowded around his desk to see.

We watched images from a security camera outside Doctor Chalmers' building, as two people, a man and a woman, walked in. The long coat the man wore was completely out of place in the Atlanta heat.

"Shotgun under the coat," Kent breathed.

"Yep," Jerry agreed. I couldn't see faces clearly, but it was only moments later that both ran out the door, the man not bothering to hide the shotgun in his hand. The image shifted to another camera shot, which showed them getting into a car about a block away. I could tell the man was wounded in the right shoulder by that time; blood had finally soaked through the tan coat he wore. He didn't have an easy time opening the car door or getting the shotgun inside it, either. Once inside, he slumped into the seat as the car pulled out of the parking spot and almost hit a delivery service van.

The image cut one last time—to the dashcam on the delivery truck.

There was a very good image of a tag number on that footage. Cliff's throat rumbled at that point. He moved away, jerked out his phone and was talking to someone about tracing the tag in seconds.

"I need to get to Atlanta," he said after ending the call. I recognized the light in Cliff's eyes, now—he'd found his prey.

Cliff, Kent, Parke, Jerry, Yosuke and I were back at the house in Temperance Acres; we were still entitled to it as the lease wouldn't run out for five more months. We had an ID on the woman who owned the car; Lilith Sloane.

As for the man, Atlanta PD was still attempting to identify him. "Her husband's in prison," Parke announced as new information came to his laptop. We sat in the kitchen, waiting for updates while Cliff paced like a caged wolf and I sat watching him, feeling helpless.

He wanted to go to the crime scene, but everyone advised him against it, since others could be watching for him. We didn't need a bigger target painted on his back, or the backs of his friends listed in an old address book.

Do you need us? Rob sent.

Not now—we're holed up in the house, waiting for more information. We have ID on the woman; her name is Lilith Sloane. Apparently her husband is in prison right now, so we have no idea whether that's connected or not.

What's her husband's name?

Hold on, I had to walk behind Parke to look at the email he'd gotten. *Doyle Hicks,* I said. *Looks like she didn't take his name.*

Are they looking at his criminal connections?

Probably, but I'll ask. Looks like he's in jail for aggravated assault, attempted murder, and rape—for eighteen more years of a twenty-year sentence.

What a nice guy, Rob's sarcasm came through clearly. *I can't believe that woman is still married to him. That's grounds for divorce, right there.*

Not if she believes he's innocent. Some people are that gullible, I reminded him.

But what does all that have to do with Cliff? This makes no sense. He has no connection to that case or any of those people.

We're missing something here, I agreed. *It's a nagging feeling that this is all—wonky. I hope it isn't the reason the ice demons are coming back this way.*

I figure they logged onto Demonnet and got pulled back after Parke's post was handed to Shakkor Agdah.

That makes more sense than these people coming after Cliff.

"They've been arrested," Cliff crowed aloud, interrupting my silent conversation with Rob.

Looks like the culprits just got arrested. I'll get back with you when we know more, I told the Earth sprite.

I turned toward Parke and Cliff, who were glued to Parke's laptop screen. I moved over to stand with Cliff; we watched a live feed as the man was being loaded into an ambulance, while the woman was handcuffed and shoved into a police cruiser.

"Any news on Doctor Chalmers?" I bumped Cliff's shoulder with mine.

"In surgery, last I heard," he said softly. "Too bad I can't hand out werewolf justice on this one." His hands clenched and unclenched as we watched the ambulance drive away first, followed by the police car carrying Lilith Sloane.

"Man's name is Jinx Hicks—Doyle Hicks' brother," Parke read the information aloud as it appeared on his screen. "That makes some sort of sense, but still no idea why they'd come after Cliff."

Parke's phone rang, then. He answered quickly. "You're saying Jinx Hicks is connected to Norville Pittman?"

Cliff and I exchanged a glance. Norville Pittman—the man who'd tossed bombs on the lawn and precipitated our move from Atlanta to Gulf Tides. Hicks may have been looking for revenge for his friend's death, but why was he tossing bombs on the lawn in the first place?

"You think Pittman was in cahoots with Shakkor Agdah?" Cliff asked.

"I think they wouldn't have bothered with a human if they'd known where we were," Parke said. "Cliff, do you want to go to the hospital?"

"When he's out of surgery. I don't want a mob of press waiting to ask questions of anybody who shows up."

"We don't need your name associated with this, if we can help it," I agreed. "Shakkor Agdah will be aiming for you, and they can cause more harm than that human idiot ever could. Parke, is there any way you can be present when those two are questioned?" I asked.

"Why?" He turned his head to look at me.

"Because you'll know whether they're telling the truth or not. It's still daylight and we can't get a vamp in there for compulsion. You're the next logical choice."

"I can't force them to answer questions like a vamp can. We need to wait." His answer didn't make me feel better about the situation—I had a sudden sense of urgency about this whole mess, and I couldn't explain it.

"I can transport you back to Gulf Tides," Yosuke offered. "Cliff, I can bring you back to see your friend from there, just as easily. Like Cassie, I have an unsettled feeling about this. We should go now if Parke is unwilling to be present at the questioning."

"Fine." Parke shut his laptop and stood. "I'm ready whenever you are."

In seconds, we were back in Parke's office at the Gulf Tides estate. We didn't get the news that the Temperance Acres house exploded behind us until nearly an hour later.

Cliff

"The bombs were laid around the perimeter; when the police learned that Jinx Hicks had a direct connection to Norville Pittman, and that Hicks had been seen around the house by a neighbor, they went to check on it. The moment they forced the door open, everything he'd set out went off. One officer is dead, two others wounded," Parke sighed. His elbows were planted on the desk, with both hands now covering his face.

"So we avoided being blown up because we were transported directly inside the house?"

"Yes." Parke dropped his hands. He looked haggard, as I suppose I did. This had been a decidedly bad day, and it wasn't over yet.

We'd waited all afternoon and evening for more information, and Parke had only received this much in the last ten minutes. "We've been brought up to speed," Trey and Grim walked into the office, although Trey was the only one who spoke.

"Do you know what those two are saying? We don't have any information on the questioning," Parke said.

"They've lawyered up, which is no surprise, and both have been advised to say nothing. Jinx Hicks is still groggy after the surgery to remove the bullet in his shoulder; Lilith Sloane has refused to speak from the beginning. The only information they have as yet is Hick's connection to Pittman, and we all know the results of the intended search of the house in Atlanta."

"Yeah. We know that, all right."

"I also have a report that the truck belonging to Gorham was found by a fisherman in a wooded area between Birmingham and Atlanta. At least three vehicles were reported stolen in the same area close to that time. The Kings, Gorham and Franks could be in any or all of them."

"Fuck me," Parke moaned and leaned back in his chair.

"We have trouble," Kent walked in and shut the door. "I just heard from the guys at my station. They say there's information all over the Internet that says the gun stolen from Cliff's house was used in the Atlanta shooting, and that Cliff and Doctor Chalmers knew one another. They don't have any idea who leaked that information, but it's out there and impossible to shut down. Cliff's name is now officially tied to those two, and there's no way to know how that will play out."

"I need to get out of here," I snapped while fur stood straight out on my forearms. I was about to go fully-furred and needed a place to run.

"Parke," Cassie opened the door, almost hitting me in the nose. She took one look at me, grabbed my hand and we were both teleported elsewhere.

~

Cassie

I didn't know where else to take him that would be familiar and make it easy to find him at the same time, so I took Cliff to his acreage outside Tuscaloosa. I didn't set him down anywhere near the burned-down house, but instead put him in the ravine where I'd turned the first time.

His clothes were flung away and he was wolf in seconds, before charging out of the ravine and running toward the nearest stand of trees. After gathering his clothing and folding it to avoid wrinkles, I sat down to wait for him.

Cassie? Where are you? Rob sent.

In Cliff's ravine. He's ah—out running off his anger and frustration, I replied.

Understandable. We'll be there in a few.

All right.

In moments, all four sprites and Will arrived.

The sprites sat around me while Will wandered up the ravine.

"You can see so many more stars out here," I looked up into the clear, summer sky overhead. "When I was little, I always thought the night sky looked like a luminous, blue bowl overhead with twinkling lights and glitter set in it."

"The universe is indeed magical—when you see it from this far away," Ebb agreed. "Perhaps there is someone near one of those stars in the distance, with their own set of troubles, who've stopped to study us and the beauty around us for a few minutes."

"*No human thing is of serious importance.* Plato said that," Rob breathed as he studied the sky beside me.

"Unless you're in the middle of it, fighting for human survival and the survival of all species on the planet," Zephyr said gently. "If Shakkor Agdah succeeds, all will die and the planet will be overrun by their race. Then they will fight themselves for dominance and survival. It is their way."

"It's a stupid way," Ebb offered. "You don't mow down the garden that feeds you."

"High five," I held up a hand. Ebb had to reach around Rob, but we slapped hands and chuckled.

Cassie? Parke was calling.

Is something wrong?

No—Trey says Doctor Chalmers is out of surgery and the doctors are optimistic about his recovery.

Thank goodness. Cliff's wolf is out running. I'll let him know when he comes back.

Trey wants Yosuke to take him to Atlanta in the middle of the night to ask Lilith Sloane questions. Yosuke can get us into her cell and put up a shield while he places compulsion. We need to find out what's going on, and Trey's supervisor has given permission. Mostly, he wants to know if those two are aligned with Black Myth.

I want to know that, too. Are you going with Trey?

Yes.

Be careful and listen to Yosuke if he says things aren't right.

I will.

What about Jinx Hicks?

We may check in at the hospital, depending on what we find out from the woman.

All right. Call if you need me. I think I may have this teleportation thing almost worked out.

I used to say traveling by sprite was the fastest way. That's no longer true, is it?

Not by a long shot.

If I'm not here when you get back, I'll let you know what we find out when we return.

Thanks, Parke.

"What's up?" Rob asked after Parke and I finished our silent conversation.

"He and Trey are going to Atlanta later to question Lilith Sloane. Trey got permission from Director Logan, because they want to know if Shakkor Agdah is involved in this, too."

"What about Hicks?"

"He said they may go to the hospital afterward, depending on what the Sloane woman tells them."

"Cliff wants to rip that man's limbs off," Rob snorted. "Followed by his head."

"I don't blame him," I said. "An innocent woman is dead, and Doctor Chalmers' life is still hanging in the balance. I feel responsible for this, you know. If I hadn't needed help—well." I shifted uncomfortably.

"This is not your fault." Will had returned just as Rob opened his mouth to say something similar.

"Will, don't even try," I held up a hand. "My friend Binita and my favorite law professor died because of me. Other people died because of me in the Christmas War."

"The Christmas War would have happened, with or without you," Blaze said. "Ross Diablo wanted the Chancellor's seat and was willing to do whatever it took to get it. Had you not been there, he would now be in charge and in league with Shakkor Agdah. Admit that much, at least."

"Every war has casualties, Princess," Rob said gently. "You did not start this war; it has been going on for a very long time. All we can do is stand strong and endeavor to put Shakkor Agdah back in their place, if not outright destroy them. Do not put additional burdens on yourself; instead, take these deaths as a cause to bring their killers down."

"Rob is correct," Will said. "This war has been going on for a very long time. Longer, even, than they've been on this planet."

"What?" I stared at Will's dim figure nearby. "Say that again," I demanded.

"Princess Cassandra King, I tell you now that there were six Earths in this cluster. We stand upon Earth IV. V and VI were destroyed when Shakkor Agdah attempted their takeover on each of those planets. What I am about to tell you is something that until now was only known to the wizards."

"What's that?" I barely got the words out, my voice trembled so badly.

"There is an energy bridge connecting each of those six planets. In the case of V and IV, the protective pyramids have been buried to limit Shakkor Agdah's power, after VI fell. Of all those worlds, VI had the most talented and the most powerful beings. Shakkor Agdah is descended from some of them.

"When they destroyed VI, they located the bridge to V because they'd killed everything else, including the plants and animals. My kind planted four pyramids on V to keep it from suffering the same fate as VI. Still, Shakkor Agdah eventually located and destroyed the pyramids, then destroyed V before crossing the bridge to IV. Do you see where I'm going with this?"

"You say VI had the most powerful and talented beings?" I asked.

"Yes. As the numbers go down, so does the power and talent. We cannot allow Shakkor Agdah to reach III. It has very little talent, and will be destroyed quickly, just as II and I will be, if we fail to stop them."

There was information he was holding back, but I didn't ask what it was. Something in me said everything else he'd said was true, which made things so much worse, and so much more urgent. We were the last hope to destroy Black Myth. If we failed, all would die, just as Zephyr said.

"Fuck." I buried my face in my hands. "We really, really, need to find these assholes."

Cliff as the wolf trotted in, grabbed his clothes in his teeth and trotted away. I guess he was ready to go back, now. Five minutes later, he was back and dressed.

"Parke says Doctor Chalmers is out of surgery, and they're hoping for a full recovery," I said.

"Good. Thank you. Is that true—what you said?" He rounded on Will.

"It's true," Will said. "You may as well know what Yosuke and I have known all along. If another wizard wakes, well, you'll know the end of this world is upon us."

"We've always heard that a third or fourth wizard means the actual apocalypse," Blaze stood and dusted off his slacks. "It's why the sprites acted during the plague and have set aside differences now. Kings and Queens are equally concerned."

Rob stood and offered me a hand. I took it and rose, with the others following suit. "Are you ready to go back, Cliff, or is there anything else you need to do, here?" I asked him.

"I'm good for now, but if possible, I'd like to see Doc tomorrow if he's awake."

"Somebody will take you," I agreed. "It's the least we can do."

"Let's go, then," Will said and transported us to the estate.

Parke

Right after Cassie and I finished our mindspoken conversation, Trey and I were given permission to question the Sloane woman by Atlanta PD. Trey's boss had pulled a lot of strings to do this for us. Yosuke transported us immediately to the jail where she was being held; her arraignment was scheduled in the morning.

"Trey," a man stood and offered his hand to the vampire when we were led into an office at the Atlanta facility.

"Lou, I didn't expect to find you here," Trey shook his hand.

"Georgia Bureau for two years." Lou, who had to be in his fifties, grinned at Trey. "Got too old to go running after you guys, so I'm here, now."

"Their gain, then," Trey said. "Lou, this is Parke Worth, from Seattle."

"I've heard of your father, I think," Lou offered me his hand.

"Dad died a couple years ago. I took over his business."

"In every way?" Lou asked, a thoughtful expression on his face.

"In every way," Trey confirmed.

"Should I bow?" Lou asked Trey.

"No," I held up a hand. "But you're welcome to sit with us while we question the Sloane woman."

"Thank you—I'd prefer to be included. This mess makes no sense, and we can't get anything out of her."

"I think we should hurry," Yosuke said, stepping from the shadows and startling Lou. Until then, he'd kept himself shielded at Trey's request.

"Let me grab ID badges and a couple of guards," Lou said. We followed him out the door and down a hallway.

Dalton King

Lilith Sloane's lawyer was dead—we'd seen to that after we questioned him. Neither of us had any idea why Vaalenn wanted this woman taken, except she'd targeted Cliff Young, who'd escaped Ruudann in the past. He was a willing disciple of the Chancellor, and therefore an enemy of Vaalenn's.

I had misgivings about this assignment, but the rune on my shoulder burned every time I felt like arguing, so Morton and I went to get the woman out of jail and take her to Vaalenn.

Gorham and Franks had the easy job—they were sent to the hospital where Hicks was being treated. It was a hell of a lot easier to get in and out there than it would be in an Atlanta jail.

"You think we ought to go up the wall and find a crack to get through on the third floor?" Morton asked as we studied the building we were about to break into.

"Probably better that way than going through the front door, don't you think?"

He and I stood less than half a block away, staring at the targeted third floor of the jail. "Come on, we have work to do." I turned to ice and adhered myself to the sidewalk, before moving faster along it than any normal ice could ever move.

With Morton right behind me, we attached ourselves to the outside wall of the jail and began sliding upward. Along the way, I felt plenty of cracks in the outside stone wall that we could exploit to get in.

Maybe this wouldn't be so hard after all.

Parke

"Since we have permission to question her, we have to follow procedure," Lou insisted as we filled out forms to receive our visitor badges. "Trey's connections will get the rest of you in," he added.

This is taking too long, Yosuke informed me. I'd never gotten mindspeak from him before, and it surprised me.

I don't know what else we can do about it, I told him. *I doubt she's going anywhere.*

Yosuke didn't show his impatience outwardly; he wore a stoic expression as we signed the visitors log and then followed Lou through a door that opened with his key card.

"She'll be brought down to the visitor's lounge," Lou said. "We'll stay inside; I'll post the guards outside the door. Normally, they're in the room, but that regulation has been waived this time."

"I appreciate what you've done for us," Trey said.

"It's no problem, especially if we can get information we didn't have before."

Trey, Yosuke's getting antsy, I sent.

This will take time—we can't rush through this or we'll never get this kind of cooperation again.

I understand that—just passing along the message.

Lou didn't hasten his footsteps as he led us toward a visitor's lounge. Two guards nodded to him as he opened the door and allowed us inside.

Clean. Clinical. Just like any other facility one might visit inside a jail.

"They'll be here in a few minutes," Lou indicated chairs at a table. "If you want water, coffee or soda, I can have that brought in."

"Nothing for now," Trey waved away the offer. Yosuke remained standing; Trey and I took seats to wait for Lilith Sloane.

~

Lilith Sloane

I wasn't telling these bastards anything. I wasn't the one who shot the receptionist and the doctor. Jinx the moron had. My attorney confirmed my decision not to answer questions when he arrived earlier in the day.

Arraignment tomorrow, he'd said after sitting through several hours of questioning.

Arraignment. A foreign-sounding word to me. They'd probably railroad me into jail time, just like they'd done to Doyle.

Without my phone, I couldn't do a video visit with Doyle, either, although I'd used up all my allotted time with him for the month.

Doyle didn't know anything about what Jinx and I did; I deliberately kept that from him in case somebody made a connection and asked him questions.

Besides, my lawyer suggested that with my cooperation later on, the whole thing could be pinned on Jinx and I'd get off with little or no jail time, maybe.

"Lilith Sloane, you're being called down for questioning," a guard knocked on my door.

"Go to hell. I'm not in the mood," I yelled at him.

"You're going anyway. You can either walk along and behave yourself, or we can drag you. Your choice."

"Where's my lawyer? I want him present before anybody asks me anything."

"We've left a message; he's not returning our calls. Warden says all you have to do is refuse to answer the questions from these guys and you'll be back here before you know it."

"Good. Why can't you tell them I refuse?"

"Has to come from you."

"Fine." I rose from the bed affixed to the wall and stood at the center of my cell, waiting for the guards to enter.

And that's when a guard screamed and the wall of my cell caved inward.

~

Parke

The whole building shook, accompanied by a loud boom. Lou shouted; Yosuke transported all of us to the third floor of the jail, where two familiar ice demons held Lilith Sloane between them.

"Stop," Trey shouted compulsion at all of them.

Compulsion is dicey with demons, and Trey was too far away for compulsion to be completely effective. Dalton King's ice demon laughed at him.

Without realizing it, my rock demon jumped forward and roared, throwing a punch at Morton, who was closest to me. His ice shattered. Dalton, realizing who and what I was, jerked Lilith Sloane against him while she screamed, and then leapt through the back wall of her cell.

We're at Mount Isobel Hospital, Cassie's voice screamed in my mind. *It's Gorham and Franks*, she added.

CHAPTER 14

*C*assie

Gorham's ice demon held a screaming Jinx Hicks against him, while Franks' threatened Jerry, Pete and me with Jinx's I.V. stand. Jinx was still attached to the line and screeched whenever Franks brandished the pole.

Jerry had the sense to block the door so nobody else could get in, but outside, police guards were shouting at us to let them in.

If we did, they'd become hostages, too if we weren't careful.

"Set him down, or so help me, you'll die here," Pete gritted at Franks.

"Get back or *he* dies here," Gorham shouted.

"Kill them," I told Pete, my voice as cold as if I were made of ice, too.

"With pleasure." Pete and Jerry turned to rock demon and leapt at Gorham and Franks. Franks swung the pole at Pete, but not hard enough to harm a rock demon. The swing resulted in another shriek from Jinx as the I.V. was torn from his hand.

Pete and Jerry turned toward Franks, since he was now lifting the bed to throw at them and Gorham had backed up as far as he could against an inside wall.

"No," I screamed as Gorham's ice broke through the wall, and then the wall leading to the hallway outside from the adjoining room.

"On it," Jerry yelled as his rock demon raced after Gorham. Pete put a giant fist straight through the bed and connected with Franks behind it, shattering ice demon shards everywhere.

By that time the cops had managed to shove their way through the door and came in with guns blazing. Bullets bounced off Jerry's rock demon; I got hit twice before becoming fire and rendering their guns and bullets useless.

~

Parke

This time, I followed Yosuke's advice and went straight to the prison where Doyle Hicks was incarcerated. Yes, we were about to facilitate a jail break, but he would be far from free after we took him.

And, since Cassie got wounded trying to save his idiot brother, I didn't care if Doyle died in my custody.

"Who are you?" Doyle Hicks demanded as Yosuke, Trey and I appeared in his cell.

"A nightmare, come to life," Trey grinned, showing Hicks the full length of his fangs. "You will come with us. You will not speak while you're with us. You will not be able to tell anyone how you arrived at your destination. You understand?"

Doyle nodded his head, his eyes wide and unfocused.

"We have a nice cell waiting for you in a federal prison in Washington State, where nobody will know your real name and no visitors or calls will be allowed," Trey went on. "Yosuke?" Trey turned to the wizard.

Doyle Hicks disappeared with us, leaving his name behind in a Georgia prison.

~

BlackWing X

Zarigar

"You're sure she's all right?" Denevik demanded. I'd recreated the images of the attack on Cassie inside the hospital. She'd been hit by two bullets before stripping the guns from the police and turning them to useless, melted metal.

"She is fine, although the wounds may be sore later," I explained. "Her fire destroyed the bullets when she turned, and the wounds cauterized themselves."

"Damn, this is nerve-wracking," Denevik complained. "I have to sit here and watch, when I could be helping her."

"Now is not the time to interfere," I reminded him. I didn't like it any better than he did, but rules were rules.

Cassie

"Stop fussing—the bullets vaporized when I became fire, and the wounds were cauterized," I held out my right arm so Rob and Gina could survey the damage.

"Does it hurt?" Gina asked.

"It aches, but I don't have to worry about infection."

"I'm still interested in how you pulled guns away without frying police officers, and didn't burn the hospital down in the process," Rob's arms crossed over his chest.

"I don't know," I warbled. "It just happened, okay?"

"Jinx Hicks is dead," Zephyr walked into the bedroom. "Didn't survive the internal injuries sustained after Gorham's ice demon threw him at Jerry's rock demon."

"At least Gorham and Franks are both dead, now," I shoved hair away from my face with my left hand.

"As is Morton King," Cliff strode in, followed by Ebb. "Just got a call from Parke; he and Trey are settling Doyle Hicks into his new abode and asking questions. Parke asked about you, and then told me that he killed Morton King when he and Dalton broke into the jail to take Lilith Sloane."

"So Dalton got away with Lilith. Damn," I sighed. "Cliff, we've got a lot of damage control to do."

"Trey's department is handling it," Cliff said. "That's the other thing Parke told me. No idea how they're going to explain all this, but I'll be waiting to hear what they say."

"Should be interesting, all right," Rob said dryly.

"Do you think this means that Lilith Sloane and Jinx Hicks are associated with Shakkor Agdah?" Ebb asked.

"I don't know what it means," I said. "Somehow, if they weren't connected, I believe they are now. Too bad two of them got away. We still don't know the connection between them and Cliff."

"I'm just glad Doc is in a different hospital. They could have gone after him, too," Cliff said.

"I hope not—I hope he's out of this. Does he have guards? We can move him," I said, struck suddenly by the truth in Cliff's statement.

"Police are outside his door, but recent events," Cliff shrugged.

"Yeah. Look, can you find out if we can move him elsewhere? Might be safer for all involved."

"I'll ask. Word is he's coming along. It's the werewolf in him, you know."

"Uh, this raises questions," I began.

"Don't worry—it's been covered," Cliff reassured me. "His Packmaster is on the job."

"You could bring him here to convalesce—if he's agreeable," Rob suggested.

"That—may be a possibility," Cliff sounded thoughtful. "I'll suggest that to him. I was planning to see him later this morning, but my transport's on the fritz." He winked at me and smiled.

"At least you can tell him how his attacker died. That ought to bring a smile to his face," I said.

"Not many people have been tossed by an ice demon trying to stop a rock demon," Cliff agreed. "I hope he sees the humor in it."

"Me, too." I let my head flop back on my pillow. "Is anybody hungry?" I whined.

"I think we can find something to eat," Cliff said. "I'll even join you."

~

Parke

"Too bad Lilith didn't tell him a damn thing about what she was doing—he's never heard of Cliff Young before," I complained. Trey, Yosuke and I sat in a Japanese restaurant in Seattle, waiting for drinks and sushi. At least Yosuke and I were. Trey didn't care; he'd had his bag of blood earlier.

"If she tries to reach him, she'll know soon enough that he's been moved," Trey said. "If we dangle him in front of her like a carrot, maybe she'll turn herself in—if she's not in Black Myth's clutches, anyway."

"If they have her, you'll probably never see or hear of her again," I agreed. "If they're working to get information out of her, Cliff's name is all she has. That fucking address book is now in the hands of Atlanta PD."

"Perhaps we should take that bit of information back—they've already compromised the jail and a hospital, using demons," Yosuke suggested.

"Do you want to go right now?" I frowned at Yosuke.

"I've asked Will to retrieve it. He'll let me know when he has it."

Less than five minutes later, just as Yosuke was served his hot tea, he received word that Will had taken the address book and returned it to Cliff. "He says," Yosuke told me when our server walked away, "that someone should be watching the evidence cage, in case Shakkor Agdah shows up."

"On it," Trey rose while pulling his cell from a pocket. "I'll be back in a few."

"Gyoza," our server was back, setting the appetizer in front of us. "Soup," she added, putting bowls of steaming miso soup on the table.

"Man, this smells good," I sighed and lifted my chopsticks to nab a gyoza dumpling. We were nearly finished with our meal by the time Trey returned to the table. His face was a mask.

"Black Myth attacked the police station holding the evidence," he grated. "They tore the place apart when they didn't find what they wanted. Four officers are dead, and three others may have the disease. They're all en route to the nearest hospital with enough quarantine space to take care of them."

I stared at Trey, a piece of tuna roll halfway to my mouth. "That's not all," he sat down with a heavy sigh. "Somebody on the street took video of part of the attack on the station with a cell phone. There are images of black cloaks out there, now, and my department is scrambling to deal with all this."

"I believe the phrase is, you've been outed," Yosuke said calmly. "From now on, things will be different on this world. It will be your choice whether to tell the truth—or a lie."

"Fucking hell." I dropped my chopsticks on my plate and swore again as I rose from my chair. "Damn. Fuck, shit, damn, and fuck again."

"I'll take care of the bill," Trey reached for a wallet. "Go outside. Make calls if you must, and it looks very likely that will be necessary. Yosuke and I will be out after he finishes his meal."

I stalked out of the restaurant while my rock demon wanted to manifest and tear the place down. Humans were so easily frightened, and one glimpse of a real werewolf, vampire or demon would send them into hysterics.

How the hell would we contain this? We were just as much citizens of this world as the humans were, but how to convince them of that?

I needed to speak with Cliff, Cassie and the sprites. *Cassie?* I sent.

Oh, hey, Parke.

Shit has hit the fan, baby. I think Shakkor Agdah just outed all of us.

Cassie

Trey?

Cassie? He sounded surprised to hear from me.

I think I know how to approach this whole outing thing.

If you have suggestions, now's the time.

Introduce Shakkor Agdah, first. Put it out there that they're responsible for the disease. These are alien invaders from long ago, according to Will, and I believe that's true. Tell everybody that these are the ones trying to destroy everything.

And then what?

We will come forward voluntarily, tell our side, which is that we were born here, same as the humans, and we've been fighting Shakkor Agdah since day one, because they threaten us, too.

Damn. Have you discussed this with Parke, yet?

No, and I didn't want to argue about it with him. That's why I wanted to run it past you, first.

I'll be on my phone in five seconds, talking to my department.

Thank you.

Parke

Yosuke came out of the restaurant, but Trey had yet to appear.

"What's he doing?" I sounded irritated to my own ears.

"Speaking with his department superiors. There may be a better way to handle the situation than I first thought," Yosuke admitted. "I like this place," he said. "It's cool, here. I prefer that climate."

"It rains a lot; that's why there's a coffee shop on nearly every corner."

"Sleep is seldom overrated," he observed.

"Yeah, but keeping your job is important, too."

"We may have a solution, now, but it will require a great deal of cooperation," Trey said as he stepped outside the restaurant door.

"Whose cooperation?" I asked.

"Yours, the Grand Master's and the Vampire Council's."

Cassie

"Look, if you don't need me, I'm going to bed," I grumped at Parke. Cliff, the Vampire Council and Parke could kick around what to tell the human population and when. Trey's department was already putting short informational videos together, and someone in the FBI was being interviewed by several news organizations and newspapers, foreign and domestic.

Shakkor Agdah, whether they wanted it or not, was about to be splashed onto every television, computer and phone screen around the world, with a detailed description of what they'd done to release prisoners and spread their concocted disease across the country. That would be accompanied by the video of the attack on an Atlanta Police Department.

Then, either later in the day or the following day, or night, as the case would be, Parke, Cliff and a Vampire Council member would appear on screens everywhere, explaining their part in removing the threat last time, and that they were combatting Black Myth this time, too.

Whether Trey's department would admit they existed was anybody's guess.

"Should I wake you if we need your help?" Parke asked.

"If you must. Damn, my arm still hurts." I walked out of his study, leaving him, Cliff and Trey staring after me.

"I've contacted Averill. It will be up to the sprite kings and queens whether to join Parke and the others," Rob joined me as I walked toward my bedroom.

"I know. Go to bed, Rob. Tomorrow is gonna be a busy day."

Lilith Sloane

"You are a stupid bitch, and I will only allow you to live as long as you are useful to us," the cloaked woman pointed a finger at me.

They'd taken me from one cage and put me in another, and I was still shivering from being carried by the icy asshole who'd grabbed me in the first place. To top it off, all the black-cloaked people around the big-mouthed bitch had ugly blisters all over their skin, like they had the plague or something.

I drew in a painful breath.

The plague.

These—they had it and they were giving it to—everybody else.

What had I gotten myself into?

"Tell me what you know about the Grand Master," cloaked bitch snapped at me.

"I don't know who that is," I snapped back. "Grand Master of what?"

"The werewolves, you trollop. Clifton Young."

"What? You're a crazy whore," I shouted at her. "Werewolves are a fairy tale."

"Why were you following him? Why did you burn down his house? You know him, and I want that information." Her words were hissed at me. "Who are his friends? We failed to find the address book you mentioned, or was that one of your fairy tales?"

"Let me kill her now, for calling you that name," a man approached my cage and snaked a boil-covered hand through the bars. I shrank away from him.

"If she refuses to give me information, we will allow her to starve for two days. If she is not cooperative then, you may do as you wish, Werlekk." The woman stalked away while others fell in behind her, leaving me in this dark pit with little light and the man who threatened me.

"We are Shakkor Agdah," the man hissed. "We are not human and have never been. Humans are insects to us, and we will kill all of you."

He turned and left me, too, walking away into the darkness until I heard a door shut and a bolt slide into place.

～

Cassie

"What did I miss?" I scuffled into the kitchen the following morning, yawning and still dressed in my pajamas.

"I think we should install a revolving door in this place, the way folks have been coming in and going out since five this morning," Beverly pointed a spatula at me. "How's the arm?"

"It's fine." I turned my right shoulder toward her so she could see the pink puckers where I was shot the day before.

"Too bad humans don't heal that fast," she shook her head. "How do you want your eggs?"

"Over easy, please." I walked toward the coffee pot to pour a mug for myself.

"Hey," Jon and Richard walked in together.

"Beverly, where are your helpers this morning?" Richard asked.

"Carmel and Liesl took food and coffee over to the guest house, where Parke and the others are still hashing out some business," Beverly replied. "They'll be back in a few."

"Good," Richard sounded relieved.

"They're fine workers," Beverly waved her spatula at Richard, now. "They know what to do and when to do it, so I barely have to tell them anything."

"This job pays well," Richard nodded as he accepted the mug of coffee I handed to him before pouring one for Jon.

"It sure does. I hope Cassie wants to hire a permanent cook, too, since that house in Atlanta got destroyed. Damn good kitchen, too. What the hell was that hellion thinking?"

"Not sure thinking was high on his to-do list," I said. "Want coffee, Beverly?"

"Sure."

"Coming right up."

"Never had a boss get me coffee before," Beverly grinned.

"I never had such a good cook before," I handed Beverly a fresh mug of coffee.

"Then here's to good cooks and good bosses," Beverly lifted her cup.

"Cheers," Jon raised his mug, as did Richard.

"Come on, you're embarrassing me," I said and took the barstool next to Jon's.

"Oh good, you're up," Cliff walked through the side door from the garage.

"What's going on?" I asked him.

"It's raining," he said. "How about taking me to Atlanta around nine?"

"I think I can do that," I said. "Have you been up all night? Want coffee?"

"I've only been up half the night. After the Vampire Council agreed with Trey's plan, I was on board, as was Parke. They've been hammering out particulars since then. I checked in with them just now, and they're still arguing minutiae."

"Parke's an attorney, he just can't help himself," I said as Beverly put breakfast in front of me.

"That's part of the agreement they've been working on," Cliff said. "That humans can't rescind educational degrees, or fire our kind from jobs and the like, if they discover that we've been working among them for years with zero repercussions."

"They do love to hate what's different," Beverly plopped Richard's plate in front of him.

"Yeah," I nodded as Beverly's eyes locked with mine. "They do, and it's wrong."

Carmel and Liesl walked back in. "We'll finish this," Carmel offered to take over Beverly's spot at the stove. "You've been on your feet for three hours. Time for a break."

"You had breakfast, yet?" I asked her.

"Help eats last."

"Not anymore. Take a chair. I'm sure these lovely ladies can fix something for you."

Beverly settled onto the barstool next to Cliff's, and soon enough, we were all eating breakfast, drinking coffee and talking about nothing in particular, which was just fine with me.

We'd had enough hard news in the last day or so, and light conversation was more than welcome. Was it bad that I had absolutely no reaction to Morton King's death? I'd have killed him myself if I'd been in Parke's place. Too bad Dalton got away, but Gorham and Franks got what they deserved, too, even if they killed a source of information before dying.

It meant, too, that Shakkor Agdah was down three demon servants. "Do you suppose they'll go looking for replacements for Gorham and Franks?" I said aloud.

"Huh?" Jon asked.

"Sorry—I was just thinking about Gorham, Franks and Morton King, and whether Shakkor Agdah will go looking for demon replacements. Until now, those demons have been useful to them."

"Or they could find human slaves, maybe. Money or blackmail can be big motivators," Cliff said.

"Damn. That's not a comforting thought," I replied. "They did have help with Fli-Bi-Net—shifter help," I added.

"That company had something to do with this?" Jon's eyes widened as he stared at me.

"Hmmph. Ask me what happened to Geoffrey and Annabel," I snorted.

"Uh, what did happen to them?"

"They were shifters and helped kill Parke's father. Geoffrey's pig got chewed to death by a werewolf. I boiled Annabel's shark in her own swimming pool."

"They deserved it," Parke walked in with Jerry and Pete behind him. "They were also involved in the attempted coup against the Chancellor, trying to further their aims and that of Black Myth at the same time."

"I hope you're thinking about sleep," I told him. "You look exhausted."

"I am. I intend to be up when the Vampire Council wakes and convenes, so we can get the public announcements recorded. Today, Trey's department will be putting out information about Shakkor Agdah and the disease they're spreading."

"So look for widespread panic," Cliff said.

"When are they scheduled to make the announcement?" I asked.

"Noon, today, but they're already running chyrons on all television stations that a live statement from the President will be broadcast then."

"He'd better have plenty of guards, and not just the human kind," I said.

Parke went still. "I'll make a call," he said and walked out of the kitchen.

"I should have kept my mouth shut," I mumbled as Cliff, Yosuke, Rob and I joined the President's Secret Service cortege two hours later. The President was scheduled to speak in less than half an hour.

"We're relying on what we've been told by the President's Secret Department," the Chief of Staff told us as we were led into a briefing room.

"You mean that we're good enough—and safe enough—to guard the President?" Cliff asked.

"Yes." The man was brusque and straightforward, at least.

"He'll come to no harm from us," Yosuke said quietly.

"That remains to be seen. I've arranged for you four to be in the second tier around POTUS, with his best guards close about him. They will be ready to employ their sidearms if anything unusual happens."

"Look, I got shot yesterday by the police. I'd like to make that an infrequent occurrence if possible," I retorted. This guy was making veiled threats, when we were here to help him.

"You were in the hospital room when those two—creatures attacked?" He focused an intense frown in my direction.

"Yes. We were trying to save the witness, but that, as you know, didn't go very well after the police broke through the door."

"You're calling that man a witness?"

"He had information we needed. He was also a murderer and an attempted murderer, but the information he carried was vital. Now, we no longer have Lilith Sloane or Jinx Hicks to explain things to us.

Black Myth has Lilith, and I imagine she'll be dead soon enough at their hands."

"Are those creatures real—the ones you call Black Myth?" an agent asked.

"They're real—and they're deadly," Rob said. "I was there when they used the Black Death against humans. That disease may not have been designed by them, but they saw its usefulness and spread it quite well."

"You were there?"

"My race is immortal, unless we are killed in battle by someone stronger."

"Damn," the Chief of Staff swore. "This is more complicated than we thought. Look, no insult is intended, but we have the President to protect."

I have not had time to lay a perimeter shield around this building, Yosuke informed me. *It is larger than what I normally protect, so it will require more time.*

I think we can do that together after this is over, I suggested.

Thank you.

Parke

I stood inside a room connected to the Communications Director's office, where several large screens lined the walls. For now, all of them showed the same scene; the President's desk in the Oval Office, where the President would give a preliminary statement, before cutting to the video of Shakkor Agdah attacking the police station in Atlanta the night before.

Then, he'd read a statement prepared by Trey's department, with input from me, Cliff and the Vampire Council. He'd caution them to be watchful, but not to panic. At least not yet.

Jerry and Pete stood by the door, watching everybody who came in and out of the room. They were here to protect me while Cassie, Cliff and the others stood near the President.

Cliff, Rob and Yosuke weren't willing to let anyone else stand with

Cassie. I'd told her to go, since she was the best bet we had against a sudden attack by Shakkor Agdah. They'd attacked the police in Georgia last night; there was nothing to prevent them from trying the same here.

Especially if there were a leak somewhere, telling them the subject of today's press conference. Maybe this was their new strategy—rather than hiding, they were coming into the open to cause mass panic.

This announcement would be a two-edged sword—verifying Black Myth's existence and trying to control the resulting panic at the same time.

At least Cassie's disguise and new identity were in place—here, she would be Beatrice Chaumont, with blonde hair and brown eyes. I had to keep my fingers crossed that she wouldn't need her fire on live television. That would tell Black Myth exactly who and what she was.

We're about to walk into the Oval Office, Cassie informed me.

I'm watching the live feed from the Communication Director's video suite.

In case I didn't tell you before, she began, *thank you for killing Morton King and saving me the trouble.*

Uh, you're welcome.

I watched as people filed into the Oval Office on the screens; no doubt secret service agents lined the walls already. Cassie, Cliff, Rob and Yosuke came in, just before the image narrowed and focused exclusively on the President's desk.

He'd be in the shot; the others wouldn't. Made sense—I was too tired to think properly after being up for nearly forty hours.

When the President walked in, I was surprised to see the Vice President with him. So were several others; the murmur wasn't shut out of this live feed I watched.

The President sat behind his desk; the VP, hands crossed at his waist, stood behind the President's left shoulder.

This is an unplanned addition, Cassie sent. *I have no idea why they're here together. Wait—oh, shit.*

What? What's wrong? I demanded, just as I watched the VP pull a knife from a pocket and attempt to stab the President in the neck. He screamed when the fire hit his hand the same moment a secret service agent shot him in the shoulder.

Jerry and Pete had to hold me from running out of the room and straight to the Oval Office.

Cassie

"They have his family," I snapped at the President. Yeah, I could get shot myself for yelling at POTUS, but if I hadn't burned the VP's hand and knocked the knife away from him, the President would be bleeding and on his way to the hospital right now, instead of pacing back and forth.

"How do you know this?" The President stopped in his tracks and turned to stare at me.

"I saw it—a vision when he moved his hand to get the knife from his pocket."

"It is something she is becoming adept at," Yosuke came to my defense. "Some of us can see visions, although we cannot command them."

"His family was taken two hours ago," the Chief of Staff was back to make a report. "Three guards are dead—the other is in the hospital. All were in contact with the disease, Mr. President. A message was left behind, sir."

"Where is it—the message?"

"They wrote it on the wall of the VP's residence, sir. In blood." He pulled a phone from his pocket and approached the President.

"Kill the president or we kill your family?" POTUS blinked in disbelief at his Chief of Staff.

"The ah, physicians say the VP has also been exposed to the disease."

"Did he give it to me?" POTUS demanded.

"We have to get you to a safe place, and then run tests," the Chief of Staff murmured.

"No, dammit. I'm doing this announcement. If they can get to the VP, they can get to anybody. We have to do this, now. You can test me afterward."

In ten minutes, everything was back in place, the President seated himself behind his desk and the message began.

"Good afternoon, my fellow Americans. Today, I must tell you the most difficult thing any president has ever had to tell his country; there is an alien race among us, whose goal is to kill everything human on the face of the planet."

CHAPTER 15

*C*liff

"They say there wasn't enough contact from a newly-infected VP to give the President the disease. There are no leads on the VP's family, and he's been sedated after screaming his head off about evil invaders at the hospital."

Trey's announcement had come after sundown, on what had proven to be a terrible day. News reports were filled with interviews from doomsday groups saying *we told you so,* and refusing to take anyone else inside their hidden bunkers.

"Thank goodness for some better news," Cassie said. She'd found me and Trey on the back porch where I was having a beer and staring at Sandpiper Lagoon.

"I need to get back inside; the announcement will be televised tomorrow and we're making sure everything is just right." Trey walked into the house, closing the French doors behind him.

"Grocery stores are running out of everything, since people believe that locking themselves inside their homes is the best way to stay safe," Cassie told me.

"I wonder what they'll do tomorrow, after our press conference reveals werewolves, vampires and elemental demons?" I took another swig of my beer.

"At least they hadn't started broadcasting when the VP attacked," she shrugged.

"The only bright note of the day."

"Well, Yosuke and I managed to put a shield around the White House. Doesn't include the Capitol building, though, since they're two miles apart."

"If he leaves the White House, he could be screwed," I pointed out.

"I know." Cassie pulled a camp chair over and flopped onto it. "I'm tired and wound up at the same time."

"We could go visit Doc Chalmers."

"We could do that. Want to?"

"I'd love to." I tossed my beer bottle in the trashcan somebody had thoughtfully left on the back porch.

"Let's go. Maybe you can convince him to come here when they let him out."

Seconds later, we were at Bournemouth Hospital, checking in with the staff. We had to be cleared by the guards posted outside the room, too, but it didn't take long.

"Cliff," Kirk Chalmers grinned at me when I walked in the door first. "Good to see you. Tell those white coats outside I'm good to go home."

"Doc, how the hell are ya?" I grinned back and held out a hand to shake.

"I'm great. Heard the asshole who shot Muriel and me got what was coming to him."

"Yeah. That's a story I'll have to tell you later."

"Muriel's family isn't doing so well right now, what with all the mess on the TV today, and the funeral scheduled for tomorrow."

"Something else to discuss later," I said, sitting on the chair beside his bed.

"I'd like to go to the funeral, but I don't know if I can," he changed position on the bed, as if the admission made him uncomfortable.

"You can leave against medical advice," Cassie said quietly.

"Huh? I guess I could do that," Doc admitted. "I'm fine—the wounds are almost healed, too. No reason for me to stay here."

"What if I told you we can take you somewhere safe, and still get you to the funeral tomorrow?" I said.

"I'd say that sounded great," Doc said. "But I need clothes, first. The ones I wore when I got here were trashed."

"No doubt," I said.

"What sizes?" Cassie asked. "I think I can get you something that'll make you decent in public. Enough to leave, anyway."

"Large sweatpants and a T-shirt is good enough. Maybe slippers, size eleven," he told her.

"I'll be back," she said, and disappeared.

"Tell me she didn't just disappear," Doc blinked at the space Cassie occupied moments earlier.

"She did. It's a relatively new development. Don't worry about it, though. She and I will get you to that funeral tomorrow the same way."

"Well, we better put the doctor on notice, then," he reached for the call button.

"Wait until Cassie gets back, first," I warned.

"Probably a good idea," he conceded.

Cassie

"I love your hair," the girl at the department store in Gulf Tides told me as I set socks, sweatpants, a package of T-shirts and a pair of slippers on the counter. "Did you get it done in Gulf Tides?"

"No," I touched the hair that to her looked blonde. "I had it done in Atlanta."

"Figures. I can't find a good stylist anywhere close."

"That's too bad," I told her. She rang me up and bagged the merchandise. "Keep looking—there's bound to be somebody here who can do your hair," I said. "Thanks," I held up the bag before heading for the door.

"No problem," she waved.

I made sure I was blocks away before ducking into a dark corner and pulling my disappearing trick. I didn't need people noticing me. Especially now.

"This is nice," Doctor Chalmers said as Cliff and I showed him to his bedroom at the estate an hour later.

"We can have food brought up if you're hungry," Cliff offered.

"I just came from the hospital. Of course I'm hungry. Got anything decent?" He sat on the side of the bed and bounced a time or two. "Good mattress," he said.

"I think we can do better than decent," Cliff said.

"I'll get it," I told Cliff. "Get him settled in while I round up food."

Rather than run downstairs and through a warren of rooms and hallways, I took the easy route and teleported to the kitchen. I found Gina and Kent sitting at the island having a drink.

"Want a margarita?" Gina asked.

"Nah. I need to grab some food for Doc Chalmers. He's complaining about hospital grub."

"Sounds just like a werewolf," Kent grinned.

"It does, doesn't it?" I opened the fridge and pulled out roast beef, mashed potatoes and brown gravy. "I hope he likes hot roast-beef sandwiches," I said, grabbing a plate and placing bread in the toaster.

"No self-respecting werewolf would turn down Beverly's roast beef," Kent said.

"Does he need anything—medical-wise?" Gina asked.

"I doubt it—I think his doctors just wanted him to stay so they could gawk at him a little longer," I replied. "He's walking on his own, didn't sound winded and his color's good."

"I'll still check on him tomorrow," Gina said. "Unless he needs something tonight."

"Sounds good." I set slices of roast beef on a plate, covered them with wrap and heated them in the microwave.

The gravy and potatoes went in after that. By that time, I had the toast cut into points and arranged on the plate, set the roast beef over them and added gravy and potatoes when they came out of the microwave.

I took the quick way back to the doctor's room, too. He smelled the roast beef the second I appeared and moved to a chair beside a window to eat.

Cliff pushed a side table around so I could set the plate in front of Doctor Chalmers. "Excellent," he said after taking his first bite.

"Oh, I forgot a drink. What do you want?" I asked.

"Sweet tea?" He looked hopeful.

"I think there's some in the fridge," I said.

"This is the south," Cliff teased. "You get your southern card revoked if there's no sweet tea in the house."

I teleported back to the kitchen to get the good doctor sweet tea.

Parke

"The Council's message is recorded," Trey informed me. "Now it's your turn, and Cliff after that."

"The sprites have something ready, too," Rob walked into my office. "The decision was made this morning, and a joint message was finished less than an hour ago. I have it here," he held up a flash drive. "If you want to see it before creating your own."

"I do," I said.

"Good. We can watch it together."

The message was clear, and each sprite monarch was dressed in royal regalia as they recorded their joint message. "Many of you may have difficulty believing we are real, and not some electronic wizardry," Averill spoke last. "For now, it doesn't matter whether you think we are real or not. In the coming days, however, please keep your minds open, as we combat Black Myth with the others you will be introduced to this evening. Nothing less than the survival of all life on Earth hangs in the balance."

"Damn, he's good," Trey breathed.

Rob didn't say anything, but pride showed in his eyes.

"Now it's my turn. I can't guarantee eloquence," I said, pushing my desk chair back to stand and stretch.

"Just show them the rock demon. I think they'll get the idea," Rob grinned.

"Not at first," Trey said, making me snort a laugh.

"Their first idea will be to run," I said. "So a brief warning, perhaps?"

"That's better than having to stand behind a waist-high barrier before changing to wolf," Cliff said. "My top half has to remain visible, so there won't be accusations of a switch."

"There will still be accusations and doubt," I said. "If we can convince enough people that we're looking out for their best interests, maybe they won't gather the townspeople with pitchforks and torches to kill us."

"We're outing ourselves to the entire world," Cliff agreed. "That means we'll be subject to species-ism, at the very least. I hope it doesn't cost us, work-wise."

"I've already considered that," I agreed. "I hope you've got plenty of diverse investments to carry you through."

"I do. Don't worry about me, Chancellor. Besides, I can always lose myself in the Canadian wilderness and live off the land."

Trey's cell phone rang the same moment that Cassie, Yosuke and Will appeared simultaneously in my office.

"There's trouble in D.C." Trey barely got the words out before we were all transported to the Capitol steps leading to the National Mall, which was now being overrun by Shakkor Agdah.

I barely had time to consider where they'd all come from before Cassie's fire demon blazed to life and went to work.

Yosuke and Will had disappeared, only to reappear with reinforcements—Rob and the sprite guards, Kent, Benjamin and our other wolves, Jerry, Pete and the other rock demons, and all the vamps.

They'd emptied the estate except for the humans, Mom, Destiny and Doctor Chalmers.

We need help, I sent to any other sprites in the area, before changing to rock demon and charging down the steps to follow in Cassie's wake.

~

Cassie

Black cloaks fled before us; they imagined we wouldn't arrive so quickly, I think, and they'd have at least half of the House of Representatives held hostage.

I wasn't about to let that happen.

They'd already killed too many of the Capitol Police; bodies were strewn around the perimeter of the Capitol. They'd attempted a coup, and they had more black cloak warriors than I could have imagined.

They truly had been building their army for centuries, and we were seeing the results of their efforts now. Pulling my anger and fear together, I released it in a massive wave of fire before me, while black cloaks screamed and burned.

In my peripheral vision, I saw rock demons rushing down the tree-lined sides of the mall, crushing trees in their path as they hastened to destroy the black cloaks seeking refuge there. Cliff and the other wolves followed them, sniffing and hunting for those the rock demons missed.

The vampires moved so swiftly between wolves and rock demons I could only sense the wind recording their passing. With extended claws, they'd behead anything that survived rock demons and the wolves.

Another wave of fire flew before me as black cloaks raced toward the Lincoln Memorial at the opposite end. They'd almost reached the major thoroughfare of 14th Street, where vehicles were hitting the running army. Forcing myself to run faster, I knew I needed to avert more disaster, if those drivers got out of their cars.

≈

Yosuke

Will and I prevented car doors from opening—although it panicked drivers who'd hit fleeing Shakkor Agdah. Some attempted to roll down windows; we disabled the mechanisms. If they came in contact with only the slightest trace of the poison covering black-cloaked bodies, they'd die in three days.

Traffic was therefore backed up on both sides of the street, while Shakkor Agdah, in numbers I hadn't imagined before, fled before the approaching fire demon.

Cassie was so large by that time she leapt across the road with little effort and continued burning the fleeing enemy.

Our combined effort to shield the White House kept Shakkor Agdah from running in that direction, at least, but they were nearing the reflecting pool. Would they save themselves by diving into it to avoid Cassie's fire?

I transported myself to the pool, knowing that there wasn't enough time to lay a shield over it that would hold the enemy back. As expected, Shakkor Agdah dived into the water by the scores, and began swimming their way toward the Lincoln Memorial.

Cassie reached the edge of the water and paused for only a moment.

Then I saw what I never expected to see; she set the water on fire and destroyed the last of the attackers. More than five hundred died in the water, after she'd killed at least a thousand on the ground.

And then suddenly, like a snuffed candle, the fire disappeared.

Cassie? I sent.

I'm at the estate, she said. *If you need me, let me know.*

≈

Parke

Director Logan and half his department had arrived to sort things out. The National Mall looked like a wildfire had run over it, which was a pretty good description of what had actually happened.

Trees had been knocked down and destroyed by rock demons searching for escaping Shakkor Agdah, and the reflecting pool was dry as a bone and filled with the burned bodies of Black Myth warriors.

Jerry, Pete, Landon, Liam and a handful of vamps were guarding the bodies in the reflecting pool; they could still be contagious enough to infect humans. Frankly, I was thankful Cassie evaporated the water; it could also be used to spread the disease.

"What should we do with the bodies in the reflecting pool?" Director Logan asked as he cautiously approached my rock demon.

"I think we can move them wherever you want them to go," I said. "If you'd like your forensic scientists to examine what's left of them, this is an ideal situation for that."

"Hold on, I'll see if we can find a suitable building," he said, jerking his cell phone from a pocket.

All around us, firetruck and emergency vehicle lights flashed. Their personnel, dressed in HAZMAT suits, were gathering human remains carefully after being instructed not to touch anything wearing a black cloak.

"We're doing our best to keep the media away from the scene," Director Logan spoke into his cell phone.

"Don't," I interrupted his conversation. "Let a few in. This will go a long way in explaining what we are and how we're trying to help. In fact, I'll volunteer like this to do an interview."

"Trey, Grim," Director Logan shouted. Both vampires arrived in a swirl of ash.

"Let three journalist in, with their camera crew only. The Chancellor has agreed to an interview regarding the events tonight."

"We'll be right back," Grim said.

⁓

Cassie

"These are bodies of the aliens known as Black Myth," Stephanie Emmings, the journalist I was watching on television pointed toward the reflecting pool, where bodies of toasted Shakkor Agdah lay. Lights had been brought in to illuminate as much as possible for the camera crew.

"We're not allowed to get closer, as these bodies are still capable of transmitting their disease to humans," Stephanie continued. "You've already seen video images taken by a few who were here when these black-cloaked invaders arrived. They were racing toward the Capitol, which was initially placed on lockdown. At this time, all have been evacuated and everyone inside the building accounted for.

"Six officers died attempting to protect the building, and more could have been killed had the Chancellor of all things paranormal—that's what he calls himself—had he not shown up with a small army at his back to combat these invaders."

I was watching a split screen, now, between the anchor at the reporter's news station and the reporter herself. The chyron at the bottom kept repeating that an attack had been made against the government earlier.

"Jennifer, I am still trying to come to grips with the reality of these —supernaturals, as Chancellor Worth calls them. He spoke to us in an alternate form. It is quite difficult to associate that image with the photograph we're showing now."

A photo of Parke from his law school yearbook was flashed onscreen.

"I'm still attempting to get information on those warriors who were seen wielding swords—we only have a few images of them, and the Chancellor refused to tell us anything. He says that they are in charge of their own media releases, and whether that will happen is anyone's guess."

"He said that the fire we saw was a fire demon?" The anchor sounded doubtful.

"Chancellor Worth did say that," Stephanie agreed. "Although that is difficult to imagine at this time."

"Shakkor Agdah didn't imagine it—they died from it," Destiny grumped beside me. "Parke did a good job, didn't he?"

"He sure did. All that legal training was put to good use tonight."

Not only had Destiny chosen to watch the news with me, Chet had curled up on my lap, his ears twitching now and then at the voices coming from the television.

We're on our way home, Parke informed me.

Good. Want anything to eat or drink?

Both would be nice.

"Want to help make sandwiches for Parke and the others? They'll be here any minute," I patted Destiny's shoulder.

"Sure."

I even teleported Chet to the kitchen. He seemed fine with that.

Lilith

Something had happened, and it wasn't good for the ones who surrounded my cage in the middle of the night. Earlier, other cages had been brought in that held a woman, a young girl and a teen boy.

They looked familiar, but I couldn't recall the name and the woman refused to talk. Right now, too many black-cloaked individuals crowded into the room, and the young girl began to cry.

The woman attempted to hush her, although I understood the fear in her voice. Was this where we were killed or exposed to the disease these bastards carried?

As for asking them questions—that would be stupid and draw their attention solely to me rather than the crying child.

Once the girl stopped crying, one by one, our cages were lifted by as many as it took to carry them. We were hauled out of the room and down a long hallway, until we reached a door and rough, stone steps reminding me of a cellar. The smell was the same, too. The bricked space around the steps was barely large enough to accommodate our cages; much grunting and hefting occurred before we were carried upward and set on the ground. Outside it was night, and not far away an owl hooted.

We were in a field, or what I imagined was a field, but in the distance I saw what looked like a pile of rubble. The weak light of the moon cast little illumination on the pile, destroying my hope of identifying a landmark of some kind.

Whispers around us began, as if our captors were discussing where to go from here. That made no sense, so I discarded that idea. Soon enough, they lifted our cages again and began to move a second time, while the earth-covered door to the steps and the warren below was closed behind us.

Cassie

Chet sat on the counter near the coffee pot, watching as Destiny and I put sandwiches together for the ones Will and Yosuke brought back from D.C. I sneaked him a bite of roast beef—he meowed his thanks before eating it.

"I guess we'll see if everything goes to hell tomorrow, after people wake up to all this," Parke said as I set his sandwich in front of him. "The recorded interviews will be aired as agreed, but at an earlier time. What a mess," he shook his head and bit into the sandwich.

"We stopped 'em, though," Destiny pointed out. "You sounded great in the interview. I think you all did a good job," Destiny stated, handing Cliff two sandwiches on a plate.

Jerry, Pete, Liam and Landon got their plates next, followed by the werewolves, who were all starving. We ran out of roast beef, so we switched to ham and turkey. "Mom in bed?" Parke asked after finishing his sandwich.

"Yeah. She said you could handle things just fine," Destiny informed him. "I stayed up with Cassie and Chet to watch the news."

"Who found clothes for you?" I asked Parke, who was dressed in an unfamiliar T-shirt and jeans.

"Director Logan. He came prepared," Cliff said. "If he hadn't, all of us would be naked right now."

"Did he have the ladder the guy stood on to talk to you?" Destiny asked Parke.

"One of the news crews had that in their truck. Good thing, too, or I'd have had to sit on the ground to look him in the eye."

"What happened to all the bodies in the reflecting pool?" I asked the question in an off-handed manner, but I was worried they hadn't taken proper precautions.

"They're in an old airplane hangar on a nearby military base," Will explained as he reached over Cliff's shoulder to give me his empty plate. "I told Director Logan it would be best to burn the place to the ground after they finished their forensics work."

"What if they extract that poison and recreate it?" I asked. Parke's eyes locked with mine as that thought hadn't occurred to him until then.

Don't worry about it, a voice I'd never heard before sent. *It's been neutralized,* the male voice added. *We hope they'll believe its efficacy died with its carrier.*

We? We who? I demanded.

Nobody you should concern yourself about. Please believe me when I say we only have your best interests at heart. Ask yourself—and the wizards this; did Shakkor Agdah employ disease warfare before they reached Earth Four, or is this the first world where it was employed?

I almost said *huh* out loud, but I caught myself. "Uh, Will, Yosuke," I began, "before Shakkor Agdah reached this world, had they ever used germ or disease warfare before?"

"No. This is something new to this world. Until now, our kind believed they weren't savvy enough to create something like this," Yosuke replied. "Why do you ask?"

"Because if they could create something like that, wouldn't it make sense that they could do other stuff, too? Technologically advanced stuff?"

Will and Yosuke looked at one another. I imagine they were having a mental conversation about it. "That should make sense," Will agreed.

"One would surely follow the other, but they have been attempting all along to regain the power that the pyramids have suppressed. Perhaps they haven't experimented outside the disease because of that. With the power and talent their ancestors were born with, they can accomplish many things."

"Or they could have been working all along to do or create things in other ways," Parke nodded his understanding. "Doesn't make a lot of sense, now that you mention it."

"They didn't create the Black Plague; they only found ways to spread it easily and quickly," Yosuke noted. "This disease is definitely not the plague—that has already been determined."

"The CDC says it could take years to develop a cure or antidote," Cliff said. "Everybody understands that."

"I'm becoming concerned about where this disease came from, and how they managed to create it," I said, pushing away from the cook's side of the kitchen island. "If nobody else needs anything, I think I'll go to bed."

"Go ahead. We can stack plates and fill the dishwasher," Zephyr said.

"Thanks. Destiny, are you tired, or do you want to stay up with the others?"

"I'll go to bed."

"Come on, then."

"Don't forget Chet."

"Of course not." I scooped the cat off the counter and headed for the bedrooms upstairs. He was purring, his head tucked beneath my chin as we made our way to bed.

Dalton King

Vaalenn was pissed. Royally. If I thought she'd listen, I'd have told her it was senseless sending an army against the Capitol. After her attack against the Vice President and the kidnapping of his family, even I knew that anything connected would be carefully watched by

Demonkind, Wolfkind and Spritekind.

They'd all shown up to combat Vaalenn's forces, and she'd lost every fucking one of her soldiers, most of them to the Chancellor's new fire demon.

It was best to make myself as invisible as possible while she railed against her generals. All of them had done her bidding, as they hadn't wanted to argue with her. Many of their subordinates died in the attack, but they didn't point that out. Vaalenn held rune sigils on all of us, and our lives were in her hands.

"We have a message," a trembling underling approached Vaalenn, who'd become rabid as she cursed her generals.

"From whom?" She turned toward the underling, her voice colder than my ice and his life a thread away from ending.

"Ver'Dak, your worship." I saw a change come over Vaalenn that I never expected to see. Was that fear in her eyes? Did her hand tremble before she hid it?

Who the hell was Ver'Dak?

"You will deliver the message in my private chambers." Vaalenn marched out of the meeting hall with as much dignity as she could convince others to believe.

I wasn't fooled—*she was scared shitless.*

BlackWing X

   Zarigar

"Ver'Dak is now on Earth IV," I told Captains Travis and Trent, while Denevik nodded his agreement. "Until now, he has controlled Shakkor Agdah's actions from the shadows. Now that they've revealed themselves, something changed."

"Enough to pull him out of his hidey-hole? Whatever it was must have been really important," Trent said. "We've been looking for the bastard for over a year, and suddenly he decides to appear in the light of day? Out-fucking-standing."

"Is now the time to interfere?" Denevik lifted an eyebrow as he posed the question.

"I believe it is," I smiled at him. A slow grin spread across his face. He'd wanted this almost from the moment he'd seen Cassie the first time. I understood his motivation completely.

Cassie

"Mmmmm—coffee," I breathed as I walked into the kitchen the following morning.

"The shit has hit the fan, as folks say where I come from," Beverly was wagging a wooden spoon at me while I poured coffee in a mug.

"What shit and which fan?" I sipped from my cup, hoping my eyes would be convinced to stay open while I walked from the coffee maker to a nearby barstool.

"All shit, all fans, all the time," Beverly whacked the top of her oatmeal saucepan with the spoon. "Folks everywhere are either convinced you're a hoax or that they're all gonna die."

"The first is obviously not true. The second, eh," Rob shrugged as he got his coffee and joined me at the island.

"I think Beverly wants to smack them with her spoon," I turned to Rob, who grinned.

"Might do some good," she said and whacked the pan again. "You want oatmeal and sausages, or an omelet?"

"Oatmeal with brown sugar and sausages," I said.

"You got it."

"There's a crowd of humans outside the gate of the Seattle house," Parke stalked into the kitchen.

"Is that good or bad?" I asked.

"Both. Some of them are calling me the devil. Some are calling me their hero. Hell, some people are waving signs saying they want to have my babies."

Rob laughed so hard he almost fell off his barstool.

"Are you thinking about taking them up on their offer?" I teased Parke. Beverly whacked the pan again.

Dalton King

"Who is Ver'Dak?" I asked Werlekk. I didn't really want to talk to Vaalenn's closest sycophant, but he was the best source of information in this case.

"Ruudann and Ruudann's father struck a deal with that one," Werlekk grumbled. "He gave us the poison disease and the means to manufacture more, and the demon killer guns come from him, too. Ruudann always said that with Ver'Dak's help, this world would be ours. Ver'Dak would not have returned if something hadn't gone wrong with the plan."

"What is Ver'Dak's stake in this?"

"He only wishes to help us. That's all I know." I watched as Werlekk stalked away from me, his shoulders set and stiff beneath his black cloak.

Nobody did something like this out of the goodness of their hearts. Ver'Dak wanted something. I wanted to know what it was. After all, someone who could provide demon killers could kill the entire demon population if he wanted.

Whenever he wanted.

And, if he could kill demons, he could kill Shakkor Agdah just as easily. What the hell did he want out of this?

Who the hell was he? I paused a moment to consider that he certainly wasn't human. He was covered in scales that resembled plate armor. As for the goggles he wore, I wondered if those were night-vision glasses to enable him to see in the underground warrens that Shakkor Agdah called home.

What if they weren't? What was he hiding?

Something was very wrong with this picture, and I cursed the day I involved myself in it. Morton was dead, and I hadn't realized before that I'd miss the fucker. Hell, I'd settle for a decent conversation with Gorham and Franks, but they were dead, too.

The whispers began, then, as Vaalenn emerged from the meeting, her eyes downcast, followed by Ver'Dak and at least twenty more who looked very similar to him, except they didn't wear goggles.

What in the hell were they, and how had so many arrived from nowhere?

"They're taking over," Werlekk hissed as he passed me. "If I were you, demon, I'd get away while I still could."

The nearest wall was three feet away. I became ice and plastered myself against it in a thin sheet. Taking Werlekk's advice, I got the hell out of there while I still could.

CHAPTER 16

*C*assie

"There's a delegation of demons who want an audience with the Princess of Alabama," Rob handed an envelope to me.

"Who?" I asked.

"The same ones who made a request to Greenville, only he never got around to it."

"Do we know what they want?"

"Not yet."

"I suggest a reception of sorts at a neutral site," Jon offered his advice.

"Good idea," Rob said.

"If it's a reception, you can invite others who are guaranteed to be sympathetic to your holding the position—in case anybody thinks to get out of hand," Yosuke walked into the room. "Princess, may I speak with you privately?"

"Yes. I was just about to send mindspeak, but you're here instead," I told him.

"We'll leave you alone," Rob herded Jon out the door and shut it behind him.

"Something's wrong," I said, as Yosuke spoke nearly the same words.

"Something has shifted, and I feel it is not in a good direction," he agreed.

"It feels—more malevolent, if that's possible," I said, holding back a shudder. All afternoon, the feeling had grown steadily worse, until I was ready to scream.

"Yes—certainly that. The dynamic has changed, and I have no idea how or why."

"Cassie," Cliff burst into the room, as if Shakkor Agdah were behind him. "We have trouble, and I need your help."

Lilith Sloane

"I made the call for you. What else do you want from me?" The woman wept inside her cage.

The woman. The Vice President's wife Jessica, actually, because she'd placed a call to the White House for those who held us.

Only they hadn't asked for a ransom or an exchange of prisoners.

No.

They asked for Cliff Young's phone number.

Strange that I was no longer interested in Cliff Young, or anything else except getting out of my cage and escaping my captors.

I understood that the people Jessica spoke with wanted to keep her on the line to trace the call, but once they had what they wanted, our captors turned off the phone. And, to make sure we couldn't be tracked, they were now preparing to move us.

Then they intended to contact Cliff Young. I waited to see whether they'd demand he exchange himself and others for us, or if they wanted something else, instead.

Parke

"As you can see, we have prisoners. For now, they are safe. What we ask is to speak with you and the Chancellor if possible. It is most important that we meet. We have information necessary to the survival of all."

They'd texted their message to Cliff, complete with video of Jessica Brown and her two children—and Lilith Sloane.

All of the captives appeared healthy, if a bit pale, but all were in cages set beneath an oak tree. Black cloaks stood guard among the cages, their hoods hiding faces from us.

"What the hell do they want with us? A prisoner swap?" I shook my head at Cliff. We stood inside Cassie's office, watching the video over and over, looking for clues. So far, nothing had presented itself.

"I think we should meet with them," Cassie said.

"I agree," Yosuke chimed in.

"We could be walking straight into a trap," Cliff growled. "After last night, they want revenge, I'd bet my tail on it."

"I don't get that vibe from these," Cassie appeared thoughtful.

"What vibe do you get?" I rounded on her, my words harsher than intended.

"Fear," she snapped. "They're afraid. Everybody in that video is scared witless."

"Cassie is correct—I feel what she feels," Yosuke nodded.

"What the hell is going on, then?" Cliff growled.

"Text them back. Tell them we're willing to meet as long as the prisoners are kept safe," Cassie said. "This may be a tiny beam of light in what has suddenly gone darker than dark. I'm willing to go with you, in case things get out of hand."

"I will go, as will the sprite guards—to witness this meeting," Yosuke said.

"Or this massacre, whichever it turns out to be," I complained.

Cassie

"They want to meet here." Rob was back, with a tablet depicting a map.

"The demons?"

"No. The Shakkor Agdah who want to talk."

"Let me see," I moved to stand beside him, so I could see the map. "They want to meet at Stone Mountain?"

"None of our feet will be on soil, making it more difficult for anybody to detect our whereabouts. Even the air sprites would have to be told to specifically search there to find any of us."

"What does Zephyr say?"

"She says the decision is yours whether Queen DeLeah is notified before or after."

"When do they want to meet?"

"Tonight, at half past midnight," Rob replied. "After the park closes."

"You know there's more to this than meets the eye, don't you?" I asked him.

"I get that feeling. Probably not as strongly as you do, but there is something to this that isn't obvious."

Vaalenn

"Of course they took your prisoners. I allowed it," Ver'Dak hissed at me. "Do you think I wasn't aware of their defection? I've been watching you, Vaalenn, every since Ruudann perished. You've settled for petty revenge and have lost sight of the bigger picture. I gave your race everything it needed to destroy the humans here, yet you settle for the smallest of crumbs."

I had to rely on other facial features to convey his real mood; he kept his eyes covered always, whereas his minions didn't bother. "We lost the demon killers," I said. "How are we supposed to proceed without them?"

"You let a single fire demon take them away. I warned Ruudann to destroy all of the fire demons, did I not?"

"Ruudann died destroying the last one capable of fighting us," I sniffed, refusing to show Ver'Dak my fear. "And yet, another one steps forward who is even stronger than the last. At least the two remaining in Europe are crippled and can no longer make fire—we saw to that."

"Well, you'll have your chance to destroy this one, then. Your deserters are arranging a meeting with the Chancellor and his minions after midnight, tonight. You and I will be there, as will friends I've managed to make in the country's military."

"What do you mean, friends in the military?"

"Oh, they aren't my willing friends. Let's say they couldn't refuse my suggestions and leave it at that. Regardless, they will back us up when we attack in Georgia tonight. I intend not to lose this battle, so they've been equipped with the demon killers this time. They will sacrifice themselves before they hand these weapons to the enemy; I've made sure of that."

I wanted to scoff at this armor-plated pig who dressed himself in leather and fur. I didn't. He could kill me as easily as he intended to kill our mutual enemy tonight. I bided my time; after all, if the desired result was achieved, perhaps he would leave us here to reap the benefits.

With Ver'Dak here, perhaps the lessening of my power would go unnoticed. It should be waxing rather than waning, but Werlekk and the others hadn't spoken of it, making me think it could only be my own power draining away.

Regardless, with hundreds of new demon killers provided to my army, along with the armed military vehicles Ver'Dak intended to supply, we would win this war with little effort.

Still, I wanted those who'd deserted me to feel my anger. They'd cut the runes away that had been placed on their bodies, and that was an act of treason. Perhaps I should consider how their impending deaths might be prolonged—to increase their suffering.

Ver'Dak Dis'rai

"We only have a small window of time to act, before those who hunt us detect our interference," Powl, my First-In-Command, informed the other officers in my Krelk army. "We have not successfully hidden from our enemy this long just to reveal ourselves now. This means we kill the fire demon, the demon Chancellor and those who stand with them, leaving the other demons leaderless and in disarray."

"It makes them easier to capture and imprison for the cage fights," I grunted my agreement. "Once they're out of the way, the werewolves and other shifters will be easy to capture."

"What about the vampires and sprites?" Hannet asked.

"Those who refuse to join us will die—with the rest of the planet."

A light appeared in Powl's eyes; he wanted to use the larger weapons as much as I did.

~

Cassie

"Doctor Chalmers, good to see you up and around," I said. I found him and Cliff sitting on Cliff's favorite part of the back porch. They were talking and watching the neighbors and tourists from rental cabins half a mile away boat, kayak and jet-ski around the lagoon.

"How are you doing, Cassie?" He countered.

"Uh-uh, no doctoring while you're recovering," I told him. "Besides, I'm feeling halfway better, I think."

"She hasn't killed Will yet, so that's a good sign," Cliff shifted to a more comfortable position in his chair.

"He's here? I haven't seen him, yet," Doctor Chalmers admitted.

"I think you're safe enough; he only murders fire demons," I said.

"Um, Cassie?" Gemma opened the French doors and poked her head out to blink at me. Dressed in a bathrobe, she'd covered half her face with a hand towel, so I could only see her eyes.

Without makeup.

"Gemma?" I asked. She'd sounded afraid for some reason.

"I found Chet, he got into—some of your stuff," she finished quickly.

"Is he okay?" I immediately walked to the door.

"Come with me—he made a mess," she said.

I followed Gemma as she wandered through rooms and hallways before reaching the steps leading to the bedrooms upstairs. Once we reached my suite, I discovered what Chet had done, because he was still at it.

Tampons were strewn across the bedroom floor, all of them in some stage of cat-clawed-destruction.

"Chet," I scolded him. "Bad kitty. Bad. Stop that right this instant."

Chet went still, carefully let go of the tampon he was clawing with his back feet and stood, shook himself and walked away, tail high. Gemma and I both watched him leave the bedroom as if he owned the place.

"Mom told me there'd be days like this," I quipped, before picking up scattered tampons, wrappers and bits of fluff strewn everywhere.

"I can do this," Gemma offered, lowering the hand towel. "I ah, needed to borrow one of them—that's why I came here in the first place. Chet beat me to the box."

I forced myself not to stare at the deep scars on her face. This was what she'd been hiding all along. "Oh, honey," I said, heading for the bathroom where I'd hidden the box of tampons. "Take as many as you need. I'll clean this up."

At least the box was still intact, as were more than a dozen tampons on the bathroom floor. Scooping those up, I handed them to Gemma. "If you need more, let me know."

"Thanks. The grocery order won't come until tomorrow, and it sorta couldn't wait."

I lifted the large box that Chet had opened, and felt the weight of the pyramid inside it—except now it felt heavier than it had before. Gemma turned to leave.

A flash of understanding came the moment I reached inside the box to check on the pyramid itself.

Themselves, I corrected myself.

"Gemma?" I called out to her.

"Is there something else?" She came back to ask.

"Who attacked you? It was Doyle Hicks, wasn't it?"

Her face blanched at the mention of his name. "After you take care of business, I'll get you set up with Doc Chalmers," I told her. "He's in the proper mood to help you, I think."

"But," she began.

"No—you need this. So does he, okay? They just buried his assistant, and he needs to help somebody. By the way, Jinx Hicks, Doyle's brother, is the one who killed Doctor Chalmers' assistant. Jinx is dead, too, if nobody thought to tell you. I think I can guarantee that you'll never hear from Doyle or anyone connected to him ever again."

"I try not to watch the news," she whispered.

"Go take care of yourself. I'll let Doctor Chalmers know you're seeing him this afternoon."

"Thank you."

After she left the suite, I carefully pulled out four, perfectly-formed pyramids from the tampon box. I found I could read all of them.

Because they all had my name written in runes at their tops.

It took you long enough to check on your pyramid, the voice I didn't recognize teased.

Who are you? I demanded.

Somebody who will be there to help you tonight. I'll bring a couple of friends with me—you need us.

No—I refuse to accept that. I need your name.

All right. Denevik Lith, dear lady. High Demon, at your service.

If the pyramids hadn't started humming gently, urging me to accept the offered help, I'd have spent the rest of the day fretting. Something was definitely going on, and we were in more danger than we realized.

Parke

"Everything ready to go for tonight?" I pulled up an empty lawn chair beside Cliff's. I'd found him on the back porch with Doctor Chalmers. Both were talking and having glasses of sweet tea.

"Yeah. Just the waiting is all that's left," Cliff drawled.

"Have you seen Cassie?" I was considering asking her to spend some time with me, but wasn't sure it was a good idea. We hadn't had sex even once since she'd returned from the dead.

I guess we were both different people, now, and I wasn't sure how to explain that.

"Chet made a mess of some kind," Cliff said. "Gemma came to tell Cassie and both left in a hurry."

"Must be upstairs, then," I said.

"Want something to drink? We have more tea, beer and soda in the cooler."

"I'll take a soda. Beer sounds good, but I need to stay sharp."

"My thoughts exactly."

Cassie

Once I had everything picked up and tossed in the trash, I studied the four pyramids on the counter in the bathroom. Chet walked back in, wound himself around my legs and purred loudly.

As if he were proud of himself.

We're having a meeting, the one who called himself Denevik Lith informed me. *We need your input.*

Right. Where and when?

When is now. I tried to shriek—the sound never left my mouth, I was transported away so quickly. Instead, I made an embarrassing squeak after landing inside a room with a large table—where several people sat, waiting.

Beside me, someone stood.

Someone nine feet tall.

And blue.

"I am Zarigar," he informed me with a brilliant smile. "Welcome to BlackWing X."

Dalton King

I'd changed my mind about leaving—my curiosity was unsatisfied regarding Ver'Dak and what he wanted. Attaching myself as the thinnest sheet of ice on the ceiling, I turned back to follow him.

Therefore, I heard quite clearly what his intentions were regarding demons, Shakkor Agdah and every other creature roaming the planet.

Cage fights? That didn't sound good in any vocabulary. Where was the money and power we'd been promised by Ruudann? These fools sounded as if they wanted to subjugate all of us, Shakkor Agdah included.

Fuck that.

As for demon killers and slaves in the military who were set to kill those opposing Ver'Dak? I wasn't giving the Chancellor's odds of survival much thought, because even he and his fire demon couldn't stand against *that.*

Where the hell had these armored pigs come from? I was beginning to think that the Earth I knew wasn't the only inhabited planet after all. *Fuck you, Ruudann,* I cursed silently. *Fuck you and all your lies.*

Cassie

Too much information swam in my head, so much so that I almost felt dizzy from it.

"You need something to eat," the man sitting beside me said. "I'm Denevik Lith, by the way."

"You said you were High Demon," I frowned at him. "I've never heard of that before."

"They're not local." One of a set of identical Asian twins peered around Denevik with a grin.

"Trent, stop scaring her," Denevik snorted.

Wait, was that *smoke* coming from his nostrils? Holy cow patties.

"Come on, I'll take you to the galley," Denevik took my elbow, ignoring the one he'd called Trent.

"Did you just breathe smoke?" I asked, feeling stunned. I'd breathed smoke once, but it was around the time I was fire demon, so I hadn't thought much about it.

"It's something that happens when they're annoyed," the second Asian twin informed me. "Don't worry—nothing he can do will harm you—we've all seen the vids of your recent exploits."

"What do you do?" I asked.

"I turn Thifilathi. Full Thifilathi is seventeen feet, in your measurements. Smaller Thifilathi is around seven or eight feet."

"You have two forms?"

"As do you, if I understand correctly. Mine look the same, only the size is different. Yours are quite different, or so Zarigar says."

"Is Zarigar—uh," I hesitated.

"He is Larentii. He is the reason we were able to come here—to Earth IV. Earth III is on our plane of existence, so we needed Zarigar's abilities to make the transfer into another universe."

"Uh, I think I'm into information overload, now," I confessed.

"You'll feel better when you eat something. Come on, I'll skip us to the galley."

Whatever he did got us to the galley right away, and felt similar to my new talent of teleportation. When I gazed out the windows along one side of the galley, I realized why the dining room and kitchen area was called a galley.

We were aboard a ship, and far in the distance, I could see the Earth below us. "The sun will be setting on your part of the planet very soon," Denevik said.

"I have to get back," I began.

"We have Zarigar. He can bend time if it's necessary. I hope you like steak—it's on the menu and fresh-cooked to your specifications."

He took me to a small table and pulled out a chair for me. "How do you like your steak? I'll order for both of us."

"Uh, medium rare, please."

"Coming right up."

He was back in a few minutes, with two plates of food. Our steaks were still sizzling when he set them down. "Save room for dessert—we have gishi fruit and you don't want to miss that."

My steak was perfectly done, and tasted wonderful, as did the vegetables that came with it. But nothing I'd ever eaten before compared to the gishi fruit. It was heaven from a tree.

"Gishi trees are the most expensive trees in either Alliance," Denevik informed me after we'd finished. "They only grow in certain climates and in specific soils. Only two worlds can grow gishi fruit like this."

"So, you've been hunting this—Krelk—is that right? For how long?"

"We've been after him for over a year. He showed up after we managed to save Earth III from his brother. We almost had him, too, until he disappeared. Zarigar's mother was the one to suggest that we search the planets in this pod, which are in six different universes."

There was something he was holding back, but I let it go for the moment. "I'm still trying to wrap my head around this," I confessed. "Will said something about Earth III and below, but I didn't really understand what he was saying."

"Zarigar will have to answer your questions about the wizards you're referring to. He says they're an unusual lot and born for a specific purpose."

"Their purpose is to blow up fire demons, because they can't contain Shakkor Agdah any other way," I grumped.

"That wasn't always true," Zarigar appeared as if called and shortened himself to sit with us. "Once, the wizards who came from Earth VI were powerful enough to keep their more mundane brothers in check. As those wizards were killed or destroyed themselves because they became tired of living, their power dwindled. Only a few centuries ago did they discover that they could no longer battle the traitors who'd traveled from V to IV. VI and V are completely devoid of life; I don't believe the wizard has told you that, yet," he added.

"Shakkor Agdah destroyed those worlds?" I blinked at the blue-skinned man.

"Yes. With enough of them going unchecked, the wizards were outnumbered. When they crossed the world bridge from V to IV, they knew something needed to be done. Shakkor Agdah hold a power of their own, and wielded together, they can become quite destructive. That's why the pyramids were built."

"The Egyptian ones, or the smaller ones in my bathroom?"

"The smaller ones came first," Zarigar smiled. "The larger ones may have been built as a reference to the others, as they held a great deal of power. The last of the most powerful wizards from Earth VI placed their power inside all four pyramids, leaving their bodies behind as dead husks. Immediately, the pyramids worked to hold the power held by Shakkor Agdah at bay. All was well for a while, until Shakkor Agdah learned of their existence and began to hunt them."

"One was destroyed, and maybe a second one, too. A third was damaged. Now they're all whole and sitting on my bathroom sink. With my name on them," I frowned at Zarigar.

"Because things have changed. You have changed. My mother says you are the key, now, and the power that resides in the pyramids know this. She only had to *Change What Was* a little, to bring everything back to where it should be."

"Which is?"

"You've heard already that Ver'Dak has taken prisoners from the military and turned them into his slaves. They also have weapons that none on your world can combat. That's why the crew of this ship will do battle beside you tonight. We have the same kind of weapons, and Ver'Dak won't be expecting us."

"We need your help to convince those who stand with you to accept our help when it comes. The Shakkor Agdah who asked for the meeting are fleeing for their lives. We ask that you honor their courage in coming to you and offer asylum. They can be quite useful to you in the coming days, I think."

"You say that Ver'Dak is the enemy. What does he want with us and Shakkor Agdah?"

"He wanted Shakkor Agdah to destroy the human population, leaving only demons, shifters and such. Shakkor Agdah were mere tools to accomplish this much of the plan for him, so we wouldn't be alerted to his hand in this. He intends to take demons and large shifters for the Krelk version of cage fights, where opponents are required to fight to the death. What the wizards began by destroying fire demons, was taken as a viable solution to removing the only known threat to Shakkor Agdah and to Ver'Dak's army."

"Without you, all the demons you know could end up in Ver'Dak's cages, waiting for their death match while Krelk bet on which one will survive," Denevik snorted. "Socially, they're still in the dark ages, as you'd say. Technologically, they're far advanced, thanks to interference from others who only wished to cause chaos and death.

"It's like giving a caveman a machine gun," Denevik sighed. "No good will come of that, you can be sure."

"How many of Ver'Dak's troops are we facing—Black Myth and Krelk?" I asked.

"A conservative estimate is ten thousand," Denevik replied. "Plus they'll have tanks, helicopters and who knows what else. We're trying to get a message to someone in your Pentagon about those who've been conscripted by Ver'Dak, but they may not pay attention until it's too late."

"Trey can get to them," I breathed. Why don't you come back with me? Don't we need to coordinate?'

"We do. What we need to know is whether your friends will accept us, or if other methods will be needed to insure their cooperation."

"I'll make sure they understand," I said.

"Good enough. I'll bend time to deliver the crew to your home," Zarigar said. "Be safe. This is a very real battle, and none can predict the outcome."

Parke

"Parke?" Cassie appeared before me as if called, shortly after I'd asked Cliff if he'd seen her.

"What is it?" I stood, puzzled by the expression on her face.

"We're going to need allies for tonight," she said. "I found out what has changed in the dynamic. It isn't just Shakkor Agdah, anymore. If it were only them, I think we could take them on ourselves."

"What's changed? Who's in this with them?" Cliff stood, then, sounding worried.

"The ones who gave Black Myth the demon killers. The ones who convinced them that killing all humans was a good idea. The same ones who think that sticking demons in cages so they can fight to the death is fun to watch."

"What the hell are you talking about?" I demanded.

"Cassie, what do you know?" Cliff waved off my annoyance.

"A lot more than I did. I know that if we don't have help, we'll lose this fight. That's what I know."

"Who will help us? Even the military won't get involved without a lot of red tape, and time is running out," I complained.

"The other side already has some of the military on their side," Cassie snapped at me. "They're nothing but slaves, now, and their tanks and helicopters will be fitted with bigger, more powerful versions of demon killers. There's a new despot in town, Parke, and he's way more dangerous that Shakkor Agdah ever was."

"You know somebody who can help us?" Cliff asked her.

"I do, but I have to have reassurances that we'll cooperate with them. They don't have time to make nice and be sure everybody has a feel-good session. They need to tell you what they know, and when Trey wakes, he needs to tell Director Logan about the theft of military vehicles and personnel. We're running out of time, and this requires a joint effort."

"Who are they?" Cliff asked. I let him talk, because everything I said appeared to upset Cassie.

"Friends." I stepped backward when three dozen people appeared behind the house at Cassie's announcement. The tallest was nine feet and blue. The rest looked human enough, but could be anything, I realized, when one of them became a dark, scaled creature with wings and curved horns. He snorted smoke with his breath while his eyes, with flames at their depths, narrowed in my direction. Arms crossed over his chest as he studied me, then snorted another cloud of smoke that obscured his image for a few moments.

What the fuck was he?

CHAPTER 17

Cassie

"You won't believe what's on the front lawn," Daniel burst through the French doors, followed by Jerry and Pete. The three of them skidded to a stop when they saw what was on the back lawn.

Or in this case, *who.*

"What's on the front lawn?" Parke asked, the anger in his voice barely controlled.

"Stuff from sci-fi movies," Daniel sounded out of breath.

"Most of the stuff in sci-fi movies doesn't work," a tall, dark-haired man stepped forward. "What's on the front lawn does."

"He's a wolf," Cliff turned toward me with wonder in his eyes.

"I'm William Winkler—originally from Texas on Earth III," he introduced himself. "Zaria figured you people might need some help in the diplomacy department, so here I am."

"Who is Zaria?" Parke asked, still sounding as if he were about to go rock demon and smash a few things.

"My mother," Zarigar replied. "One will refrain from insulting her, or any other of my kin."

"Texas, eh?" Cliff stepped forward and offered his hand to Mr. Winkler.

"Yep." They shook; Cliff asked Winkler if he wanted tea, soda or a beer. Winkler grinned and accepted a beer.

"This is Denevik Lith, a High Demon," I introduced Denevik, the one who'd changed and now glared at Parke. "This is Captain Travis and his brother Captain Trent," I went on. "Denevik, will you introduce the others? I don't know all the names."

That required Denevik to change his appearance so he looked human again, but he did so, then dipped his head in my direction before pointing out his companions and naming all of them.

Even I drew in a breath when Denevik introduced Darzi, the lion snake shapeshifter. I'd never met a snake shifter before.

"I bite, even Shakkor Agdah die," Darzi informed us.

"That sounds useful," Jerry mumbled.

"We'd like to coordinate tonight's battle with you," Travis said. "With your permission, Chancellor."

"What the hell," Parke flung out a hand. *What have you gotten us into?* he growled at me in mindspeak.

We're outnumbered. We need the help. When you hear about Ver'Dak, you're gonna want the help, too.

"Come inside," Parke snapped. "Tell me what you think I should know."

Will, Yosuke and the sprites joined us for the meeting. If I hadn't been worried that Parke wouldn't be civil or mind his manners, I'd have sneaked out for a few minutes of calm before rejoining the group.

"We have seen your kind before," Rob bowed to Zarigar, who beamed at him.

"What do you know about them?" Parke was still in rock-demon-smash mode.

"We have visited the sprite kingdoms," Zarigar said politely. "Long ago."

"Larentii are mostly observers," Rob informed Parke. The tone of his voice warned Parke to cut the bullshit.

I don't know what Parke's problem is, I informed Rob.

I do. We'll talk later. For now, he needs to play nice with the alien who can separate his atoms if he tries to attack.

They're that dangerous?

Only to those who wish them or their kind harm. Otherwise, they're the most peaceful race ever. Averill has records in his library about a visit from the Larentii eons ago. I found the information fascinating and read it several times.

You mean you knew all along that aliens existed? And you didn't tell me?

Well, yeah. Besides, if Parke understood anything at all about the Larentii, to know that one was here with this bunch would automatically reveal them as trustworthy.

You're saying they don't hang with criminals?

They don't hang with criminals.

Who was the Larentii who visited the sprites? I asked. *Since you know so much about them.*

It doesn't mention a name, Rob replied.

At that moment, Zarigar turned to lock eyes with mine. *Lady Demon,* he said, *Larentii can bend time.* And then he winked at me before turning his attention back to Parke.

"Shall we begin?" Travis cleared his throat to interrupt the stare-down between a Larentii and a stubborn rock demon.

"Absolutely," I agreed.

Cliff

Trey was on the phone with Director Logan almost from the moment he woke for the evening. He stayed on the phone while Director Logan spoke to the President, who then blew through enough red tape to circle the Earth a few times to mobilize the Georgia National Guard.

At least the helicopter portion of it. It was too late to get anything other than ground troops and helicopters to Stone Mountain, so that's what they were sending. Emergency alerts were scheduled to be sent out beginning at midnight, for everyone to stay indoors.

"Who would have thought that Stone Mountain might be the final battleground to save the Earth from Ver'Dak and Shakkor Agdah?" Winkler shook his head and barked a laugh.

He'd asked me to call him Winkler—because *everybody does*. The name was an easy fit for him. He was certainly wolf; I'd known it from his scent. There was something else about him that indicated he was more than that.

"You had to be a Packmaster—where you're from," I said.

"I was—of the Dallas Pack. Before Lissa came along."

"Lissa?"

"Maybe someday, you'll meet her. We survive the battle tonight, I'll make introductions myself."

"You're worried?"

"Every time one of these infernal Krelk hybrids is involved, there's no telling what may happen, or what, exactly, they can do."

"What do you mean?"

"Let's say part of their hybrid lineage is powerful—and malevolent."

"More so than Black Myth?"

"Hmmph. Black Myth is nothing to them, other than a convenient means to an end. After all, you don't need to come out of your hidey hole if somebody else is willing to do the work for you. We've been hunting Ver'Dak for months."

"I figure there's more to this story. What are you not telling me?"

"That Ver'Dak's specialty, like that of his brothers, is getting rid of anyone or anything that might stand in the way of their controlling everything."

"Such as?"

"You really don't have to look much further than Cassie and the demons, shifters and sprites who follow her. They are dangerous to Ver'Dak's plans. Tell me, Cliff, who is the person you think of now, whenever there's a new emergency to deal with? Who is most capable of taking care of the situation?"

That's when I understood much more than I had before. "Cassie," I whispered. "She's the best we have."

"Exactly. The Chancellor comes in second, doesn't he?"

"He handles the rules and regulations, but if the enemy is at the door, I want Cassie to be standing at the front of our army."

"We've ah, noticed. When Zarigar told us that the pyramids were tuning themselves to her, we understood that to be a fact."

"Parke won't relinquish his position," I said, as I considered everything I'd just learned.

"We know that, too. And on any other world it might not be a problem."

"You think there will be a problem?"

"Zarigar is concerned. No Larentii is concerned without good reason. I believe he's far more worried about Cassie than the Chancellor in this scenario."

She'd only had one session with Doc Chalmers, and that probably hadn't put a single dent in the whole betrayal-death muck she'd already been through. "What's the solution?" I asked.

"I can't give you an answer to that. First, we have a bunch of crazy assholes to take care of, and all of them will be trying to kill us first."

"Yeah. First things first."

Cassie

There wasn't much time left before going to Stone Mountain and engaging in battle. I stared at four pyramids, which still lay on my bathroom sink.

"What am I supposed to do with you?" I asked them. "You're far too important to be sitting here, with anyone capable of coming in and taking you away."

I can help you with that, Zarigar's voice sounded in my head. *You're right—they don't belong here. Not because they can be stolen—that is no longer possible, as they contain a bit of your fire. If anyone else touches them, they will be burned.*

"Where can I put them?" The implications of the Larentii's words terrified me. What if Gemma or Destiny or someone else touched them? Would they die?

"Let me place them in strategic locations—and place shields about them so none will ever discover their location. This way, they will continue to protect the planet against future invaders, and as you are connected to them, you will know if the planet itself is in danger."

Zarigar had appeared behind me while he spoke, almost startling me. I could see our reflection in the bathroom mirror; he much taller than I.

There wasn't a question in my mind whether I could trust him—something in me said he would be the most trustworthy person I'd ever met.

"Will you do this for me?" I craned my neck to look up at him.

He smiled. "That and much more, should you ask."

Closing his eyes and raising his hand, Zarigar caused the pyramids to disappear. When he opened his eyes, I understood that they were safely placed where none would ever find them.

"Thank you," I told him.

"You are welcome. Now, come with me—Denevik would like to speak with you."

I found myself on the back porch again, but this time, only Denevik, Zarigar and I were there.

"Is there something you need?" I asked Denevik.

"Need? Perhaps, but that is a discussion for another time. What I'd like is to show you that you cannot harm me while I am in demon form. I will change, and you will envelope me in your fire. Zarigar says this experiment may be beneficial to both of us."

I stared at him, probably with my mouth inconveniently open in shock. "Ah, this scares me," I began.

"I know; that's why we need to do this now, under controlled circumstances."

"I will shield you from sight," Zarigar promised. "No matter what."

What happened next even I had few words to describe; I can only say that it was terrifying at first, and then exhilarating.

~

Parke

"The troops will be flown in on my command," Trey said as we studied a map of the Stone Mountain area. "There's another vampire mindspeaker who'll be with them and relay information."

"Tell them to focus on shooting Shakkor Agdah," William Winkler advised. He and Cliff had joined us once Trey had everything coordinated between Director Logan, the White House and the Georgia National Guard. "Shooting normal bullets will only piss off the Krelk."

"That means we have to take them down, then," I said.

"Tell your ice demons to spread ice between their armored plates and force them apart. That allows you to get to the vulnerable skin beneath, and that can be pierced by ice daggers—if they're talented in that area."

"I'll let Daniel know," I said dryly. "Will the Krelk be able to stand against a rock demon?"

"Only as long as it takes to throw a first punch. Crush their heads —it's the fastest way to kill them."

"This is why they want to destroy us—just as you said. We're dangerous to them," Trey breathed.

"Exactly. They're aiming at any world that could defeat them in a fair fight. Ver'Dak is more dangerous to the demons here than you can possibly guess. If he removes his goggles and issues commands, you're compelled to obey."

"Like vampire compulsion?" Trey sounded worried.

"Let's say it's vampire compulsion to the hundredth power. Very few are immune to it. I hear that some vampires can withstand the obsession, but they must be more than four thousand years old and be powerful among their own kind."

"That leaves me out," Trey shook his head.

"Can all the Krelk do that?" I asked.

"The Krelk have no talent in that area. Ver'Dak, thanks to his parentage, is able to do it quite well, in addition to folding space, mindspeaking and several other things that regular Krelk can only admire from afar."

"T minus thirty minutes," Trey shut his laptop and made his announcement. "Should we go in waves, or all together?"

"I suggest placing squads around the base; those who've deserted Shakkor Agdah must be gotten to safety first, and then we take on the army that will surely follow," Winkler advised. "Travis and Trent are talking to the rest of your crew about where they should go and what they should do when this shit show starts. By the way, if you happen to see dragons, they're on our side."

∽

Cassie

Remember—I can't shoot out my fire like you can, Denevik sent. *We'll have two fire-breathing dragons helping us—they can burn Shakkor Agdah in swaths. What we don't know is whether the Krelk will have some kind of shielding that will keep them safe from that fire. That's where you and I may come in.*

Right. Denevik, Rob and the other three sprite guards, plus Landon and Liam, stood with me in a wooded copse on the southern side of the monolith. Our other groups were scattered beneath trees all around the large, granite mountain.

The armed vehicles that Travis and Trent brought with them were situated farther down the mountain and bore weapons that would be used to combat the ones Ver'Dak had mounted on his commandeered military aircraft. National Guard helicopters had also been hastily equipped with the weapons.

The only advice Denevik and the rest of his crew gave regarding those weapons was *don't get in the line of fire if you want to live.*

I was beginning to wonder if the deserting Shakkor Agdah would show up when I got mindspeak from Trey. *They're at the base of the mountain. We'll attempt to divert them so they can be transported to a safe place.*

Don't put that Lilith woman anywhere near Gemma, unless you place compulsion first, I replied.

Don't worry. Lilith Sloane has caused the last bit of trouble she'll ever cause. For a moment that worried me, but Trey was right in this, and I did promise Gemma that Lilith and Doyle wouldn't trouble her again. I shrugged off my concern and gave my silent permission to a vampire who knew what he was doing.

They're going to kill us all, a voice sounded in my mind. *They're setting a trap. They'll put demons in cage fights!*

I drew in a breath as Denevik stiffened beside me. Until then, I'd never known that Dalton King could mindspeak. When a murderous traitor comes out of hiding long enough to warn about other murderous traitors, then it has to be serious.

Dalton King, I hope you're close enough to die in this battle, I hissed into his mind. *If you don't, I'll never stop hunting you.*

Cassie? You're alive?

No thanks to you.

I've got this, Denevik's hand landed on my shoulder. *Keep him talking. I'll be back shortly.*

I didn't have to worry about making Dalton talk—he was ready with his own brand of snake oil. *Cassie, if you can get us away from this mess, I swear I'll give you anything you want*, he offered.

I don't want anything from you, I snapped at him.

They intend to kill us—or cage us and then kill us, Dalton whined. *We're in danger. You can protect the both of us.*

Where did you dump my mother's body, you piece of shit, I demanded, as anger threatened to light my fire early. I was already in-between human and prelim.

I see you're willing to allow your kin to die, Dalton hissed. *Suit yourself. Your mother is buried at the back of Ross' property, with his permission.* The asshole didn't even sound contrite about his role in her death and hiding the body afterward. *Want to know how she*, his voice was cut off.

He's dead, Denevik informed me. *His mindspeech led me straight to him. The fool was driving a stolen truck down a country road toward*

Tennessee, Denevik landed beside me again, in what he called his smaller Thifilathi. He didn't look fazed in the least.

Thank you. I rolled my shoulders, trying to contain my fire demon. We didn't need Parke's subsequent call to do battle; Ver'Dak's commandeered helicopters could now be heard in the distance, flying in from the west.

Then, the voices of thousands of Shakkor Agdah roared a battle cry at the base of the mountain. The war for control of the planet had begun.

Destiny King

Beverly and Gemma were overwhelmed in the kitchen; the people brought to the house were starving, and three of them were the family of the former Vice President. His wife understood that he'd already died from the poison disease—the ones who'd kidnapped her told her as much.

As for the Black Myth people, they'd cut as many of the poison bubbles off their skin as they could. Their faces were covered in pock marks, like the worst acne scars anybody could imagine. I figured the rest of them could be in the same shape. They made sure not to touch anybody directly by wearing thick, leather gloves. They were thanking everybody for their rescue and the food.

Faith joined Beverly and Gemma, cooking whatever was fastest and easiest to feed them. Kate and I pitched in to help. I was pouring water and sweet tea for everybody. Will had brought them to the house but left shortly afterward, to go help the others.

It worried me that Cassie and Parke were in Georgia, fighting Black Myth and whoever they'd sided with in order to get weapons and the disease. Didn't make any sense to me to destroy the planet that fed and supported you, but they wanted to do just that for some reason.

Stupid, really.

"You have a faraway look," a young Black Myth man told me as I handed him a fresh glass of tea.

"I was just thinking how stupid it is to destroy the planet beneath our feet."

"We've been thinking the same thing," he agreed. "I hope that one day, I can be free of all this and study in a real college," he said. "Thank you for the tea. It's the best I've ever tasted."

"Then I hope college happens for you," I told him. "And you're welcome. What's your name?"

"Baarkann," he said. "And you?"

"Destiny," I shrugged.

"What a beautiful name."

I'd never thought of my name that way. Sometimes, I thought it was a stupid name. Baarkann thought it was beautiful. Maybe he didn't understand much about the English language.

Or maybe he did.

Federal Prison, Washington State

Doyle Hicks

I wasn't expecting any visitors, especially this late at night. The door to my cell opened anyway. "Who are you?" I rose from my bunk and confronted the man who'd entered. Even in the dim light, he wore a pair of aviator sunglasses.

"I'm here to get you out," he shrugged indifferently, drawing my attention away from his potential blindness. "If you'd like to leave," he added.

"How? Did my appeal go through?" I asked, squashing the excitement that threatened to overtake me.

"In a way, I suppose," the man agreed. "Come, there is someplace for you to be, I think. If you wish to go, that is."

"Let's go. I'll take anything over this cell."

"I'll remember you said that," he grinned. "I suggest you do the same."

I expected to walk out of the place with this man, but that isn't what happened. Instead, he gripped my arm and in a blink, we were someplace else.

I'd been here before, I realized. *Stone Mountain, Georgia.* Only this time, it was night and a war was going on all over it. To make things even stranger, I saw that every shot fired between armies had stopped —frozen somehow in midair.

In the distance, I saw—was that a dragon? He was in the act of bellowing fire at figures crouching on the ground. If the battle resumed, those on the ground would be toast.

Helicopters hung overhead, in the act of firing bright blasts at what appeared to be giants made of rock to the east. Wolves—huge ones—ran behind and to the side of the rock giants, attacking what looked like armored, pig-like humans.

As for the men dressed in black with foot-long claws extending from their fingers, they were attacking the pig-humans from this side. One, I saw, had nearly sheared through the neck of an armored pig-man.

"You have seven seconds to choose a hiding place before the battle continues," the man said as I studied the suspended chaos around me. "A wise choice will extend your life span, although that grows short."

"You set me down in the middle of a battle?" I shouted at him. "You lying fucker!"

"Remember, you said you wanted to come. Two seconds remain," he added. I ran.

The battle resumed.

A bullet hit me in the shoulder, knocking me down and sending me into a rough slide across granite rock and scrabble. Something stopped my forward motion just as the pain from the wound bloomed at my back and drew a pain-filled curse from me.

A body—a female body, lying against a small, tenacious tree trunk, had stopped me from falling over a sharp edge of granite. The granite had been smooth and rounded only moments before, but while I'd been sliding toward the body and the tree, a portion of the rock had been blasted away by some of the weapons being fired.

Dragging myself toward the tree trunk, I cringed as more weapons fired around me. If I could only pull the body over mine, perhaps it would shield me from more bullets.

The head had almost been severed, I noticed, as I attempted to burrow beneath the body, and it wasn't until the head lolled toward me as I moved it that I realized I knew the woman.

Lilith.

Dead.

What was the bitch doing here, of all places?

Zarigar

When the small ranos cannon blast hit the granite behind Doyle Hicks, he was attempting to shield himself with the body of his dead lover. Just as he'd spent his life doing, he'd attempted to use someone else to cover for his misdeeds.

The cannon blast split the rock and rendered it into a destructive explosion of granite shrapnel. Both bodies disintegrated in the force of the weapon's violent discharge.

Rob

Shakkor Agdah were everywhere. How had they increased their numbers like this? Of course, they'd remained in hiding for centuries, making all of us think that we'd devastated them so much they wouldn't consider coming out of hiding again.

They'd certainly had help in this, just as our new allies said—there had to be at least twenty thousand of them. As for the damage their helicopters armed with demon killing weapons could do—I'd already witnessed it, and much closer than I wanted. Half of Stone Mountain was nothing but rubble, now, although the National Guard helicopters were armed with similar weapons.

Had they not been, all of us may have died in the enemy's initial attack. The copters still aloft were now engaging one another, forgetting about the battle on the ground for now.

Shakkor Agdah ground troops had emerged from nothing by the thousands, and all of them came at us, shouting and running. Many of them wielded demon killer rifles or pistols, which they aimed in our direction, caring not whether they hit anything or anyone.

A rock demon fell with a cry, stones from his breaking body flying in every direction. Zephyr's blade never stopped moving as she spun wind about her, tossing away her kills to enable her to attack the next black robe who thought to take her down.

Ebb pulled water from the air itself and aimed it straight into the faces of his opponents, temporarily blinding them while he relieved them of their heads.

Blaze's body was encased in flames as he fought; it was fortunate he was a swift runner, as Shakkor Agdah preferred to flee from him and his blade.

As for my attackers—earth, pebbles and plants answered to my call, filling eyes and nostrils with dirt, leaves and gravel while I attacked. The four of us worked in tandem to cut a swath through the southern side of the Black Myth army.

My mistake, however, was not watching my back for only a moment. A squad of black cloaks had circled around behind me and my fellow sprites, intending to surprise us. Blaze had run ahead to take down another enemy soldier armed with a demon killer. He turned in the forceful act of slicing through the black cloak and his weapon and saw what was approaching.

Behind you, he shouted into our minds.

Swiftly I turned, swinging my blade.

Too late.

Almost.

The enormous black wolf hit my attacker like a hurricane, going immediately for his throat. Neither I nor the wolf saw the next black cloak arrive from the opposite side, his demon killer pointed directly at us.

No! Ebb flung water at the black cloak and the weapon. Water splashed the gun and the face of the enemy, throwing off his aim by inches. The weapon fired. The thin blast came so close to my face it nearly singed my nose.

And then the wolf yelped behind me.

I knew that yelp. There was nothing I could do to help or reverse the death the weapon wrought upon my friend.

Cliff was dead.

Someone else realized it, too.

Cliff! Cassie shouted.

Had I thought the battle was intense already?

I was wrong.

Cassie

It was time. Even Denevik understood it. We'd held back for the most part, as instructed by Zarigar, Travis and Trent. They wanted to ensure that all the black-cloaked army, their helicopters and the Krelk were within a certain range.

Cliff's death precipitated that waiting period—perhaps by seconds.

Remember, I can fly, and you cannot harm me with your fire, Denevik informed me. I could probably have done all this myself, but he was there as a backup, just in case. Pulling me into a tight hug, my back to his chest, Denevik *skipped* us high in the air, until we were hanging above Stone Mountain and all those who fought below us. Even the helicopters were beneath us.

Trey, I sent, *pull the helicopters back.*

Done, he said a few seconds later. As my back was to Denevik's chest, he and I watched as the National Guard's helicopters turned and flew toward the east. Wide, leathery wings flapped at Denevik's back, keeping us aloft as Ver'Dak's stolen machines flew after our retreating choppers.

We had to wait until the National Guard cleared the perimeter before we unleashed our last resort.

The attempt to destroy all the enemy at once.

Cliff was dead. Who knew how many others had fallen, too?

I had to force myself not to think about that.

Almost there, Denevik informed me. *Almost there.*

Parke

Liam was dead. Kent, Wallis and Jackson had fallen in battle. Now, Cliff was gone, too—there was no mistaking the grief in Cassie's sending, when she shouted his name.

Time to get out now, William Winkler advised. *All hell is about to be unleashed.*

Jerry, Pete, Ben and I were whisked away—by whom I'll probably never know. This was the plan—to pull us away when the moment presented itself.

I hoped it was successful—I was done with these encroachers defacing the Earth I lived on.

We found ourselves outside a lodge away from the mountain; the National Guard forces had taken it over as a command base. I could see their helicopters flying away from the scene, with the enemy in hot pursuit.

Don't let them get away, I snapped at Cassie.

She probably didn't need any prompting from me, I realized somewhat too late.

"Watch this," Zarigar's hand dropped onto my shoulder. He'd shortened himself and made his appearance human, with darker skin, dark eyes and dreadlocks.

"Colonel Brady," a man in uniform walked up to introduce himself.

That's when the sky over the mountain lit up so brightly, it looked as if an atomic bomb had gone off.

Get down, Zarigar said, sounding almost pleasant as he shoved me into the dirt, face first. The sound of the explosion, and a granite mountain cracking and then melting, almost deafened all of us.

CHAPTER 18

*R*_{ob} Stone Mountain was no longer a mountain, and, because of the heat exerted upon it, no longer granite, exactly.

The melting, followed by rapid cooling had turned it into a pile of multicolored Rhyolite. It was the pyre on which Cliff's body was consumed, and I found myself on my knees, weeping out my grief.

Someone dropped to their knees beside me and keened.

Cassie was crying her heart out with me, with Denevik beside her, attempting to soothe her pain.

Instead, I pulled her away from him, and we wept together, her tears running down my armor and soaking the linen tunic beneath. Cliff was the best friend I'd ever had, and in the end, he'd sacrificed his life to save mine.

I was already indebted to him for my life. Now, that debt would go on for the rest of my existence. How could I ever repay it?

"What the hell have you done to my mountain?" a loud voice behind us demanded.

The Governor of Georgia just arrived, Will informed us. Well, somebody else had survived the debacle. In the east, dawn was breaking and the Governor had come to survey the damage.

We hadn't chosen this battleground; it was chosen for us. We'd just risked our lives and lost friends in this war. Had we not done what we did, perhaps his mountain would have been intact but his life would be forfeit.

"Cassie?" I whispered against her ear. "Go with Denevik, now. I need to have a word with the Governor."

"I will help," Zarigar said, offering a dark-skinned hand to lift me up.

"I'm coming with you," Cassie said as Denevik pulled her to her feet. With eyes red from crying, she scrubbed her cheeks of moisture with a fist before nodding to Zarigar and me.

Denevik came with us as we walked toward the Governor, who was now shouting at the National Guard Commander about the mountain's destruction.

"In the end of all things," Zarigar spoke softly, but drew the Governor's attention anyway, "In the end of all things, it is not the fate of a single mountain that may be remembered here, but the fate of the very planet itself. Would you prefer to have your state, your country and your planet overrun by those who intended to kill you with a terrible disease? Or would you rather hold onto the past, even though you know it will destroy you and hand the planet to your known enemy?"

"Who are you?" the Governor demanded, looking Zarigar up and down. "Who the hell is he?" The governor was now looking at me—the palest-skinned male in this group.

"I am Zarigar of the Larentii." Zarigar understood what was happening and drew himself to his full, blue-skinned height. He gazed down upon the Governor, who swallowed hard and took a step backward. "As you can see, it is not the outside of anyone that truly matters."

"My friend died on that mountain, protecting your ugly ass," I added. "If you want a monument to replace it, the sprites will be happy to build one for Cliff Young, Grand Master of the werewolves."

"I, ah," the Governor backed up another step.

"You owe your life to the supernatural races upon the Earth, that you only learned of in the past day or two," Cassie said. "Plus a few who don't even live on this planet but came to rescue your ugly ass anyway. Instead of yelling about your mountain, you should be handing out thank you notes. I believe the President was informed about the battle as it happened, just as you probably were."

"The President has already extended his appreciation," the Commander joined our conversation. "For a job well done."

"As you've come to realize," Zarigar spoke to the Governor again, "Pettiness does not belong in a conversation held with those who've recently come from battle. I suggest you retreat now and regain your dignity, then plan your words more carefully in the future."

"We have friends to mourn," I said. "You do not rule the sprite kingdoms on this planet, or the elemental demons. I suggest you remember that in the future."

"Are you ready to go, dearest?" Zarigar turned a gentle smile on Cassie.

"I'm ready," she agreed, although Denevik's hand was the one she grasped before Zarigar moved us to the estate in Alabama.

Ver'Dak Disrai

They'd destroyed my entire fucking army, including the Shakkor Agdah. We were gaining the upper hand until that firebomb exploded above our heads.

At least my shields held around me at the last—for the most part.

I studied my image in the mirror; I'd escaped with only one eye and burns on my face, shoulders and chest.

I'd been at the perimeter of the blast, as something felt wrong and I backpedaled in my vehicle at the last. Had I not, the fire would have broken through and I'd have died beside my slaves.

I'd transported myself back to the compound on Earth IV, but it was empty and lifeless, now. I'd have to find another place to hide and quickly, in case this spot were revealed to those we'd fought.

If I were lucky, they'd believe me dead. If not, they'd never stop hunting me. Time to build a new army. Tapping my comp-vid, I began searching for a likely world that would welcome an overlord like myself.

~

Parke

"I'm sorry, Gina," I said, although her tear-filled eyes accused me of allowing Kent to die. We'd lost so many, I hardly knew how to break the news to loved ones about the deaths.

Daniel found me after we were removed from the mountain; he'd been busy filling cracks with ice and breaking granite into rubble beneath the feet of Shakkor Agdah. He was on the phone talking to Louise in Washington State, telling her that he'd survived, when so many others hadn't.

"I'm so sorry, dear," Mom hugged Gina, who collapsed in her arms. Feeling even more uncomfortable, I walked out of the room to leave them alone. Instead, I went looking for the deserters, who'd ended up at the estate. I wanted to kill them and question them at the same time.

William Winkler appeared beside me as I stalked through the hall leading toward the stairs; Travis and Trent arrived almost simultaneously.

"What?" I demanded.

"Now may not be the best time to do what you intend to do," Winkler growled.

"And what is that?"

"Zarigar calls it a mistake. He also says that if you don't want the remnant of Shakkor Agdah to remain here, we will take them with us. We can remove the disease from them, provide them with an education if they want, and jobs afterward, if that is their desire."

"Why would you do that?" I stopped short and demanded.

"Because they risked their lives to warn you," Travis said. "And they saved the lives of the Vice President's family." I forced myself to recall that Travis and Trent became dragons when they turned.

275

Huge dragons.

Dragons that could likely destroy a rock demon without thinking very hard about it.

"There's something else, too," Winkler went on, as if we were discussing the weather.

"What's that?"

"Ver'Dak managed to escape. Randl says he was on the radar, and then he wasn't, and the trace of his death isn't anywhere around that mountain."

"Who the hell is Randl?" I exploded.

"Somebody you'll probably never meet, considering," Trent replied dryly. "Now, you can either notify next of kin, or you can let someone else with a bit more diplomacy handle that. I think you need a drink and some rest, considering your current mood."

"That's bullshit," I hissed. That's when Winkler tapped my forehead with a finger and everything went dark.

Travis

"Look at that, it does work," Winkler studied his finger for a moment. "All right, let's go plead our case with Cassie."

"You know they won't allow it unless they're with her," I pointed out.

"I know. Come on—we have things to do and a schedule to keep."

"You got that right," I said and stepped over Parke Worth's sleeping form to reach the stairs.

Cassie

Rob, Denevik, Zarigar and I stood on the back porch, staring at the lagoon behind the house while the sun climbed higher in the sky.

Nearby, Zephyr, Ebb and Blaze kept watch while Rob and I mourned Cliff's passing from his favorite spot. I'd released every ounce of fire I contained upon Stone Mountain before daybreak, and I'd screamed Cliff's name while doing it.

I didn't care how those below me died, I was so furious at the time. Now, exhaustion and grief had caught up with me again.

"Did we get them all?" I turned toward Zarigar, who'd resumed his dark-skinned, human appearance.

"Dearest, Ver'Dak managed to escape. I doubt he is without injury, but he is powerful, and likely on the very edge of the perimeter when you released your fire. The others—they are all gone, now. That, in itself, is a very great feat."

I realized I was crying again when I unconsciously reached up to wipe the tears away.

"What now?" Rob's voice sounded raw. "Will you still hunt that bastard?"

"Of course. If we do not, he will find a new hiding place, a new army and create havoc on other worlds. I dare say he has learned his lesson on this one."

"Take me with you," Rob grated. "I will help hunt him. It is what I owe to my friend. He saved my life a second time, at the cost of his own."

"Will Destiny be safe?" I asked.

"Dearest?" Zarigar frowned at my question.

"If I go with you, too, will Destiny be all right here?"

Denevik and Zarigar exchanged puzzled glances for a moment, before turning back to me. "There is a place we know where Destiny will not only be safe, she can be herself as an ice demon, and get the best education the Alliances have to offer," Denevik said. "If you wish to help us track Ver'Dak, and Destiny agrees to leave this world for another. You've injured Ver'Dak already, I believe. Had you been closer, he wouldn't have survived your attack."

"We have taken oaths to guard Cassie," Zephyr and the others walked toward me.

"You are released from your oaths—there is no reason for you to go if you don't want to," I told them.

"You do not understand," Ebb said. "We wished to protect you. We begged for the assignment and went through trials to win it. We want to go."

"Cassie, we may not be back here for a very long time," Denevik reached for my hand. "Be sure of your decision, avilepha."

"There is nothing for me here," I said, and realized I meant it. Parke and I—perhaps things would have worked between us had I not died and been reincarnated. Things had changed. I'd changed, too, as had he.

Now, I realized he saw me as a rival. Someone others would follow and look to first, rather than him. If I stayed, he would resent me more than he already did.

"Yes," I said. "I'm going—with Rob and Zephyr and Blaze and Ebb. And Destiny, too, if that's what she wants."

"I want to go," Destiny opened the French doors behind us and stepped onto the porch, followed by William Winkler, then Captains Travis and Trent. Chet followed at Destiny's heels until he sat at my feet, looked up at me and meowed softly.

"When will we leave?" I asked, bending down to lift Chet in my arms.

"Now," Zarigar shrugged. "I can move anything else you wish to take with you."

"Oh, no you don't," Beverly came barging out the door, shaking a wooden spoon. "Those people in the black cloaks don't know a thing about feeding themselves. Who's gonna take care of them?"

"Are you volunteering?" Winkler lifted an eyebrow and grinned at her.

"I guess I am. Just leave me with them, wherever they end up."

"Then we will place them in your care on Le-Ath Veronis," Zarigar agreed. "Are there any good-byes needed?"

"I'll write a note—if you'll send it back here," I said.

"I will do it gladly. Come, dearest, your starship awaits."

Parke

I didn't wake until nightfall, when Trey and Grim lifted me from the hallway floor upstairs.

"The President and the ah, mostly-contrite-but-still-a-little-racist Governor wish to extend their appreciation to all, and to express condolences to those lost in the battle, human and otherwise," Grim explained.

"Where is Cassie?" I demanded. I hadn't seen her since daybreak, when she, Rob and two aliens took the Governor of Georgia to task for being an asshole.

"We ah, have this," Trey handed an envelope to me. "I had a note from her, too, as did a few others."

"Where is she?" I snatched the envelope from Trey's hand.

"Where you can no longer reach her, I believe," Grim said. "A shame, too. The President wanted her to come work for him."

"As what?" I growled, ripping the letter open.

"A Special Aide to the Secretary of Defense," Trey cleared his throat.

"No. Absolutely not. She's the Princess of Alabama, and as such, cannot resign unless I allow," I began before unfolding the letter to read.

Parke, it began.

By the time you get this letter, I'll be in another galaxy, or that's what Denevik tells me. Find someone else to be Prince or Princess of Alabama. I suggest either Landon, Peter or Jerry. They'd be great at the job—with a little help from an assistant or two.

Rob, the sprites and I are going to help track Ver'Dak—he escaped and we're determined to make him pay for Cliff's death. Destiny and Beverly have come with us; Destiny has been promised a place where she can grow and learn as herself, rather than hiding among humans.

Beverly is going with the Shakkor Agdah who saved the Vice President's family and escaped the yoke of their fellow black cloaks. She says someone has to speak their language and make sure they stay out of trouble. If I know her at all, they'll eat better than most people I know, too.

As for you and me—we've known for a while that things haven't worked between us since I returned from the dead. I wasn't the same, weak-willed female you met in the beginning—the one running from Ross Diablo.

No, this Cassie knows what she wants for the first time in her life. From now on, decisions that affect me will be made by me and not by someone else.

Good luck to you, Parke, and tell Kate and Louise that I love them. You have a brand-new world ahead of you, anyway; one that now knows of the existence of elemental demons, vampires, sprites and werewolves.

Have fun with that.

Sincerely,

Cassandra King.

osuke

"And so the last viable fire demon has escaped this world," Zedarius sighed.

"We owe penance," I reminded him. "She and a handful of others did our work for us."

"I know. What can we do?" He studied his feet for a few moments. "The pyramids are no longer connected to us. We have our power, but little else. The pyramids answer to Cassie, now. All along, a third wizard was awake and working to save this world, and we never realized it."

He was correct—the pyramids had chosen their own wizard and supported her in her work here. I also understood what Zedarius was thinking—that he wished to hide himself and go back to sleep, leaving the planet to sort out its own woes.

"There will be a period of adjustment between humans and non-humans, now that the secrets are no longer secret," I said. "I believe we can help with the transition. Humans are still prejudiced against one another. How will paranormal beings be viewed as a result? As you can see, brother, we have much work in front of us."

"It is a heavy penance indeed."

"And not undeserved." I frowned at Zedarius, daring him to disagree.

"Yes," he bowed his head. "Well-deserved. Indeed."

∾

Cassie

"What is this place?" Destiny breathed as we were led through a grand entrance and a wide, ballroom-sized foyer lined with the most beautiful marble I'd ever seen.

"This is our mother's palace," Travis told her with a grin.

"Who is your mother?" Destiny's eyes were wide as she blinked at Travis.

"Well, they call me the Queen of Le-Ath Veronis," a strawberry-blonde woman appeared and walked toward us. She was dressed in a beautiful tunic with trousers, and matching ballet slippers. "Mostly, though, I just herd people around and they listen because they're polite," she said. "I'm Lissa. Welcome to my home."

The End